THE
SECRET
LIVES OF
DRESSES

THE
SECRET
LIVES OF
DRESSES

ERIN McKEAN

NEW YORK   BOSTON

Copyright © 2011 by Erin McKean

5 Spot
Hachette Book Group
237 Park Avenue
New York, NY 10017

www.5-spot.com

5 Spot is an imprint of Grand Central Publishing. The 5 Spot name and logo are trademarks of Hachette Book Group, Inc.

Printed in the United States of America

First Edition: February 2011
10 9 8 7 6 5 4

Library of Congress Cataloging-in-Publication Data

McKean, Erin.
   The secret lives of dresses / Erin McKean. —1st ed.
      p. cm.
   Summary: "A tale of a girl who finally discovers herself and finds love in her grandmother's vintage clothing store"—Provided by publisher.
   ISBN 978-0-446-55572-2
   1. Young women—Fiction.   2. Vintage clothing—Fiction.
3. Self-actualization (Psychology)—Fiction.   I. Title.
PS3613.C547S43 2011
813'.6—dc22   2010015236

For the generous readers of A Dress A Day: your kind comments and enthusiastic encouragement (and sometimes, your nagging) turned the Secret Lives into a "real book."

ACKNOWLEDGMENTS

I am overwhelmingly grateful to the following people:

My agent, Lisa Bankoff (and to Scott Gold, the Shameless Carnivore, for introducing us), my very understanding editor, Caryn Karmatz-Rudy, and her patient assistant, Amanda Englander (who didn't lose her temper even when I moved across the country without telling her), and my copyeditor, Terry Zaroff-Evans, who indulged me by using a dictionary I worked on as the preferred source for all questions of hyphenization—which is awfully circular, now that I think about it!—and who made me realize just how often I use the word "band-aid" (all-lower-case, metaphorically). I'd also like to thank Isobel Akenhead for her enthusiasm for the UK edition and for her hilarious tweets.

My sister, Kate McKean, who used her own considerable agenting and editing expertise to talk me down from several ledges and out of a couple of blind alleys, and her cheerleading skills to keep me going.

My co-workers at Wordnik for their support and understanding as I tried to finish a novel while running an Internet start-up; my in-laws, Rosemary and George Gerharz, for their understanding while I spent the entire Christmas holiday in their spare bedroom undertaking revisions; Vanessa Davis and Anaheed Alani, for letting me gossip about the imaginary Dora (just as if she were a real friend we had in common) through quite a few NYC restaurant meals; and my mother, Devon McKean, who kept saying "Hurry up so I can read it!"

And (most of all) I'm grateful to my husband, Joey Gerharz, and to Henry Gerharz, the coolest kid I've ever kidded, for indulging me with Saturday after Saturday and Sunday after Sunday. (Guys: let's go roller-skating!)

Forsyth, North Carolina, may or may not strongly resemble a hyphenated town in the western part of the state, but all the institutions and characters and any geographical, grammatical, spelling, punctuation, or other errors of fact or style herein are all mine.

THE
SECRET
LIVES OF
DRESSES

CHAPTER ONE

DORA HAD A RHYTHM GOING, OR IF NOT a rhythm, a pattern, and it went something like downshift, wipe tears away with back of hand, sob, upshift, scrub running nose with horrible crumpled fast-food napkin, stab at the buttons on the radio, and then downshift again. That had been the order of things for the past two hours. The first two hours had been pure howling, crying so hard she almost couldn't see, but then it had slowed down, a torrent turning into a spitting rain. Still bad weather, but not impassable.

The cars ahead of her, shiny boxes linked like beads, stretched as far as she could see. Whatever was causing the traffic was as yet undetermined; it could be construction, an accident, the sudden declaration of a state of fascist emergency and its concomitant checkpoints and ritual presentation of papers. Or it could be that Dora had died, and that this was her hell, her punishment for all her white lies and petty sins, stuck driving in miserable traffic to her grandmother's sickbed forever, without a clean pocket handkerchief or even her iPod.

Her iPod was still jacked into the shop's stereo. She'd left the coffee shop in a rush, throwing her apron at Amy, and run for the car. Didn't bother stopping at her apartment; what could she need more than Mimi?

Poor Amy, left alone on the Friday of Parents' Weekend,

with all the boisterous alumni leaning over the counter to tell her that they used to work in that *same* coffee shop, all the freshmen trying to sit a bit too far from their parents on the off chance that their classmates would take them for strangers, people coincidentally sharing the same table and the same nose.

Amy must have called Gary, or waited until Gary came in after the lunch shift and asked where she was, because there was a text on her phone: *r u oj?* Gary was usually too impatient to finish keying a text correctly. Dora suppressed the urge to text back, "the glove doesn't fit." Gary wouldn't get it.

Dora was not going to think about her next shift now. Dora wasn't going to think about Gary, or the coffee shop, or anything that wasn't Mimi.

Another two hours of sobbing and downshifting, ignoring equally the deliberately pretty country roads near the college and the gantlet of fast-food restaurants along the interstate, until finally Dora was pulling into the driveway of the house on Yorkshire. She fumbled for her keys at the front door; it had been four years since she'd lived at home, but the front door key of the little house in Forsyth never left her ring.

She turned on the hall light and shut the door behind her. "Gabby?" she called. Maybe she was at the hospital. But Dora barely had time to walk into the kitchen and drop her bag on the counter before she heard Gabby coming down the stairs.

"Gabby!" Although her apricot perm was fluffed up and her coral lipstick firmly drawn on slightly wider than her actual mouth, Gabby looked tired. And older.

"Sweetie…" Gabby folded her in a hug. "I was just

having a little bit of a lie-down. Want me to take you over to the hospital? You must have been driving for hours...."

"Oh, Gabby!" Dora thought she would tear up again, but even the vat-sized drive-through Diet Coke she had drunk on the way down hadn't replaced enough liquids to make that possible. "How is she?"

"She's been better, honey, you know that. But the Lord will provide." Gabby usually talked about "the Lord" as if he were one of her ne'er-do-well ex-husbands, so hearing her put any faith in him at all was a bit of a shock.

"I should clean up"—Dora gestured to her bedraggled T-shirt and good-enough-for-the-coffee-shop cargo pants—"but I didn't bring anything with me."

"Sweetie, that's never a problem in this house. You still have your closet here, you know."

The closet. Dora hadn't considered the closet. She had always had two closets, ever since she was a little girl. One was for her everyday clothes: the jeans and plaid flannel shirts of a nineties girlhood. The other was the closet Mimi was—for lack of a better word—curating for her. A combination wardrobe and trousseau, constantly updated as new pieces came through Mimi's shop that she didn't want to (or couldn't) get rid of. Dora had raided it as a girl to play dress-up, and as a teenager for a prom dress or two. She probably hadn't looked in it since Christmas... or maybe even high-school graduation.

Gabby led the way upstairs, going on about how Dora wouldn't recognize the shop downtown, since the city had done over the street to make it look old-timey and all. They'd even closed off the street to cars and put in benches. "Of course, it looks even better now that Larry

Sefford sold out his old hardware store and went to Florida! It's a fancy restaurant now."

"What, you mean they have cloth napkins?" Dora teased.

Gabby grinned. "And you can't get a pulled-pork sandwich! How do they expect a person to fill up?" She flipped on the closet light.

The closet was too big to fit within the bounds of an actual closet; it took up most of the spare bedroom. Mimi had kept a guest bed and a nightstand there, because she didn't want to think of herself as the kind of person who didn't have a place for guests to lay their heads, but Dora couldn't remember anyone ever staying there. Mimi changed the sheets on the bed weekly, though they were never slept on. The closet was really a forest of rolling coat racks, with an undergrowth of stacks of plastic shoeboxes, the shoes inside misty ghosts. Two mismatched dressers held sweaters, carefully layered with cedar sachets. There were a dozen hatboxes stacked in the corner, and a dress form wearing a purple feather boa (the boa being Dora's sole contribution to the closet, bought on a whim in high school and tolerated by Mimi).

Dora elbowed aside two racks of coats (one fur and fur-trim, one good cloth, and a few brocade), a stack of shoeboxes (fifties and sixties pumps, mostly), and a laundry basket of foundation garments. Gabby stood in the doorway, making little encouraging noises. Finally Dora found the day dresses. The rack held forty or so dresses, packed tightly, but not so tightly that they'd crush, shoulders protected with sheets of tissue paper. Dora stood for a minute, not sure which one to choose, before she realized that, since Mimi had picked them all, any one of them would be just what Mimi would like to see, would be happy to find Dora wearing, for a change.

Dora put out her hand, touched a pale-blue shirtdress, full-skirted, tricked out with blue gingham piping and pockets. She had an instant of the old, familiar resentment at Mimi's attempts to dress her, quickly followed by a shiver of regret. Why hadn't she worn any of these, why hadn't she given in, just once, on Easter or Christmas, or even Mimi's birthday, for God's sake, and let Mimi put her in one of these absurd dresses? What had she been worried about? Her nonexistent high-school popularity? Ruining the distinctive sense of style she didn't have? Making her grandmother, even for a day, happy? Dora grabbed it off the rack and turned to show Gabby.

"Oh, honey, that was...that's one of Mimi's favorites. I remember her showing it to me just last week! New old stock, see, it's got the original tag pinned to the label. Mimi washed it, though, so it shouldn't be dusty. I remember about your allergies.

"You need a slip with that," added Gabby firmly, pulling one out of a drawer. "Mimi would know if you weren't wearing one, even if she were in a coma." Its satin strap caught briefly on the drawer pull, and Gabby twitched it free. "This is a good one...no itchy lace, I know you hate that." Gabby glanced down at Dora's clogs. "Shoes. Let's see. How about some heels?" Dora looked at Gabby in desperation, too worn out to argue. Gabby took pity on her. "No, you're right, not practical for the hospital. I remember a pair of flat loafers around here somewhere...." Gabby rummaged in the boxes until she pulled them out. Dora stepped out of her shoes reluctantly and tried them on. Like everything Mimi had ever chosen for her, they fit perfectly. The only thing pinching her was her conscience.

If her eyes weren't so hot and her chest wasn't so heavy and tight, it would have felt just like one of their old dress-up sessions. Dora had indulged Gabby by playing dress-up well into her sarcastic junior-high years; it was hard to deny Gabby anything once her enthusiasm got going.

Gabby was some kind of relation by marriage, in a very Southern-small-town way: her second husband had been a cousin of Dora's grandfather, or an uncle of Dora's cousin, something complicated that Dora had never been able to keep straight. It hadn't mattered, anyhow. Mimi and Gabby had been at the hairdresser's one day and fallen into conversation, and three weeks later Gabby had moved in "just for a little while," as she waited to finalize her third divorce.

Unluckily for Gabby, her third husband was Forsyth's leading divorce lawyer, and Gabby had come away with nothing. ("No house, no alimony, no kids. I knew there was a reason I couldn't get pregnant—it wasn't that I was too old, it was that demons and people can't breed," Gabby said.)

Public sentiment in Forsyth—on the distaff side, any-way—had been firmly on Gabby's side. "Nobody wants to hire a divorce lawyer who reminds them of their almost-ex-husbands," Gabby said. He had taken off to Miami, where there were more people getting divorced, and where his new wife (and former paralegal) didn't have to deal with all of Gabby's friends snubbing her in the gro-cery store.

In the ten years since, Gabby's vague family ties to Mimi had become double-knotted. She was a combination aunt and accomplice to Dora, bailing her out the few times Dora did manage to get in trouble (a double-dare shop-lifting scare here, a minor fender-bender there). Every so often Gabby made noises about getting her own place, and Mimi squashed them flat. "If you go I won't have anyone to drink iced tea and gossip with, and that will send me right into a decline," Mimi threatened. Since Dora had been at Lymond those noises had gotten much less frequent.

Gabby kept up a steady stream of inconsequential excla-mations as she moved through the closet room, looking for a sweater. ("Those hospitals are cold, and summer's a while gone, even down here.") She oohed and aahed over an evening gown, buttoned the jacket of a tailored suit, giggled at a merry widow ("I should tell you about the last time I wore one of these, now that you're older"), and pulled out a blouse printed with little cherry pies and rolling pins ("For later"). Finally there was a slip (and a bra, thrown in the pile by Gabby, Dora too weak to protest that her own bra was just fine, thank you), the dress and a perfectly matching little cardigan sweater, white with blue buttons, and the shoes, and Dora headed to the bath-room and a shower.

The upstairs shower had always been hers, but Mimi had made it over since Dora had left for college. Not a remodel, really, but an upgrade. The showerhead no lon-ger shot a finger of water out perpendicularly towards the glass door, and the soap dish carved into the wall had been slightly re-angled so as to actually drain, rather than holding a puddle of scummy soap bog. There was a new medicine cabinet, but when Dora opened it, all her old toiletries were there: an ancient pink razor and a tube of Great Lash, a bottle of witch hazel from a drugstore that had gone out of business years before. Dora closed the cabinet and turned on the water in the shower.

There was an inch of shampoo left in the bottle in the shower, and half an inch of some lily-of-the-valley shower gel: enough to scrub off the coffee shop and the car trip, at least. Dora used it all without thinking, didn't want to think, about the next day, or the day after that. It was enough to be in the hot water, smelling like lilies of the valley.

The towels were the ones Dora had insisted on in high school, a very dark charcoal gray. Mimi had wanted pale pink, edged with an eyelet ruffle, but Dora had been in a minimalist, anti-girly phase, all solid dark colors and geometric lines. That same year she had once worn a pale-gray wedge dress with red leggings, carefully planned and saved up for, bought on a trip to the big mall in Raleigh, matched with gray suede pointy flats from Mimi's store, only to have Missy Chambers ask, mock-innocently, where she could sign up for the eighties music-video tryouts, too. The next day Dora was back in jeans and a T-shirt and sneakers.

After struggling with the pointy bra's back fasteners (all Dora's bras were front-fastening racer-backs) and pulling on the slip, Dora realized that Gabby hadn't mentioned pantyhose, or even stockings and garters. She wasn't going to remind her. Then she slipped the dress from its hanger.

Buttoning up the dress felt strange, like walking into the wrong party. It felt so different from jeans and a T-shirt, so different from anything Dora had worn for years. The little blue plastic buttons, transparent and a bit glowy in the strong light of the bathroom, the hooks and eyes that held the waist stay firm—they made getting dressed deliberate and serious, something to pay attention to. The full pleats of the skirt hung around her hips, counterweighting her as she moved. Dora reached up to shove a little ancient mousse into her short curls, and felt the narrow shoulders of the dress strain slightly. Why didn't anyone in the fifties ever seem to want to lift their arms above their heads? Dora wondered. Giving up on her hair, Dora decided nothing would make her uncork that ancient tube of mascara, so she slipped on the shoes, grabbed the cardigan, and went out to face Gabby.

Gabby, predictably, was in the kitchen, watching the little TV they kept on the counter. Instead of Mimi's news channel, though, Gabby was watching an entertainment show that promised an inside look at a starlet's closet.

"Oh, sweetie, you look like a picture! I should take a picture! You look just like Mimi did at your age!"

"When Mimi was my age she was married and had a son and smoked two packs a day."

"Well, honey, I'm just saying. You do look like her, you know."

Dora did know, had always known, that the resemblance to her grandmother was close, if not actively uncanny. Only the yellowing of the edges of certain photographs could prove that they were pictures of Mimi as an infant or young girl, instead of pictures of Dora. There were pictures of Mimi, formal photographs taken at her high-school graduation, that looked for all the world as if Dora had signed up for a series of sepia-toned novelty shots. At the rare family gatherings of their clan, there would be rashes of hair-pats and choruses that involved the words "spitting image," as if Mimi had ever spit in her life.

Mimi herself had played it down. "Oh, she's much smarter than I am, and much better-looking," she'd say. "We expect great things from our little Dora!" Mimi had never made Dora play up the resemblance. She'd suggest that Dora wear a certain dress, but she'd never insist. She even let Dora cut her hair in a completely unflattering Rachel in the sixth grade.

Gabby switched off the TV and picked up Dora's keys from the counter, handing them to her. "Do you have a handkerchief? We forgot to get you a handbag...."

"No, it's okay." Dora grabbed her messenger bag, which was a Hawaiian print in shades of red and orange, and which clashed horribly with her dress. "Let's go."

Gabby drove her little Toyota at a walking pace through the neighborhood, navigating the new speed bumps as if they were frosted with meringue and she didn't want to crush the soft peaks. She waved vaguely at some of the houses, telling Dora about people she had either forgotten or never known, talking about anything and everything rather than Mimi. "The Walraths, he died and she moved to Arizona; not so much as a postcard since then! But the new folks in that house are very nice—Yankees, of course, moved down to work at the university. She's a doctor. Oh, and didn't you know Robbie Henderson in school? He got married and works at the insurance place, I forget what they call it now. And his wife had triplets!" Gabby lowered her voice. "They used that fertility-drug stuff, I'm sure of it. Real cute babies, though."

Dora tried not to feel a rising panic, a fear that they would never, ever get out of the neighborhood and that Gabby would just drive her around, telling inane stories, for hours, days even. While Mimi was lying in the hospital, waiting for Dora.

Finally they were out of the neighborhood's deliberately twisty streets and onto the parkway. Two lanes and a speed limit of forty-five seemed to throw Gabby into NASCAR mode, and she changed lanes wildly to pass cars that were brazenly keeping themselves to a sedate forty-seven or fifty miles an hour. Gabby's monologue changed topic; now she was rattling off the new big-box and chain retail stores that had come to town. "We have two Targets—or Tar-jays I should say—and we have an Anthropologie, Mimi loves that place but won't buy anything there but glasses and dishes, not like we need any more dishes, what with her wedding china, and your parents' wedding china, and all of my wedding china—I kept all three, of course. I keep telling Mimi we should go in for catering, all the dishes we've got. There's even that place with all the crazy chairs, they put it in where the K&W Cafeteria used to be, I forget what it's called. Design Within Reach! That's it. Mimi and I went in there and she said nothing was within reach if you were sitting in a chair three inches from the floor. That's a young people's store, for all that those chairs were designed before you were born."

Gabby made a quick exit from the parkway, and took her hand away from her death grip on the steering wheel to pat Dora's knee. "We're almost there, honey. It'll be okay."

Dora put her hand over Gabby's, just for an instant, and felt the warm crêpiness of her skin, the cool metal of her rings. Then she took her hand away and looked out the car window.

* * *

When had she talked to Mimi last? It must have been last week—she usually called on Sundays, right in the middle of the afternoon. Mimi had a knack of interrupting her just when she had finally settled into studying. She'd tried calling Mimi earlier in the day, but by the time Dora got up and thought of it, Mimi would usually be at church. "Not that I believe one word of anything they say," she'd laugh. "But it's a mighty convenient way to catch up with all your friends and hear all the gossip. And wear a hat. Church is the last place on the planet you can wear a hat without people making a fuss about it, unless you're royalty."

Mimi had always started with news about the shop, assuming that would be the most interesting to Dora, as it was to her. What had come in, what had sold, what she'd found in the pockets of old coats (coats always had the best forgotten items), talking about the dresses and suits as if they were living things, not quite people—more like pets. Sometimes Mimi would try, not so subtly, to add to Dora's wardrobe.

"Dora, this gorgeous brown wool skirt that just came in, it's just your size, and has the most adorable pockets.... It's a fun autumn-Saturday-errands skirt, new books from the library and crisp apples and scuffling through the leaves...." Mimi always spent more time talking about what a piece of clothing felt like than what it looked like. Dora loved to listen to Mimi's characterizations, but when Mimi paused, obviously waiting for a "Yes, I'd wear that," she'd make noncommittal noises. "Mmmm, that sounds cute," Dora would say, and Mimi would trail off. "Well, it'll probably still be on the rack next time you're home, you can try it on then...."

Dora loved the clothes in the shop. She loved to straighten them on the hangers, rebutton the buttons that the customers had undone, rebuckle the belts, and retie the ties. She remembered being ten or eleven years old, begging, on her knees for maximum dramatic effect, to be allowed to use "the dragon"—Mimi's ancient garment-steamer. She loved to watch the wrinkles fall out, like magic. As she got older, she loved to try them on, pretend for a minute that she was the elegant, confident woman that the dress belonged to. But they never seemed to belong to her. However well they fit Dora's body, they didn't seem to fit her self.

She once tried to explain it to Mimi. "I love this dress," Dora said, twirling in a pale-blue sundress with a scalloped hem. She must have been sixteen.

"Wear it to school tomorrow, then," Mimi said. "It'll be warm enough." Her face told Dora that the dress looked right. Mimi never made someone think that something looked good if it didn't.

"It doesn't feel like me." Dora frowned. "It's so pretty, but it feels—I don't know—like a costume or something. Like I'm playing the girl who wears this dress."

"Maybe you just need time to get used to the role." Mimi stood behind her and adjusted the shoulder straps slightly. "Even understudies have to start sometime." The dress looked even better, but somehow it made Dora feel worse. She shrugged her shoulders, the universal answer of the teenager. The dress went back on the rack.

Last Sunday's call hadn't included any of Mimi's wardrobe come-ons, but there had been big news, nevertheless.

"Gabby's ex-husband is back in town, did you ever hear anything to beat that?"

Dora was doing the dishes—all two bowls and two spoons—the phone tucked between her ear and shoulder. She turned off the water and grabbed a dish towel. "What, the divorce lawyer? Big Bob?"

"No, no, Jolly Jerry."

"I don't remember a Jolly Jerry...only Big Bob and Stuffy Steve...and did Gabby ever marry anyone without a nickname?"

"If she did he got one with the rest of the wedding presents. Or maybe they wrote it into their vows. Jolly Jerry was Gabby's first husband."

"Her starter husband?"

"If you want to put it that way, and I wish you didn't, yes. Anyway, he moved up to Virginia after they divorced, did some kind of work in trucking, and has come back to Forsyth to retire...."

"At the golf club?"

"No, he's got one of those new senior apartments. Mary Beth told me."

"Have you told Gabby?"

"Of course I did."

"What'd she say?"

"What she always says when she doesn't know what to say."

" 'Funny kind of world this is'?"

"Yes, but I think Jerry's arrival might have hit her harder than she's letting on. She's been even vaguer and more absentminded than usual, lately. Last week she left the water running and misplaced her keys, twice."

"Losing keys once a week seems standard-issue

Gabby, but twice—plus the water—that's not good. Do you know why they divorced?"

"She doesn't talk about Jerry much; the most she's ever said to me is that they were just 'too young.'"

Dora looked over at Gabby and tried to see her as a young bride. Dora had seen the pictures once, Gabby with an impressive beehive and a mile-wide smile, but the groom was a fuzzy blank. She considered asking Gabby about Jolly Jerry. Had she seen him yet? Why was he called Jolly? But then Gabby turned into the driveway of Forsyth Baptist, and they were there.

Gabby dropped her off in front of the automatic doors. A couple was emerging with their new baby: she in the ritual wheelchair, pushed by an orderly; he carrying a plastic car seat buckled around a red-faced squirming pink-knitted-blanket-wrapped bundle. "You go on in, honey. I'll park and meet you inside."

●   ●   ●

The hospital was even worse than Dora had feared. She'd assumed it would be like one of those hospital shows, with all the doctors and nurses in clean scrubs, all remarkably good-looking, rushing around with great purpose. Instead it was nearly empty, the doctors and nurses unglamorous, not wearing any makeup (much less the dramatic TV kind), and moving just slightly faster than the usual pace in Forsyth—a kind of brisk amble.

While the TV hospitals had one or two grieving relatives, highlighted and set off from the staff, Forsyth's hospital was crammed with them. Everywhere Dora looked, there was another person who was stiff and uncomprehending and consumed by some nervous tic, waiting for news. Everyone looked vaguely familiar, but no one wanted to force recognition.

When Dora got to Mimi's room she took a minute to shake out her skirt and straighten herself. Stroke or no stroke, Mimi would hate sloppiness. She ran a hand through her hair. No lipstick, as usual. *When Mimi gets out of here I'll let her pick out a lipstick for me. Even a red one.* She opened the door.

The bed was far too big for Mimi. She looked tiny, like some sick Fisher-Price concept toy that never made it out of the R&D department: Your Little Hospital Friend. Her silver hair was dull against the much-washed pillowcase, and her feet barely made a bump in the sheet. There were things beeping in the room, of course, but muffled somehow, like a dying smoke detector in the neighbor's apartment. Mimi's hands looked like they'd been spilled over the top of the bed, in a position that was completely without intention.

Dora moved closer and picked up Mimi's hand. She held it for a while, then arranged it gracefully, the way Mimi would have. Her heavy wedding band and solitaire engagement ring had been removed, probably to a manila envelope somewhere, marked MARGARET WINSTON, the name she never used. The diamond was probably clanking against her Tank watch, scratching the crystal. Mimi would be irritated. Dora could imagine her at the big chain jewelry store in the mall, trying to explain to some clerk that she needed the crystal polished, while he watched out of the corner of his eye for a more lucrative customer.

There were flowers in the room, late-fall ones, orange

and maroon, the real kind from someone's garden, not cookie-cutter stems shipped in from South America. Mimi would have known their name, but Dora didn't. They smelled clean and fresh and slightly spicy, stuffed in a vase that turned out to be an old teapot. From Gabby, Dora assumed. She wished she'd had time to bring flowers, but Mimi would rather have no flowers than something wrapped in cellophane from the Winn-Dixie. Mimi would want something old-fashioned for a stay in the hospital. A bed jacket, or hothouse grapes. Did they even have hothouse grapes anymore?

The doorknob rattled and a nurse came in. Her scrubs were band-aid pink, her name tag said MARIA RN, and her socks had a pattern of yellow rubber duckies. Dora pulled her gaze away from Maria's feet and smiled at her, unsure of what else to do. Did she need to leave? Could she ask questions? Maria smiled back, but not in a way that encouraged conversation. Dora felt like a teenage babysitter when the parents came home, communicating in pantomime so as not to wake the sleeping toddler.

Maria started in on her routine, following a checklist only she knew. Various things were written on a chart, other things were just scrutinized. Soft hands checked Mimi's IV and straightened the already straight sheets. Dora sat still, out of the way.

Her invisible boxes all checked, Maria stopped at the door. "I'll tell Dr. Czerny you're here." Her voice was surprisingly loud.

Mimi's eyelids fluttered and opened. Dora could see that moment of where-am-I panic, and leaned in so Mimi could see her without sitting up.

"Shhhh. Don't try to talk. You've had some kind of stroke, you're at Forsyth Baptist."

Mimi gave Dora her best "I know that" face, marred only by the slackness of her right cheek and eyelid, and the indignity of the tube in her nose. Despite that, it was still the same "you're not getting away with this" expression Dora remembered, except this time she wasn't trying to stay out after curfew or find an excuse to avoid doing the dishes.

"It's going to be okay," Dora said, reaching for Mimi's hand again. "It's going to be okay." Dora was on Mimi's left side, in the only chair. *I wonder if they put the chair here on purpose,* she thought. *So visitors would sit on her good side. Mimi would have demanded that, if she could.* Mimi's hand twitched in hers. Dora held on tighter.

The door opened again. Dr. Czerny turned out to be a tall middle-aged woman with graying russet hair swept up in a plastic clip. She was wearing a slate-blue sweater under her lab coat, and real shoes—not the plastic clogs the nurse had worn.

"I'm Dr. Czerny." She stuck out a ringless hand. Dora took it, and flailed for a minute before remembering what her line should be. "I'm Dora Winston, Mimi's granddaughter."

Dr. Czerny looked over towards Mimi, whose eyes had drifted closed again. "Would you like to step out into the hall?"

Away from Mimi, Dora felt awkward and costumey in her dress. "Can you tell me what happened?"

"Your grandmother was brought in this morning; she had a seizure in her shop. One of the customers called 911. She was brought here, and we believe she had a kind of stroke called a subarachnoid hemorrhage."

Dora had a fleeting mental image of a giant black spider, sucking life from Mimi. She pushed it away.

"How serious? Will Mimi…" Dora felt as if even asking would change things for the worse, push the fuzzy cloud of possibilities into a hard, solid wrong shape.

"There's a chance of recovery."

A chance. Dora noticed that there wasn't any kind of qualifier there. Not "good." Not "slight." Just "chance."

"How long…"

"She will be in the hospital for some time. It's hard to predict, with this kind of brain trauma. We should really have her in the ICU, but we're full up, and we didn't want to move her. If you wish to have her moved, the next-closest ICU is in Greensboro."

Dora must have looked bewildered, because Dr. Czerny's face softened. "Is there any other family who can help you? Your parents? Brothers and sisters?"

"My parents are dead." Dora was always surprised at how saying that never seemed to lose any strength, was always shiny and sharp each time it left her mouth. "Mimi has a brother—a half brother. He's in Fayre." Dora thought of her great-uncle John, two cell phones bolted to him at all times, his unpleasant habit of holding up a finger for silence whenever one of them rang. Uncle John, in the hospital, arguing with everyone, with his attitude of "I'm rich, therefore I'm right," bringing her great-aunt Camille with him to fuss over everything. Dora shuddered. "They're not…they're not close."

"I see." Dr. Czerny looked as if half brothers who weren't close could be dismissed without a second thought. "I can make an appointment with the family counselor for you; you should see her tomorrow. Right now, if you can, just sitting with your grandmother would be the best thing, for you both."

Dr. Czerny's shoes made a reassuring clicking sound as she went off down the hallway. Dora watched her turn the corner before she went back into Mimi's room.

Mimi was well and truly asleep again, or maybe sedated. Dora wished she'd thought to ask, but sank into the chair and held Mimi's hand anyway. She felt stupid and hollow. She had always thought that Mimi would go on forever, her immaculately coiffed head held high and her strong, elegant hands always busy. Why had she never realized that Mimi would someday get sick, someday maybe even die? Did she think that losing her parents immunized her against losing anyone else she loved? That bereavement, like the chicken pox, was something you could only catch once?

Dora had caught the chicken pox late; she must have been in the fourth or fifth grade. Mimi, always good in a crisis, had built Dora a nest in Mimi's big bed, covering Dora's hands with socks to keep her from scratching. On the worst, itchiest days, Mimi set a kitchen timer to go off every hour, and every time it buzzed Dora picked a card out of a bowl (it was tricky, with those socks on her hands) to find out whether she got a popsicle, a story read aloud by Mimi, or a new video to watch, or (the joker in the pack) had to submit to more daubing with calamine lotion. One of the cards had read "Surprise!" and Mimi had given her a little enamel dogwood-flower brooch, which Dora had worn pinned to her pajamas until she went back to school, and which was still in her jewelry box, on top of her bureau, back at Lymond.

Dora wished she could fix this with a pair of clean

white socks, a box of popsicles, and a week of cartoons. At the very least she'd have to stay in Forsyth for a while. She could sublet her apartment, allow some foreign student to study on her futon and make pilaf or curry or Boston baked beans or whatever in her secondhand pots. She had one last class, an independent study, more of a formality than anything else. Missing that wouldn't be a problem.

The only hitch was the coffee shop. Actually, that wasn't true. Someone else could do the scheduling and the ordering and show up to unlock the place when Priti overslept again. Someone else could close out the till and banter with the delivery guys so the shop would be the first stop on the route and tell Mark that if he played the "Gods of Death Metal" playlist off his iPod one more time those very same gods would swoop down and kill him, on her invocation. Someone else could empty the mouse-traps and refill the napkin holders. Someone else could run to the registrar's office for change and point, for the umpteenth time, to the sign that said No Credit Cards / No Dining Plan. There was no hitch there.

Dora tried to imagine how Gary would handle her absence. Not gracefully, probably. Gary wasn't graceful, at least where the coffee shop was concerned.

She had never intended to work at the coffee shop. Her scholarship to Lymond had come with (in addition to tuition) guaranteed summer employment, doing research with a professor on campus. The first summer of her scholarship Dora had spent printing copies of research papers from electronic journals for a professor who had been worried that the library's switch to digital subscriptions heralded a new Dark Ages, and who felt that hoarding of laser-printed copies of sociological research was a perfectly rational response to the possible collapse of civilization. The second summer was spent doing data entry of student questionnaires on the exciting topic of pedagogical response. (Which Dora still didn't understand, and couldn't explain.)

The third summer was supposed to be spent cataloguing catalogues of antiquities (meta-cataloguing, as the grad student who was leaving the job pompously explained) in the Department of Classical and Near Eastern Studies, but at the very last minute, her research sponsor received a grant to go to Turkey on a dig, and she was out of a job.

The woman at the scholarship office was sympathetic, but could offer no other options. All of the other spots had been filled, and there were, unsurprisingly, no other faculty members who wanted to take on a new summer research student at short notice. Dora barely argued; these things happened. It was nobody's fault (although she did treasure some spiteful thoughts about her erstwhile archaeologist). The scholarship administrator was relieved; she'd expected tears, recriminations, possibly even threats—some of the Lymond scholarship students were very well connected. She shook Dora's hand very firmly on the way out.

"Again, I'm so sorry, Dora. I hope you have a good summer in spite of this difficulty." Dora thanked her and wandered out of her office, to stand in front of the job board on the last day of the semester. All of the sheets with their paper fringes of phone numbers mostly torn off, informing you that you could work to save the environment and make good money, asking for students to babysit, to wait tables, to be interns of every kind but the medical, left Dora empty and blank.

While Dora was standing there, wondering whether or not she could still sublet her room and head back to Forsyth, a guy rushed up. A cute dark-haired guy with a roundish baby face, hauling an open box from the copy shop. Dora could see that it was full of job flyers. He tried to juggle the box and a stapler, and Dora watched, fascinated, as the box spilled from his grasp. A ream of paper fanned out over the floor.

"Here, I'll help," Dora said.

"Thanks." He smiled up at her, already on his knees, shuffling paper.

Dora went to the end of the spill, where some pages had fallen in a damp spot and were quickly getting soggy.

"Just toss those," he said. "It's stupid, anyway, I left it too late, and everyone who needs a job at this point has one." He ran an exasperated hand through his short dark hair, and it fell back exactly into place.

Dora looked at him again. "I don't," she said. "What do you need?"

"The coffee shop is rehabbing. I need someone to help me clean, paint, and redecorate it. And then restock it. And all before August, which is going to be tight, I can tell you."

"Okay."

"Okay?"

"Okay, I'll do it."

"Don't you want to know what I'm paying? Or the hours?"

"Not especially. I figure you're paying at least the

going rate, because you're trying to get someone late in the semester. And as for hours, if you have to be done by August, it's as many as possible, which is fine by me."

"Can you lift seventy pounds?"

"How many times?"

"Once or twice a day will do."

"Well, then, yes, I can lift seventy pounds."

He stuck out his hand. "I'm Gary. I'm your new boss."

Dora took his hand and shook it. "I'm Dora. I'm your new employee."

Gary swept up the rest of the sheets and dumped them in the recycling bin. He shoved his stapler into his pocket. "Let's go get your paperwork in order."

Dora followed him back to his office. Surprisingly, it was in the Music Department.

"The Music Department runs the coffee shop?" she asked.

"Well, not exactly, no. But I run the coffee shop, and I'm a grad student in musicology, and so this is where the office is."

Dora followed him up the steps. Music was in one of the older buildings on campus. In the distance she could hear a flute repeating the same lighthearted phrase over and over again, stopping and starting like someone trying to tell a joke through an attack of the hiccups.

The office was tiny, ancient, linoleum-floored. Gary shuffled through the papers on his desk, and came up triumphantly with a battered folder marked COFFEE SHOP.

"Wait—you're a U.S. citizen, right?" He looked so alarmed by the possibility that she wasn't that Dora was almost tempted to claim that she was Bosnian or Venezuelan.

"I'm a citizen," she reassured him.

"That's good; I have no idea where to get the nonciti-zen form." Gary dug around and thrust a stack of papers at Dora. Dora held them while Gary realized there was nowhere for her to sit and fill them out. He rushed out to the hall and dragged in a chair, and then shoved a stack of journals from his desk to the top of the radiator. With a last flourish, he produced a pen.

"Sign here," he said.

Dora sat, accepted the pen, and filled out the forms. Her name, her Social Security number, her complete lack of any felony convictions. It didn't take very long. Gary hovered.

She pushed the papers back to him, and stood up.

"When do you need me to start?"

"How about now?"

Dora shrugged. "Fine by me."

Gary talked the whole way over to the coffee shop. He was from Detroit, well, the Detroit suburbs. His folks were retired. He'd been at Lymond five years, with two to go. "Except two years ago I also had two years to go." Running the coffee shop was new for him; the previous manager had actually, finally, really finished her disserta-tion and left. Dora listened, amused.

Gary was fumbling with the keys to the coffee shop. Dora watched. "It's probably the biggest," she offered. "That's a Medeco key, most of the university facilities use those locks. The others are probably storeroom keys."

Gary looked at her. "You are quite possibly the best hire I have ever made."

Unaccountably, Dora blushed. "I'm the only hire you ever made, aren't I?"

"Unless you count getting my embezzling stepbrother to help at my lemonade stand, yes."

Finally he had the door open and they were inside. Gary flipped on the lights.

"Where do we start?"

Gary looked so confused by this that Dora had to laugh. "You don't know, do you?" He looked indignant for a moment, and then laughed himself. "No. No, I don't. They left me a manual, but it's for the cash register."

"First of all, we're not going to get anything done in here today. We need cleaning supplies, furniture catalogues, paint, probably some new shelving, information about distributors...." Dora stopped, realizing that Gary was staring at her.

"So we need all that, do we? You are now officially the brains of this operation. I am reduced to mere clerical support. Hold those thoughts while I get pen and paper."

Gary went to rummage around behind the counter, emerging with a coffee-stained legal pad and a capless ballpoint. He looked at his watch.

"Hey, it's getting late.... Do you have any plans right now?"

Dora realized that she should probably say yes, start off firmly on the right foot, not let herself be imposed upon, but what she said was "Not really..."

"Good!" Gary beamed at her. He really was cute, Dora thought. She tried to avoid thinking about exactly how cute he was. He was now her boss, after all. "How about we head over to the Skell? We can work over dinner. Coffee shop's buying," he added quickly.

Dora felt, unreasonably, as if the coffee shop had just asked her out on a date.

The Rathskeller was empty; the visibly bored hostess

waved them to a booth in the front. "I can't believe we got a booth without begging and pleading," Dora said.

"Summer at Lymond." Gary shrugged. "Nobody here, and the people who are here don't want to be. If it weren't for this coffee shop I'd be bumming from music festival to music festival. That's what I did the last couple of summers. If you know the right people you can work at them and get in for free." Gary polished his fork and spoon with his paper napkin. "What would you be doing?"

"Nothing much, I guess. Working a research grunt job." Dora folded her menu and set it on the table's edge to serve as a flare for their server. Gary didn't note her diffidence, or, if he did, he didn't seem inclined to pursue it. He shoved his menu aside, putting down the legal pad. He rummaged in his pockets. The pen had disappeared.

"I have a pen," Dora said, and took one from her bag.

"Thanks." Gary smiled at her again. "What would I do without you?"

"Write with the place-mat crayons."

"Yes, a list in purple crayon just screams 'efficiency.' " Gary hesitated, the ballpoint hovering over the first line.

Their waitress showed up. "Youse guys ready?" She took a pencil from behind her ear. Her Skell T-shirt, with its cartoon-skull logo, was stretched tightly across her chest. Gary seemed to be doing a stress analysis of the fabric. With his eyeballs.

"I'd like the burger, very rare, with fries, and an iced tea."

Gary's gaze transferred itself regretfully from the T-shirt to the face. "I'll have the Reuben and a Heineken."

"ID."

Gary made a big show of pulling out his wallet and showing her his driver's license.

"Huh. You're thirty?"

"Some people are, you know."

The waitress shrugged and wandered off with their order.

"Very smart, not to drink on the job. Or are you not legal?"

"I'm twenty."

"Ah, undergraduates. Otherwise known as forbidden fruit."

Dora didn't know where to look. Gary picked up his pen again. "Where were we?"

"Cleaning, we were at cleaning." Dora focused on the list. She knew she could handle the list.

"You were at cleaning. I was at beer. Okay. I can call the facilities head about cleaning tomorrow morning. Good."

Gary wrote "Cleaning" on the list. At least, Dora thought it was the word "cleaning." Gary looked up and saw her squinting at it.

"I know, I have terrible handwriting. It's a very manly failing, though."

"Do you want me to make the list?" Dora asked.

"Nah, you'll have to learn to read my scrawl eventually." He turned the pad around and pushed it across the table. "But move over—I'll sit next to you, and then at least you won't have to read it upside down."

The booth was slightly too small for two adults to sit side by side, but Gary didn't seem to notice. His leg pressed against hers.

Dora went on. "Furniture."

Gary wrote down "Furniture."

"What's the budget? Is any of the stuff there still good? Does the university have preferred suppliers? Who has the catalogues? What's the delivery time? Eight weeks is cutting it a little close to have commercial-grade stuff delivered."

"How do you *know* all this stuff?"

"My grandma owns a store...." Dora trailed off.

"My grandma plays bridge in Florida and calls me on my stepbrother's birthday. She's kind of losing it."

"I'm sorry." Dora looked down at the list again.

"You have nothing to be sorry about. You're a lifesaver. I should stop on the way home and buy a lottery ticket, as I'm obviously the luckiest guy at Lymond today." He looked around the empty restaurant. "Of course, there's not all that much competition...."

Dora didn't know what to say. She took a sip of water.

"Hey, where's your iced tea?"

"Over there." Dora could see it on the counter.

"Don't worry, I'll get it."

Gary hopped up and walked over to the counter. The waitress intercepted him, and he gestured back to the table. Dora couldn't hear what they were saying, but the waitress smiled. Gary grabbed the tea and came back, grinning, to sit across from her again.

"I told her I was going to make you tip *me*."

"I don't think you tip your boss."

"Even if he waits on your table?"

"That might be a special case."

Gary pulled the list across the table. "What's next?"

"Stocking. Do you have any invoices from previous years? Catalogues? Does the shop have credit accounts anywhere? What do the students like to eat? Who delivers the hot food, and from where?"

Gary scribbled. "I think I have a big file from the previous manager."

Dora looked at Gary. "I could come by tomorrow and look at the file...maybe make some calls. I bet some of them have online catalogues. I could call the suppliers while you figure out the cleaning stuff."

"Sounds like a plan." Gary looked at her consideringly. "I am beginning to think that you are the kind of girl a man could come to rely on, Dora Winston."

Before Dora could respond—not that she knew what to say—the waitress swooped in with their plates, giving Gary the hamburger with something that looked suspiciously like a wink. She put the Reuben in front of Dora like an afterthought. Gary let her walk away before switching the plates.

"I think you made the better choice," he said. His sandwich was oozing Russian dressing and sauerkraut. He took a bite, and winced as dressing dripped onto his shirt. Dora laughed.

"Hey! Laughing at your new boss is not a good career move." Gary grinned, and swiped a French fry from Dora's plate.

"So you want my letter of resignation? Already?" Dora smiled back at him. She couldn't remember the last time she had felt so at home with a person. With a male person. A male person whose last name she didn't know.

"I wouldn't even know how to address it," she said. "Dear Mr....?"

"If I don't tell you my last name, you can never quit! This works out great. It's like 'Rumpelstiltskin' in reverse." Gary stole another one of Dora's fries to mop up the Russian dressing on his plate.

"No, really. You must have another name, you're not famous enough to have only one."

"Ouch. Okay, it's Dudas. And whatever joke you can make out of it, I already heard. In the third grade."

"All right, Mr. Dudas." She smiled across the table at him.

"C'mon, it's Gary." He looked at her a bit too long, and there was a tone in his voice that gave her a little shiver.

The waitress came back for their empty plates, and dropped the check on the table. Gary covered it with a couple of bills, standing to go.

"Don't you want a receipt?" Dora asked. "So the coffee shop can reimburse you?"

"You are really gunning for employee of the month, you know? I see a very shiny plaque in your future." Gary waved the waitress over.

Dora scooted out of the booth. "I'll be right back." As she turned the corner to the ladies' room she saw the waitress laughing at something Gary must have said.

When she came out, Gary was hanging over the hostess station, still chatting with their waitress.

"Dora! Thanks again for everything tonight. I'm so glad I found you. You're a miracle worker, possibly even a miracle....So I'll see you in the morning? Not too early. Maybe ten?"

"Um, sure." Dora stood there maybe a second too long, wondering why Gary was saying goodbye now, lingering in the restaurant. Then the waitress tossed her hair and smiled again, a deliberate smile, focused to a pinpoint, directed squarely at Gary.

"See ya," Dora said, and stumbled out.

Dora had been stumbling around Gary ever since. She was always off-balance with him. Just last week she had been sitting on the counter in the coffee shop (in a blatant violation of health-department policy), swinging her legs and talking to Amy, who at that point was just called "the New Girl." Nobody at the shop bothered to learn a new hire's name until they'd been there three weeks. It was a tradition. You were either the New Girl or the New Guy, and Gary had even (on Dora's suggestion) made name tags with those sobriquets. It was one good way to sort people out; if the New Girl got huffy at wearing a New Girl name tag, you could be sure she wasn't going to work out in the long run. The ones who relinquished their New Girl name tags reluctantly after the three-week period were the ones that turned out to be the most fun to work with.

Amy had been loading the coffee machine, and Dora had been sitting on the opposite counter in part to stop herself from taking over. Amy had to learn, and if learning involved getting up to your elbows in wet grounds because you didn't seat the filter right, well, that was all part of the process.

"So—where are you from?" she asked Amy. Being able to answer customers while fiddling with the machines was a necessary skill. Since the shop was nearly empty, Dora had to step in and provide the distraction.

"I'm from Chicago...." Amy almost had the clip in place.

"Chicago-Chicago, or Chicagoland-Chicago?"

"You got me." Amy didn't sound defensive, like that guy last semester who had claimed New York as his stomping ground and then turned out to have been from the mean streets of Old Lyme, Connecticut. "I'm from Lincolnwood. Lincolnwood cozies up to Chicago, but it's not Chicago. Lots of fancy houses and nice schools. Golf courses. You know the kind of place?"

"I think so."

"How about you?" Amy had finished setting up the machine, and was now looking at it in a puzzled way. Dora jumped down and walked over to flip the switch that would start the coffee brewing. Letting people learn from their mistakes stopped short of actually running out of coffee.

"I'm from Forsyth. Little town in North Carolina?"

"Oh, I went to North Carolina once. Chapel Hill. I was thinking about going to school there. Or, actually, I was thinking about a boy who went to school there. A total *Felicity* moment, but it passed."

Dora smiled at Amy and turned to wipe the counter where she'd been sitting.

"*Felicity* had a lot to answer for. Stalk-friendliness as criterion for college admissions, cruelty to hair . . . Forsyth's a bit farther west, almost in the mountains."

"Is it pretty? The whole time I was thinking about North Carolina, everyone said, 'Oh, it's so *pretty*,' like they didn't have anything else to say about it. It was the state version of 'She has a nice personality.' "

"It is pretty; they weren't lying."

"Do you miss it?"

"I don't miss the place as much as I miss my grandma. I can't get her to come up for a visit; she doesn't like to leave her store."

"What kind of store?"

"She runs a little clothing boutique down there. It used to be a department store—her family ran the town department store for years. They kept it going well into the 1980s, but then my grandpa died. She decided to sell the old building to a condo developer, but kept a ground-floor retail space for her own little shop."

"What kind of boutique is it? My cousin works in one of those four-hundred-dollar-jeans places in Chicago. She always looks like she mugged Mary-Kate Olsen and stole her clothes."

"It's weird, actually. It was a little-old-lady place for a while; Mimi—my grandma—would go up to New York for buying trips, get those coordinated beaded-top-and-skirt things that mothers of the groom always wear, but she hated it. She doesn't like to travel, and she doesn't really like modern clothes—she always says that if Jackie O wouldn't wear it, she wouldn't, either. She was the last woman in Forsyth to stop wearing white gloves in the daytime. So about ten or twelve years ago she turned it into a vintage boutique. She sells a lot of deadstock that she had in their old warehouse, and other stuff she gets from folks she knew from the department-store days—there used to be a lot of old family department stores in the South, and she knew everyone, so when people have stuff to get rid of they come to her—and she buys vintage from estate sales and old customers and pickers who bring her stuff from the eastern part of the state or from Virginia."

Amy had stopped to look at Dora, completely ignoring the guy trying to buy a Coke at the register.

"You're kidding. Your grandma runs a vintage store? Your closet must be to die for!"

"Not really. I'm not that into clothes, actually." Dora looked down at her khaki cargo pants, baggy at the knees, and her scuffed clogs. Her brown T-shirt had a pinhole near the hem. Mimi would be clucking her tongue and shaking her head at everything Dora had on. Not in a mean way, but just to show sympathy, in the same way that she would have clucked at a skinned knee or some junior-high drama. Mimi would feel sorry for Dora, beset by some accident that had resulted in clogs. Dora missed Mimi terribly, right at that moment.

Amy finally took Coke Guy's eighty-five cents. "I can't believe it. If my grandma owned a vintage store, I'd look like Doris Day, every day." Amy was wearing a yellow polo shirt and a pink cotton skirt under her apron, and black ballerina flats. Her hair was held back by a gros-grain headband striped in pink and yellow. Dora realized that if she ever needed someone to stand under a sign that read "Coed" she could grab Amy.

"I don't know.... I love the clothes, I just never end up wearing them, somehow."

Just then Gary came in. Dora felt a moment of panic, the same flush that always came over her. The shop was fine—all the tables clean, the counters wiped, the music not too loud, the bakery case stocked, and the coffee hot. Dora was even sure that her hair was neatly clipped back and her hands were clean. Not that it would help, at all.

"Hey, New Girl—nice headband! Hey, Dora." Gary came around the counter to the back. "Anything up?"

"All set," Amy said, before Dora could get a word out. She felt her face redden slightly, so she turned to the coffee-maker. Too bad there was nothing to do to it.

"Hey, Dora." Gary was at her elbow now, too close. She turned to him. He took an elaborate, cartoony inhale. "I love a woman who smells like coffee and doughnuts."

Dora never knew how to respond when Gary got flirty.

She supposed it was the kind of advice you went to your roommate or sorority sisters for, but Dora didn't have either. Her friends at Lymond were more of the "Hey, can I borrow your class notes?" kind than the heart-to-heart boy-trouble kind. She'd been concentrating so hard on her coursework and on keeping her scholarship that she'd barely had a date. In high school, she'd gone to Mimi with all her boy troubles, but Mimi's answer had always been the same: "If he can't see that you're too good for him, shame on him," usually followed by a rewatch of a Tracy-Hepburn movie. Dora couldn't imagine calling Mimi and saying, "My boss is really flirty, and I wish he'd make a move." So Dora settled for a dull "Hey, Gary."

"Dora, I was wondering, if you have time, could we go through some ordering this afternoon?" He smiled at her, sure of himself.

"Sure." Dora had been planning to work on her grad-school application all afternoon, but doing the ordering with Gary sounded far more appealing.

"At the office, then? Thanks!" He didn't wait for her reply, but gave them both a sketchy wave on his way out.

The rest of the shift with Amy went quickly; she was a fast worker and managed to keep a light chit-chat going. That was a good coffee-shop skill, to manage a conversation with a co-worker that could be interrupted without disintegrating; that could let in a customer who wanted to come in with a remark or a joke.

Dora wasn't working lunch shift that day, but she stayed in the shop, watching Mark and Amy deal with the rush and the crowd, eating her own slice of pizza, and reading a discarded section of the newspaper. Someone had already done the crossword, badly. She kept looking at the clock. Probably wouldn't work to go see Gary before two. At ten to two she was walking across campus to his office.

Gary's door was open, his desk covered with the ordering sheets. Dora realized on the threshold that she hadn't even reapplied her lip balm, but it was too late to back out and do it.

"Dora! You'll know—should we try out that new bakery? They've offered us a discount...."

"Sure, we could give them a shot." Dora sat down across the desk.

"Don't sit there, you'll get a headache if you read upside down. Sit here." Gary gestured to his side of the desk, and Dora moved her chair around, trying not to let it screech on the old linoleum floor.

He smelled of soap and strong coffee, and his arm was warmly companionable next to hers. She grabbed a pencil, peered over his shoulder at the menu.

"Oh, they have Rice Krispie squares; those are sure to do well."

"Sounds good. Hey, how's the new New Girl working out? Amy?"

"She's good—learns fast, nice to work with, takes initiative. She took out the garbage yesterday without being asked; I thought Bea was going to fall to her knees and kiss Amy's feet."

"Glad she's working out. Although she seems a little young to be in grad school."

"She's undergrad. I think she wants to study English literature."

"Oh, man. That means two months until she starts dressing like a French auto mechanic."

"What's wrong with dressing like a French auto mechanic?"

"They hardly ever wear skirts. Much less *short* skirts."

"You know, you should be glad I manage to keep you from saying these things where your employees can actually *hear* you."

Gary grinned and leaned over her to write a "6" next to "Rice Krispie treats" on the order sheet. "I know you have my back, Dora."

"That's pretty much my full job description. 'Have Gary's back.'"

"You're very good at your job," he said. His cell phone started playing a tinny version of a complicated piece of classical music, and he looked at it in disgust before picking it up. "Yeah…" He gave Dora a half-wave.

●　　●　　●

Back in Forsyth, in the cold hospital room, the door opened with a clack and a whoosh, and Gabby came in. Dora started to get up and give her the chair, but Gabby waved her off. "You sit, honey. Hold her hand. I know she'd like that."

Gabby's eyes filled and she turned her head away. "I'm gonna go get us some coffee, okay?" She left without waiting for Dora to answer.

Gabby had been right—it was cold in the hospital—but Dora had left the perfectly matching sweater in Gabby's car. How Mimi would have loved to see Dora looking coordinated, for once. Dora felt further away from being the right kind of person to wear Mimi's clothes than ever.

• • •

If Dora had come right out and asked if she had been a disappointment to Mimi, Mimi would have, of course, said no. Mimi would have said no with great force; Mimi would have been indignant at the thought; she would have reassured Dora with a hug, and praise, and a recital of all of her accomplishments, right down to her delivery of the only line in the kindergarten nativity pageant ("The star!"—added at the last minute because the special effect, such as it was, of a large flashlight shining through the backdrop hadn't worked out as planned), with special attention given to Dora's precocity in learning to read at three and her turn—however unwilling—on the mall's catwalk for the eighth-grade fashion show. But Dora knew differently.

Dora's parents had died when she was a baby—nervous new parents, they'd been taking a feverish infant Dora to the hospital emergency room. A cold January, too cold for Forsyth, a late night, black ice on the road, harried parents rushing to the hospital, and a skid were all that was necessary to send them into the concrete divider. Dora, safe in a car seat, had merely been teething. An hour later she was wailing, loud enough (Dora imagined) to drown out the siren of the ambulance that had arrived too late.

Dora was sure Mimi expected her to be some kind of genius, the universe's recompense for the loss of her only son. Mimi had watched carefully for signs of prodigy-hood, giving her the opportunity to learn Suzuki violin (the teacher had gently dissuaded Mimi after two years of scraping and screeching, and by then, Mimi was willing to listen, or, rather, stop listening) and sending her to math camp every summer until Dora had a stomach-ache for an entire week of it after seventh grade. ("I'm the only girl this year," Dora had explained. "And the teacher never calls on me and all the boys stare at my chest all day and I'm *never going back.*")

Mimi, around ninth grade, had started casually floating careers at Dora, like lantern boats down a river. There was the neurosurgeon Mimi had cultivated, inviting her to dinner and asking bright leading questions about her work; the doctor, tired of being Woman Role Model, started turning down Mimi's invitations after the second interminable dinner of ham and medical-school anecdotes. Undaunted, Mimi moved on to the more accomplished of her circle of friends and acquaintances: every lawyer at church, a professor of English from Forsyth College, two city-council members, and once, painfully, the principal of Dora's high school. Principal Morton, in his early sixties, hale and only slightly deaf (an advantage in a high-school principal, really), had misinterpreted Mimi's interest and brought flowers, chocolates, and an air of romantic hopefulness. When he found Dora there, a miserable realization clouded his face, reinforced by Mimi's questions about where Dora should apply to college, and, in tacit understanding, Dora and Mr. Morton both pretended the evening had never happened.

Mimi's hints, suggestions, and outright demands had never made a dent in Dora's lack of career aspirations; she remained completely uninterested in Deciding What to Do with Her Life.

"I don't understand," Mimi said once, at the beginning of Dora's senior year of high school. They were in the kitchen. Mimi was making a batch of brownies. "You're smart, you're pretty, you could do anything you wanted; why don't you want anything? Even your scatterbrained cousin Lionel wants to be a psychologist."

"Lionel wants to be a *psychiatrist*. The kind that has to go to medical school. And mainly for access to drugs, I bet." Dora had shrugged. "Anyway, I'll know what I want to do when I find it," she answered, stealing a fingerful of batter.

"You won't find anything if you don't look," Mimi said. She poured the batter into the waiting pan, and put the mixing bowl in the sink, running water into it.

"Hey, I was going to lick that!" Dora had protested. It was the closest Mimi had ever come to showing her disappointment.

College had been another sticking point. Dora had halfheartedly applied to State, and to a random college in Pennsylvania that her guidance counselor proclaimed "a good fit," but Mimi chivvied her into applying to Lymond, where, much to everyone's surprise (except Mimi's, of course), she had been offered a merit scholarship. Since she had no other place she'd really rather go, she took it. Lymond was prestigious, if sleepy and safe, and not too far away; better yet, to Mimi's way of thinking, they offered a surprising number of majors for such a small school, including a very broad, highly nonspecific, department-tasting smorgasbord Bachelor of Liberal Arts—what Mimi jokingly called "vagueness studies." Naturally, that's what Dora majored in.

*   *   *

When Gabby came back, two paper cups in her hand, Mimi was sleeping again. Dora took the cup gratefully, then held it without drinking it. Gabby stood next to Dora, drinking hers in silence. Gabby's bright lipstick left a mouthprint around the cup's rim. She unconsciously rotated her cup with each sip, leaving a fresh print and transferring all her lipstick from her mouth to the cup. Dora didn't even taste hers. When Gabby's cup was empty, and Dora's stopped leaking heat into her hand, MARIA RN came back in the room.

"You should let her rest now," she said, in that surprisingly loud voice. Mimi didn't stir.

Gabby put her hand on Dora's shoulder. Dora covered it with her own. MARIA RN started straightening Mimi's already straight sheets, fussing them out of the room. They walked back to the parking lot in silence. When they got to the car, Dora realized that she was still carrying the cold coffee; she carefully poured it out onto the garage floor, where it slicked like some machine effluent, which, she supposed, it was. There wasn't a garbage can, so she held the empty cup all the way home.

When they walked in the door of the miserably dark and empty house, Gabby made a halfhearted offer of dinner, but neither of them was hungry.

Gabby fussed with her earrings before managing to take them off and dump them in the little dish on the hall table, where they promptly tangled with three other dangly pairs.

"I called Maux today and let her know the store will be closed for a while," she said.

"Closed?" Dora was confused for a minute. It was as if Gabby had suggested that they burn the place down, then jump up and down on the ashes. "Close the *store*?"

Her throat closed. She swallowed, hard, and refused to acknowledge the tears building up again.

"Yeah—it's a shame, but with Mimi...Maux's only part-time, and she has her classes to consider, I couldn't ask her to take over." Gabby looked guilty. "I'd do it, of course, but I've got three clients scheduled this week. And I never did get the hang of the store." That was true. Gabby was much in demand as an interior designer, but had never, as she put it, had the "wardrobe knack." Mimi had started turning down Gabby's "help" in the store after she had dressed a mannequin in a leather-fringed denim jacket over a bouclé suit, combined with a head-scarf and 1980s visor sunglasses. "Lord help us if people start wandering the streets of Forsyth dressed that way, with me to blame," Mimi said.

Dora tried to remember if Mimi had ever closed the store before. She certainly hadn't ever done so deliberately. A few years back, the whole block had been closed for two days because of a broken water main, and the police hadn't let anyone through. Dora had never seen Mimi so angry. She'd come back from an unsuccessful attempt at passing the barricades, untouched plate of cop-bribing brownies thrown down on the counter in disgust. "They can't keep me out of my own store! And it's not like I can't swim," she had complained. Gabby had murmured something about possible downed power lines and water to a grim-faced Mimi, then retreated in cowardice to her own room. Mimi had spent hours redialing Duke Power's automated service-information line until Lou from the Hallmark store had finally called and said they'd given everyone the all-clear.

"I'll do it. I'll run the store." Dora sounded more confident than she felt. "Just until Mimi's better."

Gabby let that pass. "Honey, what about school?"

"Gabby, I'm all done except for one independent study—I was planning to graduate early, anyway, so even if I have to take an incomplete it won't really matter." Dora dismissed all of Lymond with a wave of her hand.

"I don't know, sweetie. Mimi would hate for you to miss school...."

"It's not high school, Gabby. There's no truant officer."

Dora managed what she hoped Gabby would think was a brave smile, and not a grimace of fear. "Listen, I can handle this. I run that coffee shop at school, right? I can at least make change and keep the doors open. I think knowing the store is still going would help Mimi—and what am I going to do all day, otherwise?"

"Study," said Gabby firmly. Dora laughed. "You sounded just like Mimi when you said that."

"But what about that grad-school fellowship thingy you told Mimi about? Don't you have to study for that?"

"No, not really—and it's a long shot, anyway. Staying down here and keeping the store open won't affect that either way."

"If you say so." Gabby looked doubtful. "Mimi's spare store keys are still on the hook in the pantry."

"I remember. And I'll call Maux tomorrow, and let her know." Dora glanced at the hall clock. "It's too late now, even for Maux."

"Okay, honey . . . if you're sure."

"I'm sure."

Gabby gave her a quick, tight hug. "Good night, sweetie. I'll wake you when I get up." She looked as if she wanted to say something more, but Dora turned quickly and headed up the stairs.

●　　●　　●

The fabulous closet held several peignoir sets and a couple pairs of really over-the-top, ludicrous baby-doll PJs, but nothing comfortable enough to actually sleep in. Luckily there were still a few of Dora's old Forsyth High T-shirts around. She picked the biggest of them as a nightgown, tossing the blue dress to the floor. She lay down on the bed and stared at the ceiling. She should really hang up the dress, she knew, but, then again, she should also brush her teeth, plug in her laptop and check her email, call some people back at school, let them know she wouldn't be back for a few days more. She should go online and read up on stroke rehabilitation. She should check her cell phone and see if Gary had called. But she couldn't bring herself to do any of those things.

Dora left the blue dress crumpled on the floor and fell asleep.

CHAPTER TWO

GABBY DIDN'T NEED TO WAKE HER UP, after all; Dora woke with a start out of an unpleasant dream that involved missing safety pins and frozen yogurt. She almost put on yesterday's dress, still lying on the floor, but stopped herself. Mimi wouldn't approve. Instead, she grabbed another cotton shirtdress from the closet, red with skinny white stripes. It was a little tight in the waist. She wore it anyway.

Gabby was up and dressed by the time she got downstairs, and remarkably chipper, despite the late night. She wore a pale-blue dress—Dora thought it was silk—with pantyhose and heels.

"Dora, I've got to rush off, but I can give you a ride to the store if you don't mind leaving now. I'll pick you up, too, and we can go to the hospital together tonight. You don't have a parking sticker for downtown anymore, do you? It'll cost you twenty bucks a day to park without it."

"Thanks, Gabby." Dora glanced hopefully at the coffeepot, but it was empty. She grabbed her bag and followed Gabby out the front door.

The slow-driving Gabby of yesterday had disappeared. This Gabby was in a rush. "What's the hurry?" Dora asked, as she grabbed the Jesus handle above the door.

"Oh, I just have a meeting with an old...client today," Gabby said. "I'd really like to have their business again.

Their place is a bit out of date, but it's got good bones. It'd be a lot of fun to redecorate." She sounded oddly cheerful. Dora thought she even heard a giggle, which Gabby never did before noon. She was not a morning person. Maybe the coffeepot had been empty because she had drunk the whole thing. . . .

Gabby dropped her off with a wave and a squeal of tires. Dora shook her head as she unlocked the store.

Opening Mimi's store wasn't as hard as Dora thought it would be. As long as she didn't stop to think, the muscle memory of walking a step behind her grandmother as Mimi went about her morning simply took over. Dora knew where the light switches were, and that the alarm code spelled out ALARMED. The register was so simple Dora thought that perhaps it had been purchased from a Montessori-school catalogue. The credit-card machine was perfectly centered above a five-step instruction sheet taped to the counter.

Opening the store was easy, even with the pounding crying-hangover headache Dora had woken up with. Being in the store without Mimi was hard. How many hours had Dora spent on the stool behind the counter, talking with Mimi or, better yet, listening to Mimi talk? Dora had grown up in the store, listening to Mimi. Mimi had a soft voice and used soft words even when—or especially when—she was angry. She had hardly ever yelled at Dora. "If you want someone to stop listening to you," she told Dora, "go ahead and yell. If you want them to listen to every word, whisper."

Dora loved listening to Mimi, and would have hung on every word even if they'd been raspy and harsh. Dora loved the long weekday afternoons after school, or in summer vacations, when the store was slow and Mimi would narrate her work, like Mr. Rogers or some PBS documentary. When she got to junior high, Dora would have a book open, but mostly just for show. Mimi was better than any book, because Mimi was real, and she knew how the world worked.

When Dora was little, she thought Mimi could explain just about anything. How electricity was made and how it made things go. Where babies came from. What the word Melissa said on the playground meant. Mimi would sit down seriously, giving Dora her full attention. "Well," she'd start, "it's a little like this...." Mimi never over- or under-explained: she always told you everything you wanted to know and not a word more. And if Mimi didn't know something, like why mufflers made a car engine not as noisy, they would stop at the library on the way home and find out, even if it meant they would be late for dinner and have to push back bedtime. "Never put off until tomorrow what you can learn today," Mimi would say.

As Dora got older, Mimi's explanations—and Dora's questions—became less Mr. Science and more psychological. Why was Adam such a jerk? Why didn't Mr. Schneider ever call on her in class? And Mimi talked more about the customers, too. Mimi never thought of her customers as strangers. "You have to know people to know what they want," she'd say. "If you don't know what people want you can't sell it to them. And not what they say they want, what they really want."

Mimi's soft words and explanations were given to her customers, too. "This isn't a thrift store," she told Dora. "We're not selling them something less expensive, we're selling them something more special. We have to tell them the story of what we're showing them. And then we have to show them how they can be the new heroine in the story."

Dora would sit quietly behind the counter, a good little girl, her schoolbook open, and watch Mimi at work. "This dress is a Paris original," she'd say to the woman who'd never left the state. "It was part of a special order that Humphrey's in Richmond put together, way back when. It was a little too forward-thinking for Richmond—such a timeless design, though, don't you think?—but that just means it's here now, for you. Why don't you try it on?" And the customer would try it on and think longingly of Paris, and pityingly of those rubes who hadn't appreciated the dress all those years ago, and—boom!—she was truly sophisticated, a woman of the world, whose clothes came from Paris.

But for another customer, Mimi would talk only about the quality of the fabric. "Good British tweed—those looms aren't even in production anymore. And just look at the handwork on the button holes...." And, standing before the mirror in a good tweed suit, the woman would see someone who knew quality, who bought from Mimi not because she wanted less expensive used clothes, but because she was a person who sought out Old World craftsmanship.

Dora loved to play customer with Mimi. "Sell me something," she'd say. Mimi would pretend to size her up. "Well, you're wearing too much makeup," she'd say, to the delight of twelve-year-old Dora, who wasn't allowed to wear makeup (and was secretly thankful she wasn't allowed to wear makeup, since she wasn't sure how to, anyway). "So you care a lot about your appearance. But your lipstick is too bright, so you're trying too hard. Also, your engagement ring is awful big—I bet your husband is a good deal older. You want something flashy to keep his attention." Then Mimi would "sell" her a sequined wiggle dress, or a lipstick-red suit with a fur collar, or a fuzzy angora sweater with mother-of-pearl buttons. Dora would take whatever it was solemnly up to the counter, and Mimi would pretend to ring her up, all the while putting Dora into the narrative of the garment. "This sweater would be just perfect for a quiet movie-date night at home—thank goodness for videos, aren't they great? And I think angora is so cuddly—don't you?—with maybe narrow black knit pants, and ballet flats, and just a drop of Chanel No. 5." And Dora would laugh because she knew Mimi hated Chanel No. 5—but her made-up customer would adore it.

Mimi could learn from the smallest of cues. A woman came in wearing a black suit, a white blouse, sensible pumps, and no jewelry. No perfume. Twenty minutes later, Mimi sold her an electric-blue bugle-beaded flapper dress. Dora was amazed.

"Oh, honey, it wasn't hard. I saw her look at it the minute she came into the store, she just needed permission to imagine herself in it."

"But do you think she'll ever wear it?"

"It doesn't really matter, as long as she loves it. She'll wear it a hundred times in her imagination before she even tries it on again. As long as she has the option of wearing it, she'll be happy. Though the best thing would be if it got her to come up with some excuse to wear it."

Later that year, Mimi had shown her the paper's society page. It was the black-suit lady, wearing the blue dress. "Roberta Armfield, senior partner at Gordon,

Gordon, and Hicks, at their annual themed holiday dinner-dance."

"What do you want to bet she suggested this year's theme? I've sold a lot of twenties gowns over the last month. I would send her a thank-you note if I didn't think she'd be embarrassed!"

Everything was in order, almost. Three dresses, tagged and priced, waiting to be hung up, were draped over the display case, underneath a huge cartwheel hat dotted with extravagant silk roses. On impulse, and to get it out of the way, Dora jammed it on her own head and went to hang the dresses on the rack. It probably wouldn't help her headache, but she didn't care.

Dora walked around the store, familiarizing herself with the stock. She turned a few hangers so that they all faced the same direction, buttoned undone buttons, and tied a loose ribbon into an inartful bow. The display cases were clean, no fingerprints or dust. The carpet had been vacuumed recently; she could see the broad brushstrokes Mimi's ancient Hoover had left in its wake.

Dora relaxed into the familiar layout of the shop. Being inside the shop was like being inside Mimi's head, everything logical and well thought out. There was a pyramid rack towards the front with dressmaker suits in black, gray, and tweed, a red number placed eye-catchingly in front. The few more fragile twenties and thirties gowns were hung high on the wall, out of reach of the casual shopper. A wishful-thinking-only fur was up there, too; it never really got cold enough to wear them in Forsyth, at least not more than a day or two in the year. Mimi probably had ten more like it in storage.

There was a circular rack of brightly colored fifties

and sixties day dresses, mostly cotton, but a few rayon or nylon, all spotless, belts included. Mimi did the best day dresses. "That's what really gets a workout, so it makes sense to buy the best." Then she'd shake her head. "What we used to wear to the grocery store, these girls wear to parties! I guess it makes a nice change."

Dora's favorite had always been the formals, in their pastel Jordan-almond colors and yards of net and tulle—not that she had ever told Mimi this, for fear Mimi would expand the closet over again by half, just to indulge her. (Dora had even let short, sniffling, hay-fever-prone David Russell take her to the prom, just to be able to wear one seafoam-colored number.) Mimi had a good selection right now, but by late March there'd be slim pickings. Forsyth's prom shoppers knew to come to Mimi's early.

The mannequins were all dressed: half in gowns suitable for the winter formals at Forsyth College, the others in outrageously garish sixties and seventies polyester—cheap stuff for Forsyth College's Halloween blowout. The mannequins were almost all that was left—Mimi used to sell right up until Halloween, but after Dora went to Lymond she gave it up as too much work, and now after the first week of October, Mimi donated two big boxes of costumey stuff to the college Columbus Day rummage and benefit sale and took the tax credit instead. "I certainly don't miss all those last-minute shoppers," she told Dora. Dora agreed, remembering a few Saturdays where she had thought she would die of polyester poisoning. Dora had helped as much as Mimi would let her, but Mimi wouldn't let her work during the week. "Concentrate on your studies," she'd say. "There'll be time enough for working when you're done with school." So Dora had brought her homework to the shop, and done it sitting at the table in the back room, instead.

Dora's head throbbed like a thumb hit with a hammer. Her eyes were scratchy and dry, and her throat hurt. She wished she'd stopped for breakfast, although, knowing Mimi, the little fridge in the back would be filled with blackberry yogurt and string cheese.

Dora had her back to the door, rummaging around in the drawer under the back counter for aspirin, when she heard the bell above the door jangle.

"Mimi!" called a deep voice.

Dora turned, swallowed. "I'm sorry, Mimi's not here. Can I help you?"

The man who had come in was quite a bit taller than Dora, and dressed in well-worn jeans and work boots and an incongruously crisp tattersall dress shirt. He looked as if he could be a college student, but carried himself with the authority of an older man. He had an aluminum clip-board under his arm, and a takeout cup of coffee in each hand. He stopped short and stood staring at Dora.

Dora knew it had to be the hat. "I'm sorry, I'm not sure we have anything in your size...."

The man barked with laughter. "Mimi said that to me once, too. But where is she? We had a date this morning." He smiled, a lopsided grin that Dora didn't want to drive away.

She took a deep breath. "I'm so sorry...Mimi...Mimi had a stroke yesterday. She's at Forsyth Baptist."

He set the coffee cups down on the counter. "Is she going to be okay?"

"I don't know. I hope so."

He looked as if he wanted to ask more, but all he said

was "You must be Dora. Mimi talks so much about you. And you have her eyes."

Dora wasn't sure she knew what to say to that. She took the hat off and put it back on the counter. She straightened the stapler and moved the box of straight pins a little to the left. She felt as if something else needed to be said, but she didn't know exactly what. She settled on a banal "How do you know Mimi?"

"I've been working on a job here for the last six months, total gut-rehab of the penthouse apartment up above us. Mimi came out once to complain about the noise, and we started talking—gossiping, really—about the penthouse people, who are God's own stirrers."

Dora almost laughed, and then she thought of Mimi leaning over the counter, gossiping with this guy, hale and happy, and she couldn't.

"Are you going to drink both of those cups of coffee?" she hinted. "And if so, could I at least watch?"

"Oh, sorry. No, I brought one for Mimi, as a kind of bribe. I hope you like it so sweet the spoon stands up in it."

"I do, actually." Dora took the cup gratefully. "I work in a coffee shop, and they all tease me about my coffee-flavored Yoo-hoo. They all like their coffee as black as their hearts. They think it's sophisticated."

"Well, it is, isn't it?" He lifted the lid from his cup to show her his, oily and black like licorice.

"I believe you're actually drinking motor oil. You should go back and complain."

"What, you think Jim's Jiffy Lube and Coffeetorium could have gotten the spouts confused? Never. Anyway, if

I complain they'll spit in it forever after. At least my motor oil is unadulterated."

That did make Dora laugh, and she choked, having just taken a sip. She sputtered, but fortunately didn't spit the coffee out.

His cell phone rang, and he waggled his head at her for permission to answer it. Dora, still gasping, just nodded.

"Hi, Mrs. Featherston, I'm just on my way in. Yes, we should be able to install the new commode today, it arrived yesterday. Which one? I didn't realize you'd had more than one sent. Yes, we can put them both in place so that you can see which one you like better—I'll upload the pictures this afternoon, and you can tell me which to make permanent tonight...or, yes, tomorrow morning. No, I don't know what the time difference is between Forsyth and the Virgin Islands; but I'm sure I can find out. Great. Talk to you later."

"Mrs. Penthouse Apartment?"

"The one and the same. I'd better get going."

"Thanks for the coffee. You never told me what it was supposed to bribe Mimi to do, though."

"I've been working on a retail project, and she was advising me. I'd like to go see her. Can she have visitors?"

Dora hesitated for a moment.

"I promise, I won't bother her about work, it's just to see her. She's been so helpful to me."

Dora smiled. "I'm going tonight, after I close the shop. How about I put you on the approved-visitors list while I'm there?"

He smiled, and his face looked as if it were most comfortable when set to full grin. "I'd like that."

He was heading for the door, juggling his clipboard and coffee to reach the handle, when he turned back to Dora. "By the way, my name's Con. Conrad, but everyone calls me Con. But not Con man. That's not good for business."

"I'll keep that in mind, Con."

His face turned serious. "And...don't worry. Mimi's tough. And worrying has been scientifically proven to be ineffective. Keep busy, keep your mind off it as much as you can. That's the only thing that helps."

Dora felt as if she might cry again, so she just gave him a tight little nod.

The door jangled again as he went through. Dora hoped he'd be back.

●   ●   ●

It was a slow morning. A few moms wandered through bearing sling-held babies, obviously out just to be out, and none of them likely to buy new clothes until after they "dropped the baby weight." Dora didn't care; maybe they would come back when they got to the point where they'd leave the babies with a sitter and go out to dinner. The phone rang a few times—once someone asking to have some red hats put aside (Mimi sold a lot to the local Red Hat Club) and once someone trying to sell ads in the high-school yearbook. Mimi had always advertised in the yearbook, so Dora said yes.

It wasn't until nearly lunchtime that Dora had her first serious shopper, if serious intent could be measured in the number of dresses tried on. Grim-faced, beautifully dressed, adorned with several shades of diamonds, she shrugged off Dora's diffident offer of assistance and continued her march through the store. At least she was wearing the right shoes, and, as far as Dora could tell, suitable underwear, and she wasn't trying on things that were desperately too small. Dora tried to think of what Mimi would do. "Customers are like children," she had once said. "They need to know you're near, for reassurance, but they hate to be hovered over." Dora left the woman alone and went back to reorganizing the already organized jewelry case.

After half an hour or so, though, she seemed to have decided on a late-1930s day dress, fairly severe in cut, with a high round collar and pockets. It was in really good shape for its age. She came out of the dressing room in it, finally seeking Dora's opinion.

"Does this work?" She gestured at the dress. The thirties cut flattered the woman's slim frame, and its deep-mauve color set off her dark-blond hair and blue eyes. For all its beauty, it gave the woman a somewhat intimidating air.

Dora tried to think of what Mimi would have said. This wasn't a woman who wanted to be reassured, or who needed to be tactfully steered towards something else. "Depends on what you want to do—that dress means business. That's a dress for extracting concessions, I would think," said Dora, truthfully.

The woman laughed. "Excellent. I'm wearing it to my divorce hearing tomorrow."

"Oh, I'm sorry," Dora said, automatically.

"I'm not. It's perfect, and I'll look great and hard-done-by, and that bastard will pay for cheating on me and then freezing our bank accounts and canceling my credit cards. Thank God I remembered this shop; I couldn't think of any other place where I could go to get a new 'screw-you dress' for the cash I had in my pocket."

"Um...I'm glad you found us?" Dora wasn't sure what to say. But the woman just laughed again and turned back to the dressing room.

Dora had rung up the sale and was wrapping the dress carefully in tissue paper when the woman reached out and turned over the tag.

"Aren't you going to check if it has a secret life?"

Dora stopped wrapping.

"A secret what?"

The woman looked impatient. "A secret life. A story behind the dress? If there's a number on the tag, then the dress has a story, and you get the story when you buy it."

Dora pulled out the top drawer of the ancient file cabinet where Mimi kept her files. The last time she had looked in this drawer, there had been decades of utility bills and canceled checks; now there were clean new manila folders. There must have been more than a hundred of them. The folders were marked by number. Double-checking the tag, she flipped through the drawer.

"One fifty-eight, two forty-three, three oh nine...five hundred twelve. Five hundred twelve." Dora pulled out the old-fashioned envelope, closed with a red string. She looked at the woman.

"I don't...Mimi didn't tell me...I just want to make a copy of this, just in case, okay?"

The woman shrugged. She pulled out a gold compact and touched up her lipstick. "Sure, whatever."

Dora untied the envelope and pulled out the sheets. Mimi had a photocopier in the back, an ancient tabletop model just one step removed from using thermal paper. It groaned as she copied the pages, moving slowly. Finally the last page chugged out, and Dora hurried back to the desk, stuffing the pages back in.

The woman looked annoyed. Dora hurriedly finished wrapping her dress and settling it, and the envelope, in the shopping bag.

"Good...good luck with your hearing," Dora ventured.

"Thanks." She smiled wryly. "If I'm lucky I might not be back soon. Much as I love this place for quirky charm, sometimes a girl just needs Neiman's, you know?"

Dora couldn't remember if she'd ever been inside a Neiman Marcus, but she nodded in agreement.

As soon as the door jangled shut, Dora rushed back to grab the pages from the photocopier. Stray toner left dark streaks on her hands.

When he picked me up from the cleaners, I was a little surprised, but not much. I try not to have any expectations. I don't think, I'm going to be worn on Tuesday, and then get all snagged because she wears the gray dress instead, you know? Makes things smoother. Anyway, he was always doing little nice things for her, like bringing her flowers he'd picked himself, or drawing her little doodles, or cutting out funny articles from the newspaper for her.

But there are some expectations you have, whether you have them deliberately or not. Like, if you leave a full closet, you expect to go back to a full closet. Not to be hanging there all by your lonesome, with only a bunch of naked hangers and a single tattered scarf for company.

He called out "Sylvie?" when he brought me back to their apartment. He had nudged the door open with his hip; I was in one hand and a shopping bag was in the other, and there was an awkward loaf of French bread sticking out of the bag that did nothing but get in the way. I thought I heard some bottles clink, too. Maybe wine, maybe that bottled beer she liked. Likes, I mean.

The apartment—it didn't really seem at first glance that anything had changed, but then you saw the holes. The silver-framed picture of her mother wasn't on the mantelpiece, and the little rocking chair wasn't in the corner. I could see into the kitchen and the new toaster was gone, although the old percolator was still there. She didn't drink coffee.

I think he saw those things, or the lack of those things, when I did, or even sooner. He dropped the shopping bag, but he held on to me. He just said "No," in a sort of sighing, resigned way. It was a "no" that never had a chance of being a "yes."

He walked from the parlor through the whole apartment, leaving the shopping bag slumped on its side just inside the open door. I didn't know why he carried me around instead of throwing me over a chair, as she usually did, but he did, even holding me high so I wouldn't drag on the floor.

Her silver candlesticks weren't on the sideboard in the dining room, and her little jars of cream and powder were gone from the bathroom. Her robe wasn't on the hook on the back of the bedroom door. Her suitcase wasn't under the bed, and the drawers of the dresser weren't shut all the way. The book he'd given her for her birthday was still on the nightstand, though. I guess she forgot it, even though she hadn't finished it. The bookmark stuck out, only a few pages in.

He looked in the closet last of all, and then he hung me

up there. I thought he would just shove me into the middle of all the empty hangers, but he hung me all the way to one side, the way she liked to.

I don't know how long I've been hanging here by myself; it's hard to tell the days when the closet isn't opened every morning. He's opened the closet twice, but the room's been dark, both times, and he isn't dressed for work when he does open the closet. I mean, he's wearing street clothes, not pajamas, but they're all rumpled and not very clean, either.

When he would go to meet her at her office he'd be very nicely dressed. "Have to compete with that clotheshorse Phil at your agency," I heard him say to her once, when she told him it was nice to see him in a tie, for a change. It was supposed to be a joke, that bit about Phil, but I don't think he was joking.

Phil really did know about clothes. He once told her that my color brought out her eyes. That was nice to hear. You like to be flattering, you know? She didn't seem to mind hearing that, either.

He didn't say that, about me and her eyes, in the office, though. He said it at the restaurant they were in. I was happy he said that, because when they went in she had said, "Oh, Phil, this place is a bit ritzy, isn't it, and me in an office dress?" and then he had said that thing about my color and her eyes. I've tried, but I can't remember exactly what he said. I remember how he said it, kind of in a low, rumbly voice, not at all the way he talked at the office.

The restaurant was pretty fancy, fancier than any I'd ever been in, with flowers on the tables, and white table-cloths, and waiters with long aprons and funny accents.

*They even had wine with their lunch. It wasn't the kind
of place where she usually had lunch while wearing me.
That's why I was at the cleaners—Phil made her laugh so
much during lunch that her glass wobbled and a couple of
drops hit my skirt.*

*The cleaners got out the spots. She'll be so happy when
she comes back.*

Dora rubbed the toner off her hands absentmindedly.
Where had the secret life come from? Mimi? It was a bit
like the stories she used to tell Dora when she was little,
on quiet afternoons after school in the shop, about the
adventures of the women who had worn Dora's favorite
dresses. Most of those stories had been full of derring-
do, girls flying airplanes in chiffon and foiling spies in
charmeuse, but some had been like this, stories told by
the dresses themselves. Those stories had always been
Dora's favorites.

Why wouldn't Mimi have mentioned them?

Dora wanted to go rummage in the file, pull them
all out and read them, grab the dresses off the rack and
match them up, one by one, but didn't. She felt that would
be cheating, somehow.

Dora stalled, looking at the clock. It was well after one,
but she wasn't hungry. The door jangled, and Dora looked
up, expecting maybe the grim divorcée, but it was Barbara
Ann, from the bookstore down the block.

"Dora! I heard Mimi was sick—I saw the ambulance,
actually, the other day, but I couldn't get down here. Too
many people in my store. Everything okay?" Barbara Ann
didn't stop for Dora to answer. "Glad you're here. You're
a good girl." Barbara Ann had taken Dora's allowance

cheerfully for years, selling her the latest installments of *Babysitting Adventures* or whatever girl-and-horse series had been available. To Barbara Ann, Dora would always be twelve. "That book Mimi ordered came in." She plopped a heavy book on the counter. "That book from the museum. From that Dior exhibit. Whew, that's heavy! Tell Mimi it's on me, a get-well present, and that I hope she feels better soon."

Dora didn't know how to tell Barbara Ann that even a book about Dior wasn't going to help Mimi get better soon. But Barbara Ann didn't seem to want to hang around. She headed towards the door. "Let me know how things go, let me know if you need anything...." On her way out she nearly collided with Maux, who was on her way in.

Maux had her cell phone clamped between her cheek and one shoulder, her other shoulder shoved up to keep the strap of an enormous bag from falling off it. She was juggling a cup of coffee and a brown paper bag of what looked like doughnuts, judging from the grease patterns. It might be past lunchtime for most people, but it was still breakfast time for Maux. She mouthed "Hi!" to Barbara Ann, and lurched towards the counter.

"Holy shit, I knew it!" she crowed. Dora stood still, not sure if Maux's comment was directed at her or the phone. She had forgotten to call Maux.

"No, not you. Dora. At the store. I'll see you tonight, Harvey."

Maux managed to get the coffee cup and doughnuts slopped onto the counter, and dropped her bag on the floor. She ostentatiously turned the phone off and shoved it in her pocket. Her face softened.

"I knew Gabby wouldn't have the cojones to shut this place up, no matter what she said." Maux made a forbidding face, made all the more terrifying by her full face of retro makeup—black eyeliner, artificial beauty mark, and a shade of lipstick that could have been called Death Row Red. "But I didn't expect to see you!"

"I'm sorry—I meant to call you first thing."

"Not a problem. It's damn good to see you! Let me shove this in back," she said, hefting her huge bag back onto her shoulder. "Then you're eating a doughnut. You need to keep up your strength."

Dora just nodded. She always forgot how overwhelmed she felt around Maux—it was like being in a huge crowd, leaving a stadium after a concert or ball game—you just felt carried away on the tide, constrained to go with the greater mass.

Dora and Mimi dated a lot of things from the day they met Maux. "That was about two months after Maux came," they'd say, in the same way they said, "That was the year after the hurricane." It had been late July, weeks after Dora's junior year of high school had ended. Her friends were at the beach or working jobs that required paper hats and left them smelling of French fries. Dora was supposedly spending her vacation helping Mimi in the store, running the steamer and refreshing the moth-proofing, but the day was just too hot. So she was camped at the counter, leafing through an old *Vogue* from Mimi's collection.

Mimi was sitting on the other stool, carefully tightening some loose silver beads on a moon-gray cashmere sweater. Dora didn't know how she could bear to touch

something so warm, even though the shop's air conditioning was on full-blast.

"I'll have to hire someone to help out in the store on
weekends, once you're back to school," Mimi said. She
tied one last knot and snipped the thread with a pair of
gold embroidery scissors.

"That seems like a lot of trouble." Dora flipped the page
to an ad for Vanity Fair underwear. The women looked
like the figureheads on the prows of ships, only with
more false lashes. "You're awfully picky, it'll take forever
to find someone before then. Maybe I should just drop
out," she joked.

Mimi wasn't amused. "It's not too late for me to enroll
you in summer school. Starting tomorrow."

"Okay, okay." Dora pulled out the folder where Mimi
kept job applications. There were only two forms inside.
"You already called both these people?"

"You might as well throw those out. One can't spell,
and one showed up to drop off the application wearing cutoffs." Dora didn't know which Mimi considered
the greater sin.

The bell over the door jangled, and Mimi put the
sweater down behind the counter. She didn't like the
customers to see repairs; she said it made them think too
hard about how old the clothes were.

A woman came in, wearing a black sundress with red
cherries embroidered around the hem—not vintage, but
definitely retro-styled. Her black eyeliner was perfect,
despite the heat, and her long Lucy-red hair was pulled
back in a high ponytail and fell in a long frizzless swoop
to her shoulders, in exactly the way that Dora had always

wanted her own hair to fall, and which no amount of flatironing or blow-drying had ever achieved. Dora stared.

"Good afternoon," Mimi said, and busied herself tidying the hat rack. No one was going to be buying a hat for six months, easy, so it was a good place to stay out of the way. She gave Dora the hairy eyeball until she closed her magazine.

The woman sorted through the rack of sundresses, and pulled out two, a white eyelet that Dora loved, the other a ruffled tangerine halter dress that clashed horribly with her hair.

"Mind if I try these on?" She gestured towards the dressing room.

"Please, go ahead," Mimi answered.

She came out a minute later in the tangerine. It fit as if it were made for her. "Jesus Christ," she said, when she looked in the mirror. "I keep forgetting my hair. It seemed like a good idea at the time, and folks are way less shocked when you swear if you're a redhead. The only downside is that orange looks like hell on me now."

"Try the white," Mimi said.

The white was much better. The straps were too long, but the woman pinched them up herself without any prompting. Dora was always surprised at how many people didn't think of doing that, when it was such an easy alteration to make.

"This is more like," she said. She dropped the straps and spread out the skirt, turning to look at the rear view in the mirror. She ran her hands down the side seams. "And, hey, pockets!" She grinned at Mimi. "Sold!"

She poked around the store a bit more, looking at some of the party dresses and peering into the jewelry case, but when she came to the register she had just the white dress. Dora rang her up.

Mimi came over with the tangerine dress. "It's a shame, this really did fit you so nicely. Want us to hold it for you in case you change your hair color again?"

The woman laughed. "I might just take you up on that. Keeping this color is a lot of work. But I'm not sure when my budget will stretch to another new dress."

"In that case, do you want a job?"

Dora boggled. Mimi sounded serious.

"Here?" The woman sounded as if Mimi were Elvis and had just given her a new Cadillac.

"I don't have any other stores," Mimi said. "It's here or nothing." She wrapped the white dress carefully in tissue paper, and fastened it with the gold "Mimi's" sticker.

"Is part-time okay? I'm a student—I have classes in the daytime."

"Weekends and some evenings are what I need." Mimi put the dress into a shopping bag. "Ten dollars an hour, plus a fifteen-percent commission on any sale over $250. Plus a forty-percent discount on anything in the store, except furs and fine jewelry."

"When can I start?" She stuck her hand out to Mimi. "I'm Maureen—Maux for short. That's M-A-U-X." Mimi shook hands with Maux, solemnly. "It's lovely to meet you, M-A-U-X. I'm Mimi, and this is my granddaughter, Dora." Maux turned and held out her hand to Dora as well. Not knowing what else to do, Dora shook it. "M-A-U-X" was tattooed in script on the inside of her right wrist. Maux's hand was perfectly manicured, with gleaming short red nails, but heavily callused. Dora let it drop.

Mimi elbowed Dora out of the way. "Let's do your

paperwork now, and maybe you can start tomorrow afternoon? What's your schedule like?" Mimi had barely raised an eyebrow when Maux explained she had welding classes on Tuesdays and Thursdays, and Introduction to Refrigeration on Mondays and Wednesdays. "I'm studying HVAC," Maux explained.

After Maux had filled out the forms (in very nice handwriting, Dora had to admit, and without misspelling anything), and left with her new dress, promising to come back the next day, Dora turned to Mimi.

"What?" Mimi said, with a look of mock innocence.

"I can't believe it! Usually you ask for eight references and practically demand a blood test before hiring somebody!"

"I just had a feeling." Mimi hung the tangerine dress on the "hold" rack. "Anyway, I need the help, and Maux looks right, doesn't she?"

Dora looked down at her shorts, scruffy Keds, and washed-out sleeveless polo shirt. She had to admit, Maux would look better in the store than she did. "Even the tattoo?" Mimi was not a fan of tattoos.

"I didn't notice," Mimi said, airily. "I'm sure it's a reasonable one."

Dora didn't say anything. She sat back up on the stool behind the counter and reopened her magazine.

Dora had resolved to be a bit aloof when Maux came in the next day, but it had been impossible. Maux threw herself into everything with such abandon, like a puppy. She was quiet around Mimi at first, but treated Dora as a kind of vintage-clothes savant, asking her question after question.

"I know this has a name, I just don't know what it is,"

she said, pointing to the peplum of a 1940s dress. "I don't know how you know all this stuff," she said, shaking her head, after Dora told her.

Dora shrugged. "I just know, I guess."

"Explain to me again how this works," Maux said, hovering over the sewing machine in the back room, while Dora reinforced the underarm seams of a cotton housedress.

"You thread the machine like this." Dora pulled the thread through the tension discs and threaded the needle. "Then you catch the bobbin thread and start sewing."

"Nah, like, how does the machine part work? Where does the needle go?"

Dora had never considered that. "I don't know the how, I just know the what," she admitted.

"I like the hows, myself, but I can see the attraction of the whats." Maux picked up the next dress in the mending pile. "Don't worry, I'll download a manual or something." She held the dress up. It was deep blue, with a winged collar and an eight-inch gap in its waistline seam. "We should fix this one next. It would look pretty good on you, I bet."

"Don't you start...." Dora backstitched and raised the presser foot.

"Ah." Maux looked thoughtful. "Never mind." She turned to the next dress in the pile. It had a huge triangular tear in the skirt. "Holy sh—I mean, how do you fix this?"

"You can't—we're just saving it for the buttons." Dora handed Maux the scissors. "Here, you can snip 'em off if you like."

Maux hadn't stopped at trying to figure out the sewing machine. She wanted to figure out Dora as well.

"Tell me, kiddo," she said one afternoon a few months later, as they were putting price tags on jewelry, "why are you here? I mean, not existentially, but here in the store. Because I know for a fact that it's Forsyth High's homecoming today."

Dora winced. She tried to pass it off as a jab from a pin, but Maux wasn't deterred.

"Oh," she said. "What's the rat bastard's name?"

"If I tell you there's no him, would you believe me?" Dora put a fish-shaped cloisonné brooch in the tray.

"If you told me it's none of my business, I'd believe you. Not that it would stop me. But you look awful glum for there to be no him." Maux looked at her consideringly. "Wait, is it that there's no particular him, or no him in general?"

"I would like there to be a him," Dora admitted. She shrugged. "I just can't get up the enthusiasm for any specific him." Dora saw Maux's head tilt speculatively, and she interrupted it. "Or any specific her, either, so that's not it. It's just...I feel like, why bother?"

"High-school boys," Maux said, rolling her eyes. "I can see why you might feel that way."

"They're way too noisy and they make really, really stupid jokes," Dora said. "Plus, or maybe minus, I don't seem to...catch their attention." Dora looked at Maux, who was wearing a sexy-secretary dress that would catch the attention of someone in a sensory-deprivation tank. "Maybe I should crank it up a notch? Or a mile?"

Maux punched her in the arm. "Nah. At the risk of sounding like an afterschool special, you should just be you."

Next to Gabby and Maux, Dora sometimes felt like

some forgotten Gabor sister, one who never married any-one and ran a small tax-preparation business, and whose name had more consonants than vowels. Not that they ever tried to make her feel that way; she just did. Dora made a face at Maux.

"That's easy for you to say, because your 'you' is cool. My 'you' is...blah."

"You're not blah, you're just not ready yet." Maux looked over at Mimi, who was deep in conversation with a cus-tomer. "Look, I've heard Mimi give you a hard time about 'your future'"—Maux imitated the way Mimi said the words, like Dora's future was a difficult and risky surgery Dora was going to have to have—"but I'm not worried about it. You're one of those folks who will wake up one morning and just know. And once you know that, all the other crap just falls together. No sense wasting your time trying to pick out accessories before you've found your dress, as Mimi would say." Maux held up a pair of novelty earrings shaped like bananas. "Although, if you wanted to wear these, I sure as hell wouldn't talk you out of it."

"I don't know what we'd do without Maux," Mimi had said in late November of that year, looking around the store. It was the Wednesday evening before Thanksgiv-ing, and Maux and Dora and Mimi had been putting up the Christmas decorations and pulling out the rack of hol-iday dresses (and a few themed sweaters, although Mimi herself would rather wear a polar-bear costume than a holiday sweater). Usually putting up the decorations took them at least five cranky hours, with Dora up on the lad-der and Mimi fluttering around, calling out "Be careful!" at the worst times. Maux had swept in like a commanding general, untangling the lights, hanging the velvet swags, and setting up the aluminum Christmas tree as easily as if it were a folding chair. They had barely made it through the first side of Mimi's favorite Sinatra Christmas album before Maux had brushed her hands off on the seat of her pants, taken a look around, and said, "Hot damn, it's really Christmas!" before wishing them a happy Thanksgiving and heading off on her scooter.

After that, Maux was family. Even Gabby had taken to Maux. "She swears enough to blister paint, but her heart's in the right place." Maux, for her part, was the president of the Gabby Admiration Society. Whenever Gabby came into the store, Maux would hound her for what she called "Ex-Husband Chronicles" (which she would later relay to Dora, who had never been brave enough to ask). "Did you know she cut the cuffs off all of Stuffy Steve's French-cuffed shirts?" Dora, wide-eyed, would shake her head. Maux and Harvey had even come over for dinner a couple of times. Harvey, shy and quiet, had said hardly anything, but his impeccable table manners and the thank-you note he sent afterward went a long way towards improving Mimi's opinion of poets in general.

Dora hadn't realized how much she'd come to rely on Maux until the second week of her classes at Lymond. The first week had been a blur of new classes and new people, but during the second week, homesickness had begun to creep in like fog, and even worse, all the things Dora had assured herself would be better in college—boys, her confidence, herself—had been depressingly, discouragingly the same. She'd been walking across campus and her phone had rung. Dora answered it fumblingly, trying to get it out of her jacket pocket. She almost dropped it, catching it just in time to hear Maux's voice.

"Dora?"

"Maux!" Dora could have cried; as it was, she had a lump in her throat. Maux might have heard it, or maybe she just knew.

"Figured I'd give you a call. Thought you might be deep in the throes of the blue meanies, now that the allure of all the sugar cereal in the cafeteria you can eat has worn off."

"Did you know Cap'n Crunch wears off the roof of your mouth if you eat it for every meal?" Dora tried to joke. "How's Mimi? How's Gabby?"

"Mimi's being very brave, and doing her best not to call you every ten minutes to make sure you're wearing warm enough clothes and to remind you to get enough sleep. Gabby keeps starting to tell stories from her college years, realizing they're inappropriate, and stopping. So, in other words, they're fine."

Dora couldn't catch her breath. She missed them so much.

"Dora? Did I lose you?"

"No, no, I'm here. Sorry, just a sec." She shooed a squirrel off a bench and sat down.

"Anyway, don't worry, I just wanted to tell you that we all miss you, and that I hope you're having fun, and, if you're not having fun, that you're not beating yourself up for not having fun." Dora could hear Maux's earring clicking against the phone. "And before you left I forgot to give you some advice, or, rather, I couldn't fit it in edgewise between Mimi's warnings and Gabby's stories."

"Shoot," Dora said. Mimi's warnings had been concerned with not getting in trouble with boys, and Gabby's stories explained how best to get in trouble with boys (Gabby's delivered out of earshot of Mimi).

"It's easy. Just set yourself a goal of talking to the one person in every room who looks as uncomfortable as you feel, or even more."

"Easy for you," Dora said. "You're like Gabby. You could talk to the president and not feel outmatched."

"Easy for me now," Maux admitted. "Maybe Gabby was born that way, but I had to ease my way into it. Which I mostly did in college, mostly by doing the talk-to-nervous-people trick."

Dora was suspicious. "You wouldn't just be telling me this, would you?"

"Even if I were, what's the harm? But I promise I'm not." Dora heard what could only be the anemic beep of Harvey's car horn. "Dora, gotta go. I'll call you in a few days, or call me anytime.... Love ya."

"Love you, too," said Dora, but she said it to dead air.

Dora hadn't quite managed to follow Maux's advice (she took exception to talking to the most nervous boy in her lab group, since he had a tendency to set things on fire when flustered), but she followed it enough to feel it working. Which she duly reported in calls with Maux, now nearly as frequent as her calls with Mimi, but with many more expletives.

Now, watching Maux emerge from the back room, Dora tried for the thousandth time to imagine her shy. It was like trying to imagine a timid bulldozer. Maux didn't walk anywhere, she strode. It might have been the tee-tering platform heels, but Maux could probably stride in flip-flops. She pushed impatiently at her carefully set sausage curls. "God, I need a haircut," she said. "Here, have a doughnut. Coconut or chocolate?"

"Chocolate," said Dora.

"Good, I got two of those." Maux settled on the high stool behind the counter. She was wearing a navy-blue men's boiler suit carefully tailored at the waist, over a white A-shirt. The sleeves were rolled up past her biceps, and the wide pants legs draped beautifully just to her ankles. She looked like a sexy Halloween-costume version of Rosie the Riveter, which was probably the idea.

"So spill. Gabby just said Mimi was in the hospital. Did she fall? Did she break a hip? I always told her she was going to break a hip."

"She had a stroke."

"Holy shit." Maux launched herself off the stool to hug Dora, shedding doughnut crumbs everywhere, then stood back to look at her.

"Holy shit again. You're wearing your closet." Dora involuntarily spread out the skirt of the shirtdress she was wearing.

"Well, I drove straight down from Lymond and didn't pack anything...."

"You should just burn all your regular clothes, honestly. I knew you could pull this off, you're Mimi's girl, after all. Hell, Dora, you look better than me! I could take you to the rockabilly show in Greensboro next week and you'd show 'em all up. Well, maybe if we gave you a couple temporary tattoos..."

Dora smiled, a bit weakly. Maux paused.

"But—Mimi—stroke? How bad?"

"Bad." Dora gulped a bit. Every time she had to talk about Mimi it felt like she was making it more real. Like if she just stuck her fingers in her ears and went "La la la, I can't hear you," if she refused to say the word "stroke," Mimi would walk into the shop and give her and Maux both a lecture about eating doughnuts at the counter.

"Okay, then. I'll tell you what. I'll skip my classes this week, come in full-time at the store. Then you can be at the hospital all day, and I'll go at night. I can get Harvey to come in, too, if we need him."

Dora thought of Harvey, with his pompadour and leather jacket, working in the store, threatening to declaim his slam poetry to the customers, and almost giggled in spite of herself.

"Maux—thank you, thank you so much—but it's okay. I can do the store. If you could just do your regular shifts, that would be the best. I just can't…"

"I get it. I wasn't thinking. You can't be at the hospital that much, can you?" Maux rummaged in the bag for the coconut doughnut, and gestured at Dora with it. "Dad was that way about Mom, when she had the chemo. Couldn't bear to see her there all tubed up.

"Anyway, you can keep busy here, for sure." Maux looked around. "You changed the jewelry counter, didn't you?" Maux stared into the case for a minute. "It's better like this. Mimi always put those tiaras on the bottom, where nobody could see them." Maux balled up the empty doughnut bag and lobbed it, underhand, into the trash. "Let's keep it going."

Maux worked Dora like a stevedore that afternoon. They pulled down box after box from the far basement shelves. "Mimi kept talking about doing a new inventory, but she kept telling me her insurance didn't cover someone on a ladder in four-inch heels. Like any underwriter pulls that out of his ass. So, if you want busy, we'll do busy."

While they worked, Maux kept up a running conversation, heavy on the monologue. Harvey's latest slam-poetry tournament win. Her HVAC apprenticeship had finally started. ("It's fucking awesome. It's like science, but it actually has some goddamn real-life applications, you know? Air conditioning—now, that's important.") A band called Big Sandy and the Fly-Right Trio, which was the awesomest, in fact, of all awesome things. A new nail polish that was just the right shade of black-red, instead of "red-black. Red-black is easy, you can buy that at Walmart. Black-red, now, that's hard."

They had just taken a break from box-hefting to wait on a customer (total purchase: one black kiss-clasp patent handbag, with a chain strap, twenty-five dollars) when Maux looked Dora full in the face. "Dora, I have been talking for hours, and you haven't said one goddamn word."

"I said I'd like to hear that Big Sandy song," Dora protested. "And I said how nice it was about Harvey's slam thing."

"You haven't said anything real." Maux frowned again. "Spill it. You'll feel better if you talk about what's going on."

"I don't think talking about what's going on—about Mimi, I mean—would make me feel any better," said Dora.

"Just start talking, then. How's school?"

"Almost done. I have one more class, and then I'm graduating early."

"Early? That's impressive. But didn't you want the big spring graduation, hats tossed in the air, and so on?"

"Actually, if I want to, I can walk in that ceremony. Lymond's nothing if not flexible."

"Does graduating early save you tuition—no, wait, you had that scholarship, right? You couldn't find four more classes to take? Might as well get all the learnin' you can." Maux grinned.

"If I have my bachelor's by the end of this calendar year, I could apply for a fellowship to a grad program at Lymond, so I rushed it through. Then I wouldn't have to wait to start grad school, I could start in January."

"Grad school, huh?" Maux looked at Dora. "This is just my opinion, kiddo, but I'd wait on grad school for a bit. No sense rushing into things. I wish I'd waited a bit before starting grad school."

Dora looked puzzled. Maux laughed. "Not HVAC school, dorkus. I was in the Ph.D. program in psychology at State. I lasted for three years, and then had to bail. I think if I'd had some time outside of school I would have known earlier that academia wasn't for me."

"It's just a master's program," Dora protested.

"So you're graduating early just to stay in school an extra year?"

"Sort of." Dora felt herself reddening.

Maux grinned. "What's his name?"

"Whose name?"

"The guy you're trying to find an excuse to stay at Lymond for."

"How do you know there's a guy?" Dora's face was a full-on fire now.

"I didn't until you turned the color of a fire hydrant. But now I do, so details, please."

"His name is Gary. He's my boss at the coffee shop. He's a grad student. And he let me know, fairly kindly, that he doesn't date undergrads. Can't. Department policy, or something."

"Aha! There's the story. So once you're a grad student, too, it's hearts and roses? Sitting in a tree, K-I-S-S-I-N-G?"

"I don't know. Probably not." Dora sighed. "I mean, he's flirty, but he's flirty with everyone."

"Oh. One of those." Maux looked sympathetic. "That's the worst, when they're set at super-flirty. You never know whether it's because he's into you, or whether it's because you have a pulse."

Dora stared at the floor. "My money's on pulse, but..."

Maux gave her a stern look. "Don't sell yourself short, Dora." Her phone trilled. "Dammit, that's Harvey. I told him I'd meet him early tonight. His parents are in town! That's rarer than an eclipse." She looked down at her coveralls, smeared with dust from the boxes they'd shifted. "Shit, I better change. He's all antsy about me meeting them. I keep teasing him about épater the bourgeoisie, and all that, but for some reason he doesn't seem all that excited about my putting on a shock-and-awe campaign."

Dora gestured to the racks. "You know you can take anything you want—Mimi wouldn't mind." Dora had a little stab of pain at speaking for Mimi. She hoped she wouldn't have to do so too much before Mimi came back.

"Thanks." Maux reached out and ruffled her hair. "I brought in a dress special—dammit, I forgot to hang it up when I came in!" Maux stomped off to plug in the steamer. It was almost time to close up anyway; Dora started putting together the night's deposit.

She was trying to reconcile a five-dollar discrepancy in

the store's favor when Maux came back, in a dark-olive wool dress. It was still va-va-voom, but it had a much subtler fit than Dora was used to seeing Maux in—and she'd even toned down her makeup slightly, trading her red lipstick for a deep berry.

Maux turned around in front of the three-way mirror. "So—what do you think? Parental approvable?"

"You look lovely." Dora felt that there was something else to say, and groped for it. "You still look like you, just like a different flavor. You're a really good cover version of you. Same song, different band."

Maux grinned. "Got it." She grabbed her bag off the floor and swooped in to envelop Dora in a perfumed hug. "Hey, I'm sorry I can't go to the hospital with you tonight—I'll go by tomorrow, though. Just hang in there—Mimi's one tough bird." She was out the door before Dora had cleared her throat to reply.

The lights had been off, and the sign turned to CLOSED, for twenty minutes, with no sign of Gabby. Dora paced the sidewalk, feeling foolish for not waiting inside the store, but being inside had been too much. At least outside she could try not to think about Mimi, but inside...inside was like seeing everything through Mimi's eyes. At least it wasn't cold. She shifted the bag with Mimi's heavy Dior book from hand to hand, and dialed Gabby again.

Being late wasn't like Gabby, but not picking up her cell phone was. "Can't keep track of the thing," she always said, and it was true. The list of places where Gabby had left her cell phone was lengthy and varied. The freezer case at the Kroger, in both the ice-cream and the frozen-peas sections. In the hymnal rack at church. ("At least I had the ringtone set to 'Rock of Ages,'" she protested, after

Reverend Horton had returned it her, on Monday.) On top of her car (twice). In the cookie jar at home, on top of a dozen oatmeal-raisin, which nobody then wanted to eat. God only knew where it was ringing (or not ringing— Gabby often accidentally turned off the ringer, too) now.

Dora was staring at her phone's screen, willing it to ring, when suddenly Con was at her elbow.

"Hey, you okay?" He looked concerned.

Dora's eyes were hot, but she had promised herself she wouldn't cry at the store today, and she was going to count the sidewalk as part of the store. Plus, drinking one coffee with a guy did not mean you could break down in front of him.

"Gabby's late."

"That doesn't sound unusual, to be frank." Con grinned down at her. His eyes had a nice crinkle to them when he smiled.

"How do you know Gabby?" asked Dora.

"A better question would be, how could I avoid knowing Gabby?" Con smiled. "She knows all, she sees all. She even told me things about the Featherstons that I didn't know. I bet she knows things about the Featherstons that they don't even know."

"She's . . . naturally curious. Neighborly," Dora offered.

"She's a relentlessly nosy busybody, and I like her a lot," Con answered, and grinned. "She doesn't have a malicious bone in her body. She may not even have a malicious cell in her body."

"I believe she lost those in her divorces. She got the china, and they got the malicious cells," Dora said, and grinned back.

"If I had been married to Gabby she wouldn't have had

any divorces....I offered, you know, but she turned me down."

"You didn't!" Dora actually giggled.

"I did. About twenty minutes after I met her, the first time. She said I was a callow youth, but that she appreciated the sentiment. She batted those eyelashes at me so hard I thought I felt a breeze. So then I told her if she ever changed her mind she should let me know. And that if she wanted to take advantage of the next Sadie Hawkins Day I would take pains to make myself available."

"She must *love* you."

"Well, obviously not, or she would have taken me up on my offer...." Con was standing close enough for Dora to know that he smelled like Ivory soap and, very faintly, of sweat and fresh paint.

"So how was today?" Con asked. His voice was soft. Dora pretended she misunderstood him.

"Good, a couple of sales. Not too bad. I rearranged the jewelry case. Maux and I did some inventory." Dora deliberately avoided looking up at his face. She didn't want to see a concerned look. She wasn't the one in the hospital.

"Not busy enough, I bet, though," Con added. "Busy is the only thing that helps."

"You sound like you know," Dora said, softly. "That was the proverbial voice of experience."

"My dad...had a heart attack last year. About this time."

"Is he..." Dora didn't know how to finish her sentence.

"It was bad. He was in the hospital for two months. He didn't come home."

"Oh." Dora felt herself go cold. "I'm so sorry."

"Thank you," Con said.

"How long did it take you to learn how to say 'thank you' like that?" Dora asked. "Don't you want to just hit people who say they're 'sorry' to you?"

"I did. A lot. Want to, I mean, not hit people." Con looked rueful. "I did hit one guy."

"You did?"

"I went back up to New York, where I had been working, and a guy said it was all for the best because I'd be back in time to get a new project, and if my dad had 'hung on'—that's what he said, 'hung on,' like he was overstaying his welcome—a couple more weeks I wouldn't have been able to get that project. So I punched him. And then I quit."

"You quit?"

"Well, considering it was my boss I punched, it seemed like the right course of action."

"Good point."

"Besides…I was going to quit anyway. The punching just made it simpler. I didn't have to give two weeks' notice. And the security guards carried all my stuff for me."

"Clever, definitely clever."

Con tapped his forehead. "I is *smart*."

"So what were you doing in New York?" Dora asked. "You were a contractor up there, too?"

"No, I was an architect."

"Wow." Dora turned and looked at him consideringly.

"What, I don't look like an architect?" Con tried to look offended.

"Well, you're not wearing glasses, for one thing. I sort of thought all architects wore glasses."

"Contact lenses. Have you heard of them?"

"Ah. So did you turn in your heavy black glasses when you left the office?"

"No, no, I still have them. In case I ever have to draw up any blueprints, instead of just holding them while posing in my hard hat."

"You have a hard hat?" Dora turned to look at him again.

"Sure, it's in my truck. I'll let you wear it sometime, if you're good." Con smiled at her again.

Dora looked at the blank screen of her cell phone again, feeling oddly flustered. "What could be keeping Gabby?" she said.

"She probably ran into someone she knew on the way. It's statistically unlikely that she wouldn't," Con replied. "Why don't I just give you a ride? We can always track Gabby down later, but visiting hours end soon. Anyway, maybe Gabby got confused, and thought she was meeting you at the hospital."

Dora hesitated.

"If you're thinking, 'What would Mimi do?' I'm pretty sure she would say take the ride, and give Gabby a piece of your mind at a more convenient date."

Dora smiled. "She would. Just let me put a note on the door, in case Gabby's lost her cell phone again and doesn't hear my message."

"Here, let me." Con opened his aluminum clipboard with a flourish and produced a large sticky note. It said MURPHY CONSTRUCTION in red letters across the top. He wrote "GABBY—TOOK DORA TO SEE MIMI. CON."

Con looked down at Dora's bag. "Let me carry your books? My truck's right over there."

It said MURPHY FINE CONSTRUCTION on the side of it.

"Is your last name Murphy?" Dora asked. "If I knew your last name, then this wouldn't technically be 'getting into the vehicle of a strange man.'"

"It is Murphy. Although, if it weren't, I'd tell you it was anyway, at this point." Con opened the door for her.

"That's...not exactly reassuring, but I am not going to ask any questions," Dora said as she clambered up into the cab.

"Good call." Con grinned and got in himself. He put Mimi's book on the back shelf seat.

The short drive to the hospital felt awkward. "I should warn you...," Dora started.

"Don't worry. I know. I bet she looks worse than she is, doesn't she?"

"I hope she looks worse than she is," Dora said.

"When my dad was sick...it was like the hospital added twenty years to him. I think it's the lightbulbs, and the food, and having people come in and ask you if you're comfortable when you've just fallen asleep." Con was quiet for a moment.

Con skipped the entrance to the parking garage before Dora could protest. "Look, I'll let you off in front, so you can go in right away, and I'll park and meet you."

"Thank you." Dora hopped out quickly. Now that she was here she found she couldn't wait another minute to see Mimi. She let herself imagine the doctor meeting her at the door to Mimi's room, with the phrases "miraculous recovery" or "tremendous progress." Mimi sitting up in bed, doing the crossword puzzle with Gabby, telling the nurse about a more flattering way to do her hair, or politely flipping through an Avon catalogue. Mimi giving her a hug, exclaiming over the dress.

But the door was closed. There was no doctor, no nurse, no Gabby. Mimi was not sitting up and doing the crossword puzzle. She was lying terribly still, and Dora held her breath for a moment, listening for the beep of the machine. She counted three beeps before she stepped all the way into the room.

Dora pulled the chair closer and reached for Mimi's hand. There was a bandage across the back of it. It made Dora feel indignant, thinking of them poking Mimi with needles, no matter out of what necessity. She sat there, holding Mimi's hand.

"You should talk to her," said Con, appearing in the doorway.

"I know. I just don't know what to say."

"What did you usually talk about?"

"Well, lately, it was how I didn't need to be working in a coffee shop while I'm in school, and, oh, by the way, what did I want to do with my life? How I should wear just a little lipstick, it would brighten my whole face. How Birkenstocks aren't really shoes. You know, the usual." Dora hated how her voice sounded.

"I agree with Mimi. Birkenstocks aren't really shoes, and I always wear lipstick when I need to brighten up my face, which is never, by the way. And if people didn't work in coffee shops, where would I get my coffee?" Con smiled. "There. We've exhausted all those topics of conversation. When... when my dad was in the hospital, we used to sit there and tell old family stories. My brother trying to make soufflés when he was ten—he's a big-deal chef now, so it was fun to tease him about how bad his cooking used to be. What my grandmother did when she found a big old rattlesnake in the garage. That kind of thing."

Dora couldn't help herself. "What did your grand-mother do when she found a rattlesnake in the garage?"

"Well, she was right by the door, and there was a little jar of kerosene there that my grandpa used for his camping lantern, and she just threw it at the snake. The jar broke and doused the whole floor. And she was a pack-a-day smoker, so she grabbed a match and tossed it down, too. Whoosh! No more snake. Then she ran back inside and called the fire department."

"Did she burn down the garage?"

"Nah, there wasn't that much kerosene. I think she just figured that if she set something on fire she'd get a bunch of men there double-quick to take care of the snake cleanup."

"Quick thinking!"

"So what are the Winston family stories? They'll have to be pretty good to top my snake-fighting arsonist grandma."

"Even if they were I wouldn't know them. Mimi didn't want to talk about my folks. 'Let the past stay past' is what she always said."

Con leaned against the wall. "Nothing? Not even a 'Your dad used to do that'? Or 'You have your mother's eyes'—actually, wait, you have Mimi's eyes."

"She never told me anything. Gabby told me once that she had been fighting with my dad when my folks died, and that it tore her right up."

"Mimi, fighting with someone? That doesn't sound like her."

"I guess my dad didn't want to take over running the department store, and they were arguing about it. And then I was born, and that made it worse—Mimi thought my dad needed a real job, now that he had a baby. And so they weren't speaking."

"Poor Mimi. What a thing to carry around."

"I never could get any more details out of Gabby—she says Mimi never talks to her about my dad." Dora leaned over the bed and brushed Mimi's hair back, away from her forehead. "She'd hate it if she knew I was telling you all this."

"I don't know about that. We talked a lot, me and Mimi."

"Really?" Dora tried not to sound surprised.

"Well, I hide in her shop sometimes, to get away from Mrs. Featherston, and we just get to talking. And I've been working on this new project—I want to convert one of those Victorians down by the university into a storefront, and she was giving me advice on what a store owner would like. She was very easy to talk to. And she didn't know my folks, which made it easier, somehow. Especially when my dad was sick."

"Everybody always knows your business in Forsyth." Dora grimaced. "Whether you want them to or not."

"But Mimi didn't make any suggestions, you know? She didn't tell me how to feel, or what to do, or about somebody's friend's cousin's father who had the same thing and was now playing golf twice a week." Con looked grim. "I hope no one is saying that kind of stuff to you."

"Not yet." Dora held Mimi's hand a bit tighter.

A nurse stuck her head in the door. "Miz Winston?"

For a minute Dora thought the nurse was talking to Mimi, but then she beckoned to Dora to come into the hall.

"It's okay," Con said. "I'll stay here until you get back."

It was Dr. Czerny again, waiting in the hall. She looked tired, or maybe it was just the unforgiving overhead light.

"Dora." Dora knew from the doctor's flat affect that things weren't good. "Mrs. Winston—your grandmother— is becoming less responsive."

"That's not good." Dora couldn't make it sound like a question.

"It's certainly not optimal, but it's not in itself a bad sign." Dr. Czerny did not look as if she was convincing herself, much less Dora. "The problem is that some of the drugs that will help relieve the bleeding in your grand- mother's brain could put some stress on her heart. So we have to keep them carefully balanced."

"I understand." Dora couldn't look at Dr. Czerny too carefully; she didn't want to see any lingering doubt that might be in her face, or any sign that things were more serious than what she was saying.

"Did your grandmother have any kind of health-care directives?"

"Like a living will?" Dora could see the carefully labeled file in Mimi's desk, floating up in her mind's eye unbidden. "She has one of those."

"If you could bring anything like that with you tomor- row, that would be really helpful. We like to be as respect- ful as possible of patients' wishes. We called her internist, but his answering service said he was out of town."

"No problem. Will do." Dora didn't trust herself to speak in longer sentences. If they wanted Mimi's living will, then things were seriously not optimal.

Con was holding Mimi's hand when she went back into the room, and talking in a low voice. He seemed to be tell- ing Mimi about Mrs. Featherston. "And she was wearing a leopard-print jeans jacket! It might have even been real fur. I mean, not real leopard, I hope not real leopard, but something definitely furry. I remembered it particularly to tell to you."

Con looked up and saw her face. "I'll go get the truck," he said. He turned back towards Mimi. "I'll see you soon, Mimi."

Dora walked over and kissed Mimi on the cheek. She couldn't bring herself to say anything.

When she got back out to the front, Con was waiting. Dora hauled open the door of the pickup and hoisted herself in.

"Bad news?"

Dora only nodded.

"I know this will sound weird, but—do you want to go to the movies? I mean, now?"

"Now?" Dora looked at her watch. It was eight-thirty. It felt like midnight.

"I thought you might want a little distraction. I saw a lot of movies—especially old movies—when he was sick. Just enough distraction to keep me from dwelling, not enough distraction to make me feel guilty for enjoying myself."

"I should take advantage of your hard-won experience." Dora's voice had a little quaver in it. "Okay, let's go to the movies."

"Great. Next decision: take our chances with the nine p.m. show at the Brew & View, or multiplex at the mall?"

"Let's take a chance on the Brew ..."

Con just nodded. Dora looked out the window at nothing.

They were quiet all the way to the Brew & View, and

Dora was grateful. Dora fumbled for her wallet at the ticket booth, but Con beat her to it. The movie was *The Princess Bride*.

"Okay by you?" Con asked, as they were finding their seats.

"Perfect by me. It's my favorite movie." Dora felt like she was going to cry again. "I've never seen it on a big screen, I don't think."

"See? The universe wants you to feel better. And eat popcorn." He waved over a waitress. "Popcorn, and a beer. Two beers?" Dora shook her head. "One beer. And a…"

"Diet Coke," Dora said in a small voice.

"And a Diet Coke for the lady. You want anything else? Wings? Jalapeño poppers? Goobers? Good & Plentys?"

Dora shook her head. "That's all, then," Con said to the waitress.

When the waitress had gone, Dora turned to Con. "Nobody eats Good & Plentys," she said.

"Shhhhh," Con hissed. "The movie's starting. I have a strict no-talking-in-movies policy."

Dora nodded. The screen wasn't very big, but it was bigger than her television set. And the Brew & View had a real movie projector, and ran real film, not DVDs. Not that Dora would have probably known the difference, but she could hear the faint and comforting whirring noise of the projector in the background. Sitting in the dark, Dora tried to keep her attention on the movie, but her thoughts kept going back to the hospital room, and Mimi. She wished she had her own Miracle Max to give her a little miracle.

When it was time to storm the castle, Con leaned over. "This is my favorite part," he said.

"Shhhhh," said Dora, grabbing more popcorn. "No talking in movies."

They stayed through the end credits and then trailed the tail end of the crowd out onto the sidewalk. Dora felt exhausted. Con opened the door of the truck for her, and gave her a hand up to the high seat.

"I think I kept you out too late," Con said.

"No, no—thank you, it was really nice. Thank you for taking me to see Mimi, and the movie, and the popcorn, and everything."

Con seemed to know the way back to Mimi's house without being told. "It was my pleasure. Lots of people did stuff like this for me when my dad was sick, and I needed distractions. And I'm happy to do anything I can for Mimi."

Gabby's car was in the driveway. "That's one mystery solved. I bet she went home for a quick nap and is still asleep." Dora sighed. "And look, there's her cell phone on the dashboard."

"Well, I'm glad she's okay, but I'm not sorry she flaked." Con smiled again. He had a particularly disarming smile, Dora thought.

"Well, thank you, again," Dora said, helplessly. Con smiled down at her. "Good night."

"Good night. Get some rest, if you can."

Gabby met Dora at the door, and smothered her in a hug.

"Oh, honey, I hope you got my message."

"Message?"

"I called and let you know I couldn't come get you tonight?" The pockets of Gabby's coral velour bathrobe were stuffed with tissues, and her eyes were red. Something looked off.

"Oh, Gabby, you're missing an earring." Dora braced herself for a desperate search—Gabby was obsessive about her jewelry.

"Oh, honey, that's not important now. Besides, I bet it's just in the car, I probably took it off when I called you."

Dora looked at the remaining one, a lentil-sized diamond surrounded by tiny sapphires. "I hope you find it—it's so pretty. I've never seen those before."

"Oh, they were a present from Jerry when we were married—I don't wear them often, they're too valuable. I don't know why I didn't sell them years ago." Gabby looked vague for a minute.

Dora wanted to ask about the mysterious Jerry, but she felt too tired. It was an effort just to take a deep breath.

"Did you call my cell? Or the store?"

"The store, I think. A little after closing, but I just figured you were in the back."

"I went outside to wait, and missed it."

Gabby looked confused.

"Don't worry—Con Murphy gave me a ride to the hospital, and then we went to the movies."

"Oh, that's fine, then." Gabby looked relieved. "I like that Con Murphy. Just like him to think of the movies." Gabby gave Dora a long hug. "You're so grown up now, Dora." Gabby sighed. "You look just about worn through. Why don't you take yourself up to bed?"

Dora didn't argue. She made her way upstairs, touching each baluster of the banister for good luck, the way she used to do when she was a little girl. She was halfway up the stairs when Gabby called out to her. But when she turned, Gabby just said, "Sleep well, honey."

Upstairs in her room she saw yesterday's blue dress

still crumpled on the floor. Dora winced. Mimi hated to see clothes treated poorly.

"I can't help but think of all the dresses I'd have in the store if people had only taken better care of their things," she said. She especially hated it when some well-meaning person at a party told her that they used to have some gorgeous piece of clothing—a mouton coat, or an Italian knit suit—and that the moths had gotten it, or that someone had put it in the basement and it had gotten mildewed. "It's like they're saying, 'Nyah-nyah, you can't have it,'" Mimi would grumble. "It's just plain rude, that's what it is."

Dora reached to pick the dress up. She'd hang it up overnight, and run a load of laundry in the morning.

As she picked up the dress, a thin slip of folded paper fell out of the pocket. It looked like airmail paper. Dora unfolded it carefully.

Some dresses are only ever worn by one person, and so that's the kind of person they like. It makes sense. If you only ever get one choice, you're happier if you make yourself believe that you would have chosen that one person anyway, even given all the people in the world to pick from.

But I've been worn by lots of people: three sisters, two friends of sisters, and one friend of a friend of a sister, plus once by someone whose name I never knew, but my point is I know a bit more about what I like and what I don't like.

I like someone who laughs, but not all the time, and not too loud. I like it when someone laughs at the world, and not at someone in particular—when some particularly absurd thing happens, not just someone falling down.

And a person should stop every once in a while, for no

reason, just stop to be still for a moment. Moments of stillness are underrated, I think. They don't have to be silent moments, just still ones. A chance to let yourself imagine you can feel the earth spinning. (I didn't make that up; Edna, the oldest sister, did. She wore me first, so perhaps I am a little biased toward people like Edna. Although she did snore.)

Singing when no one else is around is always good. I especially like belters. Good, loud singing is probably better medicine than half the stuff they sell in pill bottles, and it's cheaper, too. I also think people should never turn down an opportunity to hold a baby. There's something about the feel of a new baby in your arms that just fixes you.

I don't like meanness, especially of the mealy mouthed "Well, I wouldn't say this, but I hear..." variety. And I don't like people who eat powdered doughnuts. I don't care how careful you are, they're just plain messy. I can't believe they taste good enough to justify getting that sugar all over everything, especially me.

But when you come right down to it, I'm just like everyone else, in that I like someone who likes me. The someone whose name I never knew, the one who wore me once? Said I was the prettiest dress she ever wore. The minute she said that I wanted her to keep me forever. I wish she had.

Dora read the story over three times. It didn't seem quite finished. Maybe Mimi only wrote whole stories for the dresses in the store? Dora held on to it for a moment more, then put it carefully on top of the dresser, weighted down with a crystal perfume atomizer.

Right before Dora drifted off to sleep, she remembered the Dior book. She'd left it in the truck. She'd just have to track down Con tomorrow.

CHAPTER THREE

SUNDAY MORNING, DORA WAS AT LOOSE ends. She had woken impossibly early, and lain in bed for a good half-hour willing herself back to sleep. When that failed, she crept downstairs and made coffee, waiting impatiently for the Sunday paper to arrive. When it did, she couldn't bring herself to do more than skim the headlines. Even the comics couldn't hold her attention, and she made it all of one line into the advice column ("My husband has gained fifty pounds since we married") before throwing it down.

Dora stared into the refrigerator; there were eggs, and plenty of bacon, but making a real breakfast seemed like an impossible challenge, something worthy of *Iron Chef*. She mixed the dregs of the box of raisin bran with Mimi's shredded wheat and ate a bowlful without tasting it.

Dora considered going to church. Mimi would have liked her to go, but Dora couldn't brave all that well-meaning sympathy alone. Gabby showed no signs of stirring, and anyway, Gabby's church attendance was erratic, at best, aside from her own weddings.

So Dora wandered through the house, tidying things. She did a load of laundry, carefully hanging up the dresses and slips to dry. There was a load in the dryer, Mimi's things. She folded them and took them upstairs, but stopped when she came to Mimi's door. She took a deep breath and went in.

She put the laundry on the bed and looked around. The room looked ready for Mimi to come back. Dora had almost been expecting a thin layer of dust over everything; it felt like Mimi had been away forever. There was a stack of stamped envelopes on Mimi's desk—bills, they looked like, and Dora went to go pick them up. Mimi would hate it if she got some kind of late fee. She could imagine Mimi complaining about it: "I explained to them that having a stroke usually means you're unable to get to a mailbox, but they were just so *unreasonable.* I told them I'd close my account, though, and they took off the charge."

Mimi's desk was so tidy. Her personal checkbook in its leather case; a notepad; a file folder labeled "October," those bills, and a roll of stamps—nothing else. The folder reminded Dora of her promise to Dr. Czerny, and she opened the file drawer. There it was, as she remembered it. A folder marked "Living Will—Health Care Proxy."

Dora took it out and put it on top of the desk. The next folder, its tab now revealed, read "Funeral." Dora slammed the drawer shut.

Dora left the folder on top of the desk. She would take it to the hospital that afternoon. She closed Mimi's door behind her, and went to take a shower. Dora only let herself cry for a little while, under the too-hot water in the shower. She didn't want to use it all up before Gabby got up.

Getting dressed, she hesitated. She'd washed the clothes she'd worn when she arrived—but her old pants and T-shirt looked so strange to her now, like they were intended for a twelve-year-old boy. She went back to the closet, and found what Mimi called a "housedress," hanging ignored and out of place at the end of a rack of brocaded and beaded cocktail gowns. The steel-blue color had faded a bit at the shoulders, something Dora wouldn't even have noticed last week. Dora pulled it from the hanger and put it on; now it felt as if she'd always been wearing these dresses.

Putting her lip balm in the pocket out of habit, her hand met something else—a thick fold of paper, several sheets. Another secret life.

It started out as a hard day. The pilot light had gone out, and she had to relight it while holding her youngest, who was crying. The two older ones were howling over some toy they both wanted. The laundry had to be done, and it was the day when she usually washed the floors, too. And they were out of milk. She'd forgotten to put the bottles out the night before.

Finally she got the pilot lit, and the boy, after catching her eye, had decided it was in his best interest to be magnanimous in the matter of the toy. The baby condescended to be put down and ran on his fat legs after his sister. She turned to the sink to scrape and stack the dishes while waiting for the boiler to heat up. There was a nasty, sour smell in the drain.

She opened the window a crack to let in some fresh air, but instead of the icy draft I expected, there was that cool, delicious smell of wet earth and new green things—the smell of spring. She stopped filling the dishpan and hung the dishrag over the spout.

"Danny!" she called up the stairs. "Come down here, please." She was using her no-nonsense voice. He made it

down in double time. (He might have slid down the banister; I'm not sure.)

"Honey, go down to the cellar and find me the oilcloth, will you? The red-and-white one? Do you know it?" He nodded, perplexed, but he didn't ask any questions.

She turned to the icebox and pulled out the bread and butter, the jam, the leftover slices of the roast, and some cheese. There was an apple and a slightly squishy pear; she pulled those out as well. She cocked an ear. The girl was playing house with her little brother, who was playing the daddy. She was telling him not to worry. The icebox door closed with a slam, drowning out what the little girl said next.

She reached up behind the flour canister and pulled out a small bag of peppermints, which she must have kept back from Christmas.

The boy came back with the cloth. "Thank you, sweetie. Put it in the basket in the hall, will you? And then go put on a warm sweater. Tell your sister to do the same, and dress the baby. Not in nice clothes, in his blue overalls. And then you all should put on your rubber boots." Wide-eyed, he ran off with the bundle. She called after him: "Wear your warm socks, all of you!"

Quickly, working with the ease of long practice, she made bread and jam, and roast-beef-and-cheese sandwiches. She wrapped them in waxed paper. She cut up the apple and pear and wrapped the slices in a scrap of clean cheesecloth. She put the peppermints in her pocket.

She looked in the scrap of mirror on the inside of the pantry door. She pushed at her hair. "Oh well, can't be helped." She took her sweater from the hook and put it on.

The children were in the hall, hopping from foot to foot,

trying to pull on their boots. The baby was banging his on the floor. She put the sandwiches and fruit in the basket, under the oilcloth, then put the baby's boots on. He stood up and started clumping up and down the hall. She put her rubber boots on, too.

She darted back into the kitchen and grabbed two clean dishcloths and an empty milk bottle. They went into the basket, too.

The boy knew something was going on. "Mama?"

She smiled at him, and bent down to kiss the top of his head. She swept up the basket, and took the girl's hand. The boy automatically took his brother's hand.

"It's the first day of spring! We're going on a picnic."

"A picnic!" The children hopped up and down. "A picnic!"

"Yes. And we're going to stomp in every single puddle on the way to the park."

"Puddles!" Their eyes were wide. They'd never been told to stomp in puddles—just the opposite.

"And we're going to pick crocuses, if we can find any, and the first one of you to see a robin will get a peppermint!"

"Pepmint!" The baby crowed approvingly.

And that's exactly what they did. She stomped along with them, laughing until she held her sides like they hurt. They stopped by the dairy, mud-splashed to their elbows, and the woman there laughed so hard that she cried, and then gave them raisin buns to go with their bottle of milk.

They stayed at the park, splashing through puddles until they had nearly exhausted the available store, then ate their buns and sandwiches and drank their milk. She and the baby were the only ones who sat on the oilcloth—the boy and the girl only alighted for brief moments to eat, like hummingbirds. The children picked their crocuses (three, one each, which wilted immediately in their grubby hands) and then spotted robins for peppermints until nearly dark.

The girl was almost asleep on her feet as they stumbled home, and her brother was not much better. The mother carried the baby. Then it was hot baths all around (the pilot light having stayed lit, by some miracle), and bedtime. She tucked the boy and girl in their beds, already half asleep, and went to put the baby in his crib. When he was safely settled, she went back to distribute good-night kisses. The girl was already asleep, her damp hair curling around her face. She kissed the girl's plump soft cheek. The boy stirred, eyes fluttering, as she kissed his forehead.

"Love you, Mama," he said. "Thank you for the puddles." She stood by their beds for a moment. Then she went and did the dishes and set out the bottles for the milkman. I was put in with the rest of the laundry to soak. All the mud came out.

Dora looked at the paper—it was old notepaper of her own, with little unicorns in the margins; she hadn't had that paper since eighth grade. The paper seemed faded, and the handwriting, though definitely Mimi's, was stronger, firmer, somehow. Mimi had been writing secret lives for that long?

Dora imagined asking Mimi about the secret lives. "When did you start writing them? Where did they come from? When did you start giving them away?" She could imagine Mimi brushing her questions away, hand in the air, as if waving away a persistent fly. "Don't worry about them, Dora," she'd say. "It's just something I'm trying for the store. Tell me what classes you've picked for next semester," which would be Mimi's way of inquiring by proxy about what Dora wanted to do with her life. Which of course would be Dora's cue to find a way out of the conversation as quickly as possible, even if that meant her questions never got answered.

"Dora?" Gabby stuck her head in the door. "Everything okay?"

Dora stood up. She couldn't ask Mimi right now, but she could sure ask Gabby. "Hey, Gabby, what do you know about these 'secret lives' that come with the dresses?"

Gabby looked guilty for a minute. "I told Mimi she should tell you about them, that you'd be interested. But she never wants to tell you anything she thinks might take your attention away from school, you know that."

"When did she start writing them?"

"Oh Lord, ages and ages ago. I don't know when, exactly. She used to keep them all in the top of her closet, sometimes with a Polaroid of the dress she said 'told' her the story. Then, a while back, she said she thought the stories belonged with the dresses, so they all went to the store to be given away."

"Do you know why she started writing them?"

"Honey, why does Mimi do anything? She gets an idea in her head and runs with it." Gabby looked at her watch. "I've got to go out and run a few errands now, but why don't I come back and pick you up around one, and we can see Mimi together? They told me early afternoon's a real good time for her, not too much fussing around then. We can have a good long visit."

"Sure." Gabby headed down the stairs before Dora could ask her what errands she had to run in Forsyth on a Sunday, when all that was open were the thirty-five churches and the Harris Teeter grocery store. She felt another little prick of worry about Gabby. There was something going on with her, Dora was sure of it.

The house seemed even emptier with Gabby gone, and it was too early in the morning to call Maux and hear what happened with Harvey's parents. Dora opened her laptop; email would keep her company.

Hidden among the spam and the mailing lists were five new messages, all from Gary.

EMERGENCY was the first subject line. She clicked on it.

We are out of honey can't find it natives restless if less sticky than usual and blood sugar dropping. Call soon, ok? G. PS everything okay?

EMERGENCY AVERTED was the next subject line.

Amy found honey. Stop. Also found ants. Stop. Not a coincidence. Stop. What's the number for the exterminator? G.

MORE ABOUT ANTS. Dora clicked.

Ants are very interesting creatures, but not in a coffee shop. We miss you. Everyone sends good wishes. Especially Amy who is creeped out by ants and would like the exterminator's number asap. G.

CANDY.

We are out of Snickers. (I mean, the candy. The laugh-type snickers are out in force, accompanied by pointing. Possibly due to the ants.) How much should we order? I can't find the last order sheet. How did I not realize everything would fall apart instantly without you? G.

PLUS SNAPPLE.

Diet Raspberry. We have none. What to do? G.

PS do you ever pick up your phone?

Dora looked for her cell phone, which she'd never plugged in the night before. It was out of juice. She hit "reply."

Dear Gary,

—The exterminator number is in the green folder in the back room, on the table under the window. Call first thing on Monday and ask for an appointment the same day. In the meantime there's a box of boric acid by the sink, you can sprinkle it where you see the ants.

—Snickers—I think there's still a box, but it's in the metal cabinet to keep them away from the mice. If we don't have a box, the standing candy order is on a sheet in the red folder. Fax it to the number on the front of the folder. Delivery is next-day if you fax before 10 a.m.

—The Snapple guy comes on Mondays, tell the Diet Raspberry people to be patient. Or drink Diet Peach. We should have plenty of that. (It's gross, though.)

Talk soon. D.

Dora snapped the laptop shut. She felt antsy herself. She flipped through the TV channels idly, but there was nothing that held her attention. She turned off the set and tossed the remote to the other end of the couch. What would Mimi have done, if Mimi were the one trying to kill time before going to the hospital? She'd make cookies, Dora realized, to take in to the nurses. She would have taken them to the nurses' station, on a paper plate ("Don't want to make work for anyone, washing and returning and all that"), but a nice one, a fancy one. Mimi would have winked at the nurse and made some crack about diabetes or something. Dora didn't think she could pull that part off, but making cookies she could manage.

She'd just gotten out the chocolate chips when the doorbell rang. Dora's first instinct was to hide. She felt singularly unable to cope with random neighbor sympathy. "Coward," she told herself, and opened the door, bracing herself.

But it was Con. He was holding the forgotten book and a bunch of hardy mums. Dora looked at them blankly. Had Con brought her flowers?

"You forgot your book, so I thought I'd bring it by. And my mother wanted me to take Mimi some flowers, so I've brought them to you," he said, stepping into the hall. "I thought maybe you could take them over to Mimi later. They're from her garden," he added.

"They're beautiful." Dora took them from him. "I'll find a vase. I'm sure they'll look lovely..." She didn't want to say "in the hospital," but Con didn't seem to be bothered that she hadn't ended the sentence.

Con looked around. "It seems awful quiet around here. Where's Gabby?"

"She had to run out." Dora blushed, and looked away. She hurried over her words. "It was really nice of you to bring that book by."

"Not a problem." Con didn't seem to be in a hurry to leave. Dora decided to channel Mimi again. Nobody who came to the door within two hours of a mealtime should go away without having been offered food, was Mimi's philosophy.

"How hungry are you? We've got nothing but food— people have been bringing so much over, Gabby and I can't eat it all. I haven't had lunch yet, and thought maybe I'd heat up some ham, and I could make a batch of biscuits...."

"Ham and biscuits? A good Sunday lunch. Too bad I didn't go to church this morning to deserve it."

"Well, me, either."

"Good, we can be heathens together."

Con pushed the newspaper to one side and sat at the kitchen table while Dora fussed with the flowers. He sat at the head of the table, as if he'd always sat there.

"You want something to drink? Iced tea okay?" Dora asked. Con kept looking at her in a way she couldn't put her finger on, but it was disconcerting.

"Iced tea would be excellent." Dora dropped two ice cubes before she managed to get any in his glass.

Now she had to make biscuits. Getting out the the mixing bowl from the pantry, she saw Mimi's ruffly apron hanging from the hook. Dora looked down at her dress. It needed an apron.

Aprons were harder than they looked; her fumbling fingers had trouble tying the strings. Con got up. "Hey, let me. You're trying to do something one-handed and behind your own back."

"I'm pretty sure I was using two hands."

"I won't tell anyone." He pulled the strings tight, but not too tight. Dora could feel Con's breath on her neck. She turned quickly to grab the flour. "Thanks."

Con settled into his chair again as if Dora hadn't just flinched away from him. He was smiling.

Dora reached for something to say. "Mimi loves biscuits" is what she came up with. When Dora had lived at home, it had been her chore to make biscuits for dinner, two or three times a week.

"She told me yours were the best." Con smiled. "I can't wait to taste them."

"Wait, didn't you say that your brother is a chef? I'm never going to live up to Mimi's hype."

"My brother is a fancy chef. His biscuits are either flecked with seaweed, or the size of marbles and suspended on codfish foam. I think your biscuit rep is safe."

"Well, we'll see." Dora bent over and put them in the oven.

Con laughed.

"What?"

"It's just you, in that dress, and an apron, making biscuits. It's like I stumbled into the 1950s."

Dora stood up straight, suddenly self-conscious. "You know, I don't really dress like this. Not back at school. I just didn't bring any clothes with me, and Mimi had... has... this closet for me...."

"You ought to dress like that every day. Forever." Con looked taken aback at his own vehemence. "I mean, it looks really good on you. Not like a costume. More like... you. And—did that sound skeevy? Because I wasn't trying for skeevy, I was trying for reassuring."

"It's okay. You hit reassuring." Dora smiled. "I just don't feel like the me you think this makes me look like."

"Well, you ought to. Those dresses make you look like you know what the hell you're doing, and I think you do."

"Well, if you and the dresses think that, I'll just ignore my screaming inner panic."

"You do that," Con said. "Just hit the 'mute' button on your inner-panic remote."

"Got it." Dora sighed. "The worst part about dressing like this is that Mimi's wanted me to wear these dresses for years, and I feel terrible that she isn't even seeing me in them."

"For what it's worth, Mimi talked about you *all* the time, and never mentioned your clothes."

"That's because she hated my clothes, I think. I mean the ones I actually wore, not the ones she put aside for me."

Con shook his head. "It's her own fault. I bet if she had ignored what you wore, you would have been dressing like that since 2005."

Dora laughed. "Probably. When I was very little I used to play dress-up in her clothes all the time. Once I put my foot through a 1930s chiffon gown, and Mimi never said a word. But when I hit junior high and Mimi started dropping hints...I balked."

"Has any junior-high kid responded well to hints? And I bet if Mimi had shown an utter lack of interest in your eventual vocation you'd be the president by now."

Con put his elbows on the table and rested his chin in his hands. He looked directly at Dora. "What do you want to do? I mean, grad school, sure, but grad school for what? And I promise Mimi didn't put me up to this; I'm just curious."

"You know, 'I don't want to sell anything bought or processed, or buy anything sold or processed, or process anything sold, bought, or processed, or repair anything sold, bought, or processed. You know, as a career, I don't want to do that.'"

"Oh," Con said. *"Say Anything."*

"Nice."

"I know my eighties cinema. And it's impressive that you can recite that from memory. But...that kind of pre-empts a lot of jobs. And you don't seem to mind the store, I mean, mind minding the store. That's selling things that are bought or processed."

"It's different with Mimi's store. The clothes might be bought but they're not processed. I feel like it's not so much selling as it is matchmaking. It's like arranging for pet adoptions. People who come into Mimi's store are looking for some kind of connection with something."

"A connection with something beautiful," Con said.

"Yes, exactly." Dora felt like she couldn't meet his eyes. She started slicing the ham.

"I don't know who brought us a ham. Some friend of Gabby's, I think. Thanks for helping us eat it—who said 'Eternity is two people and a ham'?"

"I don't know, but I'm going to start saying it now. My mother always gets one for Easter, and I feel the same way. I eat ham sandwiches until I start oinking."

Dora looked at the plate of sliced ham. "This meal needs something green," Dora said. She threw some lettuce in a bowl and sprinkled cherry tomatoes on top. "There. Green and red."

Dora had just put the plates on the table when the oven timer and Con's phone buzzed simultaneously.

Con looked at the screen and grimaced. "You mind if I take this? It's Mrs. Featherston."

"Oh, sure. No problem." Dora started mixing the dry

ingredients for the cookies. They could go in while she and Con ate and still be cool enough to take to the hospital. She could hear Con's voice as a low murmur from the other room. He had a nice voice, she thought. Not deep, but rumbly. She thought about him tying her apron strings again, how warm and safe he'd felt, behind her. She shivered.

"Dora?" She jumped, hearing his voice, as if he'd known what she'd been thinking. "I'm so sorry....I can't stay. Mrs. Featherston put her thousand-dollar handbag on the wet sealant on her new countertops, which I'd not only told her not to touch but fenced off with strips of bright-blue tape at six-inch intervals." Con rolled his eyes. "So now I have to go smooth it out—if it can be smoothed out—and settle the ruffled Featherstons."

"Oh, no!" Dora felt her eyes get hot. Was she going to cry over every little thing now? She gave herself a little shake. "Can I at least make you a couple of ham biscuits to take with you?"

Con grinned. "I'd like that. I'd be really sorry not to have a chance to try your biscuits. Can I get them with mustard?"

"Of course." Dora felt her face get hot, and was glad her back was to Con. She rummaged in the fridge for the mustard.

Dora put the biscuits together in record time, wrapping them in a paper towel.

"This looks delicious—thank you." Con smiled. At the door he paused. "Good luck today, at the hospital." He took a Murphy Fine Construction card out of his pocket. "Call me if you need anything." He looked stern. "That's my cell. Call anytime. I mean it."

"Yes, sir," said Dora. She gave him a mock salute. "Thank your mother for the flowers for us, please?"

"Will do." Con paused. "And I'll try to stop by the store tomorrow, if I can. Just to see how you're doing, and to hear about Mimi."

Dora watched him walk out to the truck. She wasn't hungry anymore. She put the ham and biscuits away. She didn't feel much like making cookies, either, but the butter was already soft, so she made them, mechanically. She didn't even taste the batter.

The last sheet was coming out of the oven when Gabby came home.

"Smells good in here," she said. She nabbed a cookie off the cooling rack. "Ooh, still hot." She stopped. "These must be for the nurses, aren't they?"

Dora nodded. She had felt dull and blah since Con left. "That's okay—there are plenty. Go ahead. Did you get your errands done?"

"Errands?" Gabby looked puzzled for a minute. "Oh, sure." She looked mischievous. "I got everything I needed, and a bit more, I think." She gestured down to the cooling cookies, which Dora had started packing into an old Tupperware. "You want my help with those, honey?"

"I'm okay, Gabby," said Dora.

"Well, I'll just grab a sweater, and then we can head on over."

* * *

On the way out, Dora made a slight feint towards her own car, but didn't push when Gabby offered to drive. "The parking guy there knows my car, so if we stay a little longer than we plan we won't get a ticket." Dora leaned back in her seat, the cookies warm on her lap. For once, Gabby didn't seem to want to talk, and they rode in silence.

The hospital was busy and bustling. It made sense that Sunday would be a busy day. But Mimi's room was quiet. She didn't seem to be awake. Gabby grabbed for the box of cookies.

"I think I know the nurse on duty," she said. "I'll go drop these off while you sit with Mimi, so they know where they came from." She scooted off.

Dora sat down in the too-familiar chair by Mimi's side. She reached out for Mimi's hand, and took a deep breath. If she pretended they were talking at dinner...

"The store's going well. Maux is doing inventory. I rearranged the jewelry case, but we can put it back if you don't like it. I also sold a bunch of stuff, including a dress with a secret life." Dora paused.

"I didn't know about the secret lives. Maux knew. And a few of the customers knew, too. Did you write them?"

Mimi's eyes were still closed. Dora felt a sudden urge to ask Mimi to blink once for yes, twice for no. But Mimi was probably asleep.

"I think it's funny that the dresses know more of their history than I know of mine," Dora said. Her voice sounded overbold in the quiet room.

"I've been thinking about asking you about my parents. I know you don't like to talk about them, but I'd like to know something about what they were like. Where was my mom from? Where did they meet?"

Mimi's eyes stayed closed. The beeping from the machines stayed steady, her only response.

Dora squeezed Mimi's hand, gently.

"It's not like I feel you weren't enough, Mimi. You were more than enough. Are more than enough. I just wish I could know."

Mimi hated a lot of words. She didn't like the word "moist," even when it was about cake; a Duncan Hines commercial could make her gag. She hated the word "hapless"—"What's a hap, and why should I care that you don't have one?"—but didn't feel the same way about "feckless," which she used more frequently than perhaps she should: all dogs, most men, their newspaper delivery boy, the governor, Dora's American-history teacher who misplaced one of her college recommendations; they were all feckless. Mimi hated the word "quality" without a modifying adjective. "Everything has a quality, and most of it is bad," she'd say. She also hated the name "Jerusalem," for no apparent reason, but Dora suspected it had to do with some far-off, long-ago forced hymn-singing.

Dora didn't mind any of those words (and secretly loved "hapless"). Dora only hated one word, and that word was "orphan." Dora didn't remember her parents, had not even realized she had once had parents that were now missing until she was four, maybe five. There was Dora, and there was Mimi, and that was what the world was like. When she saw other families, they seemed crowded and unwieldy; how were you supposed to get anyone's attention, with all those people hanging around?

Of course, school introduced the word and the word's problems. At Happy Hours Preschool they drew pictures of their families, for proud display on a bulletin board. Dora drew herself, of course, and Mimi. They were eating ice cream, which Dora felt was a masterly touch: how could Mimi refuse a trip to the ice-cream parlor after seeing them so happy together, eating ice cream?

Stupid red-headed Adam (who went on to plague Dora all through elementary school before his parents mercifully relocated to Atlanta) was the first to point it out. "Where's Dora's mama and daddy?" Miss Angela blanched. "Dora lives with her grandmother, Adam," she announced, in the same tone she used to announce that their classroom rabbit was going to stay at Amber's house over break. "But *where* are Dora's mama and daddy?" persisted Adam, who had always shown remarkable staying power on those topics Miss Angela liked least, such as why they were having apples for snack again, and what had happened in the bathroom.

"I don't need a mama or a daddy," said Dora, who was carefully adding sprinkles to her ice-cream cone—if you were going to invoke ice cream through art, there was no sense in not going all the way. "Only stupid people have mamas and daddies." Dora thought Adam was stupid, and everything he had was stupid, from his stupid red tennis shoes (blue was so much better) to his stupid toy truck. So, if he had a mama and a daddy, they had to be stupid, too.

"Dora," said Miss Angela, warningly. "Stupid" was a word that Miss Angela hated.

Adam only got louder. *"Where is Dora's mama? Where is Dora's daddy?"* Adam, reeling from the introduction of a baby sibling, was having some adjustment difficulties.

"Adam," said Miss Angela. Then the *o*-word happened. "Dora is an orphan. She doesn't have a mama or a daddy. It is not kind to talk about it."

Not kind to talk about it. That was the phrase Miss Angela used to talk about Evelyn's foot brace, and the stinky man who sometimes wandered down the street shouting and drinking from a brown paper bag. Dora blanched. She was a stinky person now? She was a person that it wasn't kind to talk about, for some reason? And there was a special word for it, too? Evelyn didn't have a special word. The stinky man didn't have a special word, at least not one that Dora knew. It was too much to take.

Dora stood up and threw the entire shoebox of crayons at Adam. *"I am not an orfin!"* she shouted. Adam sat covered in little flakes of crayon and crayon paper. The red had gone into his open shirt collar. Miss Angela was stunned; the rest of the class was delighted. Every single one of them had wanted to throw something at Adam since school had begun.

Miss Kristin, the assistant, ran over and began fussing over Adam, who realized that it would be in his best interests to start crying. Miss Angela took Dora to the kitchen room. Dora sat on the chair you sat on when you needed a band-aid, and Miss Angela crouched beside her.

"Dora, you know we don't throw or hit in our school. I understand that Adam was talking about things that might make you feel sad, or angry, but we don't throw things at people who make us feel sad or angry."

Dora squinched her face tight, to keep from crying. Her eyes were full, but anger was holding them as reservoirs for some future need. If Adam was going to be a big crybaby, Dora wasn't.

"It's not true, it's not true," Dora gasped. "I am not an orfin. I don't need a mama, I don't need a daddy, I have a Mimi."

"Dora, Dora." Miss Angela was giving her a hug. "It's

okay. Why don't you sit here for a minute, and then we'll see how you feel."

Dora was left in the chair while Miss Angela went to the phone.

"Dora, guess what? Mimi is going to come, and you are going to go home for the afternoon. We'll see you again tomorrow."

"But my picture!"

Miss Angela didn't understand. "Don't worry, Dora, we can put your picture up with all the others."

Dora hadn't even considered that the lack of a mama or a daddy would be cause for her picture to be rejected; Dora had been upset that she had only finished one color of the sprinkles on her ice-cream cone, and everyone knew that you couldn't get one-color sprinkles, unless they were brown, and Dora's were green. Who had ever heard of one-color green sprinkles? If the details weren't right, the picture wouldn't result in actual ice cream, Dora was sure of it.

It was useless to ask to go and finish her picture—she'd thrown all the crayons, first of all—and anyway, she could see Miss Kristen lining everyone up to go out on the playground. Dora took a book from Miss Angela's chair and read it to herself, even though it was a baby book, about teddy bears.

When Mimi came, not ten minutes later, she was incandescent. Dora had never seen her so angry, and for a moment wondered if throwing crayons was worse, even, than lying or forgetting to brush your teeth, the two things Mimi always told her not to do. But Mimi's angry face was turned towards Miss Angela, and there were words coming from the office that sounded like "allow" and "irresponsible," and then Mimi was coming to get her, with

Dora's jacket and schoolbag. Dora reached up her hand to Mimi, and Mimi took it, just like in her picture.

And Dora's picture must have worked, because as soon as they were out of the door of the school, Mimi kissed her and said, "Let's go get some ice cream."

The ice-cream shop was only a couple blocks from school, so they didn't bother to get back into Mimi's Volkswagen; Mimi carried the schoolbag and Dora carried her jacket. Mimi didn't even ask her to put it on. The ice-cream place was deserted; they went straight to the counter. Mimi said, "One sugar cone of butter pecan, please, and one sugar cone of strawberry." Mimi looked down at Dora. "With sprinkles," she added.

Dora had thought then that if throwing crayons at stupid boys resulted in ice cream she would do it every day.

Mimi paid for their cones and they went outside, to sit on the bench in front of the store. She took one bite from her cone—Mimi never licked her ice cream, but ate it, like you would a banana—and looked at Dora.

Dora looked back, and then realized what Mimi expected. "I'm sorry I threw crayons at Adam," she said.

Mimi laughed. "I wish I could have seen it! That Adam is a pill, and his mother is a horse pill. But, yes, you shouldn't throw things at people." Mimi took a deep breath, then another bite of butter pecan, then another deep breath.

"Miss Angela was right, Dora. I should have talked to you about this before, but I guess I didn't think about it. You are an orphan. Your daddy"—and here Mimi's voice caught—"and your mama...they died, Dora, back when you were just a baby." Mimi's ice cream was melting, a rivulet of butter pecan coursing down the cone. "Your daddy was my little boy, and he loved your mama very much, and they had you, and they were so happy. But they had an accident, and that's why you live with me. And I am very happy that our family is you and me together. But our family is a little different than other people's families, and that's why boys like Adam will be stupid about it, because they don't understand different. But we do, and that's why we're not stupid." Mimi's ice cream was soaking the napkin wrapped around her cone, but she didn't seem to notice. "Well, one of the reasons we're not stupid."

Dora had been carefully licking all the sprinkles off her cone before giving in to the Mimi-impulse and biting a big chunk of strawberry out of the ice cream. She wasn't sure why Mimi was upset, or if she should be upset, too, about a daddy and a mama that she used to have when she was a tiny baby and who had died.

"Like Semiramis?" Dora asked. Semiramis had been Mimi's cat, who had also died when Dora was a baby. Mimi had a picture of Semiramis on her desk.

"Yes, Dora, like Semiramis."

Reassured that Dora understood, Mimi finally turned her attention to her ice cream. Dora finished hers.

And that had been the last discussion they had had about Dora's parents.

•   •   •

Dora had been sitting quietly, holding Mimi's hand, for about an hour when Maux came by. Maux was wearing a tight 1940s cream-and-brown printed rayon dress, with tights and brown work boots. Dora thought she vaguely recognized the dress from the store. It looked great on Maux, but, then, everything did.

"Hey, Dora. Mimi." Maux's voice dropped to match the quiet in the room. She came over and sat next to Dora in the other chair.

"I'm sorry Harvey didn't come with me, Mimi." Maux didn't seem to be dissuaded by Mimi's lack of response. "His parents are in town. I can't stay long—we're taking them to that fancy French restaurant tonight. Or, rather, they're taking us, I hope. They took us to the new Italian place last night, and, Mimi, their pumpkin ravioli are divine. It's got some kind of sage sauce that will curl your toes. I ate the whole thing, plus I asked for extra bread to go with it. I had the tiramisù, too. Which was excellent. And two glasses of wine. Harvey's dad ordered it, and he knew what he was doing."

Maux patted her stomach. "Harvey's parents must think I'm a pig—but it was so good!"

Dora stood up. "I'm going to go find Gabby, and some coffee. You want some?"

"No, no, I'm good. You go right ahead. I'll be right here. Harvey's not coming to get me for a good while." Maux picked up Mimi's hand and held it, just as Dora had.

Dora wandered out into the corridor. There was no sign of Gabby. There was a coffee machine at the end of the hall, by the stairwell, but Dora passed it by. She stood and looked out the window instead. It was getting dark, and the trees looked bare and shivery outside, even though she knew it wasn't cold out. Dora felt dark and shivery, too. She stood there, watching the cars go in and out of the garage. If she unfocused her eyes just right, they were mere patterns of light and dark. She shoved her hands into her pockets. There was a handkerchief in her pocket. Mimi had kept a huge stack of them on the dresser in her closet room, and Dora had put one in her pocket this morning almost without thinking. Mimi had always carried a handkerchief. Sometimes two—"one for blow and one for show," she used to say. Dora took out her handkerchief and tied a knot in it for luck. Mimi used to do that, too, whenever she felt she needed luck particularly badly.

Dora stopped outside Mimi's door, steeling herself to go back in. She could hear Maux talking. "You'd be proud of Dora," she was saying. Dora stood still. "She's so good in the store. No surprise, considering how much time she spent there with you. She barely has to think about it, just does whatever needs doing." Dora felt a lump in her throat. She went in.

"No Gabby? No coffee?" Maux asked Dora. Dora looked blank. "Oh. Yeah. Couldn't find either."

Maux talked a bit about her apprenticeship—"We're redoing all the ductwork in the high-school auditorium. You won't *believe* the stuff we've found"—and retailed a few items of gossip about some of the other storekeepers on the block. "Barbara Ann told me she's found a bunch of liquor bottles in her garbage. She was more upset about the lack of recycling than the possibility of a secret drinker, but I thought you'd want to know."

Gabby burst in with a couple bottles of water. "I thought you'd want some water, Dora. It's so dry in here! You'd think they'd run a humidifier or something." Dora just knew Maux was gearing up to talk to Gabby about legionnaires' disease and air-recycling systems, and headed her off at the pass. "Maux, when did you have to meet Harvey, again?"

"About now," Maux said, checking her phone. "Oh yeah, he's downstairs. Gotta go have another ceremonial parental dinner." She gave Dora a big hug, and Gabby one that was only slightly smaller. "I've got work at the auditorium from seven to four tomorrow, but I can always call in, or come by later. Don't hesitate—you call me if you need me." Dora nodded.

"Has she...," Gabby whispered.

"No," Dora said. She sank back into the chair, and took Mimi's hand again. Gabby sat there with her, as the light died in the room. Neither of them made a move to turn on the light.

They were sitting there in the dark when Dr. Czerny opened the door. Dora rose and followed her out into the hall. Dora spoke first. "Has there been any...change? The nurse couldn't tell us."

"No, no change. I stopped by to see if you'd brought in any of the health directives you mentioned?"

Dora felt stricken. "I'm so sorry. I found them, but I forgot to bring them."

"It's fine—just bring them next time you come in, if you can." Dr. Czerny gave her a searching look. "You should go home, and get some rest. There's not much you can do here, and I know your grandmother wouldn't want you to exhaust yourself."

Dora just nodded. She felt as if she'd been carrying a heavy backpack for hours. Her neck and shoulders were tight with the stress of it.

Gabby came out. She blinked in the light.

"I think she's breathing better," she said. Dr. Czerny didn't comment.

Dora took her chance. "Gabby, I think I'm going to go say good night to Mimi." She went back in the room.

Dora held her own breath and listened, but she couldn't

hear any change in Mimi's breathing. She squeezed Mimi's hand, gently. "Oh, Mimi," she said. "I love you so." She kissed Mimi's cheek. Grabbing her bag, she pushed back into the hall.

Gabby and Dora were quiet on the ride home, ignoring each other's sniffles through tacit agreement.

Dinner was ham and some of the leftover biscuits. Gabby didn't even bother to turn on the television. Dora washed the two lonely dishes and the butter knife, and Gabby wandered into the hall to look at the mail.

"Oh Lordy," Gabby yelped. "I'm sorry, honey, but if you'd told me your aunt Camille was coming, I'd have found three good reasons to be elsewhere. That woman puts my back up."

"Camille?" Dora ran into the hall and looked out. Gabby was staring at the front walk as if it had suddenly become paved with rattlers. Camille was rolling up to the front door like an ocean liner, dragging a suitcase, the old-fashioned square kind, on a leash. It was upholstered in a pattern that suggested that a dentist's waiting-room couch had been skinned and tanned.

Camille didn't bother to ring the doorbell, or even knock. She opened the door and shouted *"Dora!* You here?"

"Right here, Camille." Camille flounced into the hall and smothered Dora in a heavily perfumed hug. She pointedly didn't greet Gabby.

"Baby, how are you holding up?"

Dora fought the urge to say, "I was fine until you got here." Gabby was right; if Camille had a superpower, it would be making everyone near her sullen and unresponsive.

Camille didn't notice that Dora hadn't answered.

"I can't believe I had to hear about Mimi from Joanna; she volunteers over at Baptist, you know, and when she saw Mimi's name on the list she just turned on her cell phone, right there in the hospital, and called me. Didn't even care that she could have turned off some poor man's pacemaker."

"Pacemaker?"

"Intensive-care machine or whatever it is that's hurt when you use a cell phone in a hospital. But never mind, never mind, I know you must be just prostrate, *pros*-trate, so I came as soon as I could. Now that Lionel's at Duke, you know, I'm free as a bird. Although I like to be home at the weekends, you know, for when the kiddos need me to do their laundry."

Camille gestured to her suitcase. "Would you be a doll and take this up to Mimi's room for me?"

Dora flailed, recoiling at the notion of Camille in Mimi's room, among Mimi's things.

"I'm not sure if that's a good idea, Camille; she could be home any day, and I want everything to be ready for her...."

"Honey, Mimi's gonna be in that hospital for a good long while, at the very least—you know that, don't you?"

Dora didn't want to listen to Camille. She didn't want to talk to Camille. She didn't want to look at Camille, in her designer tracksuit and flip-flops, her elaborate pedicure (three colors of nail polish!), and her birthstone jewelry.

"You know, you should really stay in my room. There's a dog, next door—right on the side of the house by Mimi's room—who barks all night; I can sleep through it—since college I can sleep through anything—and besides, my room has the newer mattress. And I know how a bad night's sleep affects your back. I'll stay on the bed in the closet room; I should really spend some time cleaning in there, anyway."

Camille didn't look convinced, but she acquiesced with a show of grace.

"Whatever you need, honey, that's fine with me. I know that space is tight, here, too." She looked pointedly at Gabby, and then her suitcase, which crouched like a large dog, senile and angry, at her feet.

Dora took the hint and the suitcase (ignoring Camille's snideness; Camille had petulantly, often, and at great length complained about Gabby living with Mimi and "taking advantage") and hauled the awkward beast up to her own room. She cleared away her few things and made the bed quickly while she was there, and took a perverse pleasure in not changing the sheets for Camille.

"Gabby said she had to go out, and not to wait up," Camille said. She had poured herself a drink from the liquor cabinet, and was now flipping through the channels with the remote.

Coward, Dora thought, and resolved to get even with Gabby later.

Camille continued with her whine. "Doesn't Mimi have more than basic cable yet? I told her about all those fashion channels, you'd think she'd be interested, you know, professionally."

"You know Mimi...." Dora trailed off. It seemed like a safe thing to say, but Camille's face darkened briefly.

"Oh, I know Mimi," Camille sniffed. "Mimi's always gone her own way. If John's given her advice once, he's given it a million times, not that she ever listens to any of it." She clicked off the remote.

Dora looked at the floor. If Mimi could ignore Uncle John, she could certainly ignore Camille. "Are you hungry?" she asked. "There's some leftover ham and biscuits in the fridge."

"Ham!" Camille slapped her midsection, and her slap resounded a little too loudly. "Can't do that, nosirree. Some of us are watching our girlish figures."

Camille hadn't been girlish since the Nixon administration, but Dora let it pass.

"I could run out…," Dora offered, weakly.

"Oh, that would be darling of you! Here's what's on my diet." Camille rummaged in her purse and came up with a shopping list. "I print these off the computer, always have a couple in my bag just in case! Such a timesaver." Dora took the sheet, which was printed on both sides. "Don't worry, it's a long list, if you could just grab a few things to tide me over until tomorrow or the next day.…Wait." Camille grabbed the sheet back and scribbled something at the bottom. "I think I'll just take a quick bath while you're gone; I hate being in the car!"

Dora looked at the list again. What Camille had written was "Ben and Jerry's Chubby Hubby."

Dora skulked through the Kroger. First of all, Camille's list was embarrassing, a huge assortment of the most plastic and artificial of diet foods, to be topped off with ice cream. Dora took a handbasket and was strangely comforted by the weight of the frozen dinners and the artificially sweetened granola bars. She managed to make it all the way to the checkout without encountering a single acquaintance.

At the checkout she froze. She forgot that half the checkout clerks would be friends of Mimi's.

"Dora!" Faye called. "Over here, dear, I'm open!"

Dora set out Camille's provisions on the belt. Faye looked at her sympathetically.

"I heard about Mimi, honey. She's on our prayer list, so don't you worry," she said, scanning the frozen dinners in a stack. "Oh my, don't tell me Camille's here, ruining your visit."

"How did you know?"

"Mimi always complains about having to buy this stuff for her. I don't ever see that Miss Camille running out to the market. It's a shame, you don't need anything extra to do right now. You let me know how things are going, you hear?" Dora swept up the crinkly plastic bags and nodded. She shoved her shoulders back and carried herself and the bags out of the store.

When she got in the car she realized she'd forgotten the Chubby Hubby, and tried to smile.

Camille was lounging on the couch in a dingy white terrycloth robe and pink slippers. The robe said, very plainly, PROPERTY OF SANIBEL ISLAND RESORT over the right breast. The pink slippers were a bit worse for wear.

There was a suspicious tang of sour-cream-and-onion potato chips in the air—Mimi's favorite.

Camille followed Dora into the kitchen and kept up a string of meaningless chatter while Dora unpacked the groceries. Her stories all involved the peccadilloes of the girls she had gone to high school with, who, if Dora knew them at all, she knew only as the mothers of people Dora had barely known in her own high school. Camille had never really left high school, Mimi had once told Dora, after Dora had come home from the tag end of her freshman year of high school, miserable about something—a dance, or a basketball game, or some other iconic high-school experience that wasn't playing out like a John Hughes movie.

"I know you don't want to hear this now," Mimi had said, making Dora cinnamon toast. "But you will look back on this as being completely unimportant."

Dora had answered this with a noncommittal gulp.

"And to give you incentive to believe me, I bring forth as an example your aunt Camille."

"Aunt Camille?" Dora hated Aunt Camille. "What about Camille?"

"Camille has never, ever, left high school. She graduated, but she didn't leave. She still lives there, in her head."

"And I don't want to be like Camille."

"And you don't want to be like Camille, so you won't live in high school in your head. You might have to live there in your body a few more years, but your head should be high-school free."

Dora never could make cinnamon toast like Mimi's. Mimi's was perfect.

*   *   *

Camille, still talking, started rummaging around in the bags. "Where's the ice cream?"

"Oh," Dora lied, "they were out of Chubby Hubby. I wasn't sure what else to get that would work for your... diet, so I just came home. I'm sure you can pick up some tomorrow."

Camille sniffed and went back to sit on the couch and cycle through the channels. Dora put the emptied plastic bags in the pantry.

"Well," Dora said, "I've had a long day, I think I'll go up to bed...."

Camille muted the television. "We should talk about tomorrow," she said brightly.

"Tomorrow?"

"Well, I thought I'd go see Mimi in the morning, then come by the shop and give you a hand. Then we can talk more about what we're going to do."

"Do?"

"About the shop, and the house, and everything."

"Mimi's not *dead*." Dora stared at Camille. It would be so much more straightforward if instead of dyed copper hair those red twists on top of her head were actual horns.

"Honestly, Dora, you're so morbid. I don't know what you were reading at that granola school. All those modern novels where everyone is an alcoholic must do something to you. I don't know why you aren't majoring in business, like my Tyffanee. But you have to face reality. Mimi's very sick, and she won't be able to do everything she's always done. And you've got your life ahead of you. We just have to be practical."

"I don't want to talk about this now." Dora turned to go upstairs.

"I know, I know, you're overwhelmed. We'll talk tomorrow," Camille called after her. Dora trudged upstairs with the canned laughter of a sitcom pursuing her.

CHAPTER FOUR

DORA MANAGED TO GET UP AND OUT of the house before Camille was awake. At least sleeping in the closet room made it easier to get dressed; today she was in a brown cotton shirtdress with appliquéd patch pockets in the shape of golden maple leaves, with a matching golden belt and brown Weejuns. Today she almost didn't scare herself when she looked in the mirror—her T-shirts and cargo shorts seemed to belong to a different life.

Dora brewed a pot of coffee and left a note beside it for Camille: "Don't worry yourself about coming to the store today—just take it easy and relax." She didn't think this would keep Camille away—it was like using a flyswatter to repel a shark—but she had to try.

Parking by the store was always a mess on weekdays, so Dora took her old bike. It was an ancient black Raleigh, rickety and noisy, but Dora loved it. She had a newer, shinier bike up at Lymond, but this was the one Dora thought of as her real bike.

Even on her bike, Dora got to the store twenty minutes early. Saturday she'd seen a pile of cotton dresses that needed buttons replaced, or steaming, or both, so she had planned to get that set up so that she could work on it all day, between customers. Mondays were slow; even without Maux's help, Dora should have plenty of time to fix them all.

Mimi's button box was completely extravagant. It was the Taj Mahal, the Buckingham Palace, the Smithsonian Institution of button boxes. It wasn't really a button box at all, but a huge steel rolling tool chest from Sears, with a dozen drawers. Each drawer was partitioned with teeny plastic dividers, gone yellow with age, and in each corral was a set of buttons, no fewer than six of the same color and design. The bottom two drawers were for the rogues and the strays—light ones in the uppermost drawer, and dark ones in the very bottom. Mimi could never make up her mind as to whether she should put the red ones in with the light or the dark, so there were flashes of red in both.

The drawers were labeled—Mimi had once bought one of those plastic-tape labelers and labeled everything in sight, up to and including a piece of hunter-green tape reading "refrigerator" on the refrigerator. The top drawer, the smallest, was labeled RHINESTONE, the next one down METALLIC, and the one below that WOOD. Then the drawers were in ROYGBIV order. Dora rolled the whole thing a bit closer, and pulled out the much less impressive old candy box of needles and thread. She plugged in the steamer and opened the front door.

It was a slow morning. A few mothers came in to browse, obviously on a pre-naptime circuit of the shopping area. Dora wondered if she had to be officious about their lattes, but they left them on the front counter of their own accord—Mimi must have her customers trained well. A student from the college came in looking for an interview suit, and Dora helped her choose between two lovely wools from the 1950s, mint condition.

"The navy is a slightly better fit, but you'll have to

spend some time finding navy shoes," Dora pointed out. "Better to buy black shoes—you probably already have good black shoes, right?—and spend the extra money to get the gray taken in a little at the waist."

The student took a last look at the navy and put it back. "You're right, I should get the gray one—my dad gave me a black briefcase, too, so that will look better with the gray than with the navy."

Dora smiled and took the gray suit over to the counter. "Once you ace that interview, you can come back for the navy one," she pointed out as she wrapped the suit in tissue. She packed it in one of Mimi's hatboxes, the ones that were supposed to be for formal gowns only. She saw the student smile at the hatbox, and knew she would love it.

Dora checked for a secret life for the gray suit, but there wasn't one. She made a note to look to see if the navy suit had one.

Between customers Dora managed to repair and steam three dresses. Two print shirtdresses got entirely new buttons. Dora tried to keep the replacement buttons in the same family as the old ones, taking her time to match colors and sizes as closely as possible. Mimi could change the entire personality of a dress with new buttons. She'd add rhinestones to a housedress and turn it into something ready for dinner and dancing, like it had never been accessorized with a vacuum cleaner. Dora had just fixed the zipper in one acetate afternoon dress, damaged after a too-enthusiastic try-on, when the bell over the door jangled. It was Camille.

Camille was wearing a different velour sweatsuit, in a paler pink. She looked like an underdone hot dog, wearing rhinestone flip-flops and a tangle of necklaces.

"Dora, I've come to help yoooooou," Camille trilled, gesturing at the store. Her coffee sloshed dangerously in her lidless paper cup.

"Camille, please put your coffee on the counter before you spill it." Dora watched nervously as Camille negotiated her bulk, including a large pink leather designer handbag, dripping with charms, towards the counter.

Camille set her cup down with a splash and caught Dora's wince. "You're so funny to be worried about stains on a bunch of old clothes!"

"Since most of these managed to go fifty or sixty years without getting *any* stains, it seems like a shame to break their streaks now," Dora muttered.

"What can I do? This is such a big project, you know, and I am so happy to help. With Lionel and Tyffanee finally off to college, I have so much free time, and I've just been *longing* for a project that will use my creativity! Of course, I do need to get back home every once in a while—you know how Lionel loves to come home for his mama's cooking and her washing machine—but otherwise I can *devote* myself to this."

"There really isn't very much to do," Dora said, wiping up the spilled coffee with a paper towel.

"Oh, baby, I'm not talking about the store as it is *now*, I'm talking about the store as it *could be*."

"Mimi likes the store as it is now."

"Oh, yes, of course, but wouldn't it be a great surprise for her when she's out of the hospital, to liven it up a little?"

"Liven it up?"

"Exactly! Bring in some more modern merchandise, some fun novelties, a few souvenirs of Forsyth...."

"Souvenirs of *Forsyth*?" Dora tried to think of what those might even be.

"Dora, you've been away for a little while, you haven't seen what a tourist mecca Forsyth has become. People looking for a relaxing weekend in North Carolina, staying downtown and shopping our quaint little district. They don't want to take home moldy old dresses; they want..."

"T-shirts?" said Dora, sarcastically.

"Yes! T-shirts! My friend Jeanette has a store out by the beach, you know, just north of Hilton Head, and you would not *believe* how well she does from T-shirts. And she's only open March through November!"

"Camille, we're not going to sell T-shirts. Mimi would hate that!"

Camille sniffed. "I've known Mimi since before you were born. And I think she'd be touched and grateful to us for helping out in the store."

"Helping out, yes. Making it into a tourist trap, no."

"Well, I know this is a lot of change for you, all at once. But let's just sleep on it, m'kay? We can talk more about changes tomorrow." Camille tilted her head. "What *is* this music?"

"It's the Andrews Sisters."

"I thought so! My mama used to listen to them. But don't you want to play what the young people listen to, to draw them into the store? My Lionel loves Maroon 5, and Tyffanee loves that Justin what's-his-name."

"Well, no. They can listen to modern music anywhere. The Andrews Sisters provide atmosphere, get people in the right mood."

"If you say so... I still think kids like their own music. But I came here to help you, so what can I do?"

"Can you sew?"

Camille laughed. "Sew? I haven't sewn in years. Why would I sew? I can buy a new dress for less than the cost of the fabric!"

Dora gritted her teeth. "But what if you can't find what you want in the store?"

"Honey, my trouble has always been finding *too* much of what I like. Well, you know, not at Target or places like that, mass-market places, but in the nicer shops. I'm known as something of a tastemaker in Fayre, you know."

Dora took another look at the plastic-doll pink of Camille's tracksuit.

"You know Mimi asks that people working in the store dress in vintage, right?"

"Oh, honey, that doesn't apply to me—how could a real woman fit in these little doll clothes? I think they promote a negative body image, don't you?" Camille held up a dress from the nearest rack, which happened, by chance, to be one of the racks of larger sizes. Mimi made a point of hunting down as many large-size dresses as she could, and the dress Camille held up was a gorgeous light wool sheath and at least a size 48. Camille looked disconcerted. She put it back hastily.

"Mimi won't mind," she said decisively. "She'd hate for me not to be expressing my own style."

Dora considered. "Well, if you're not dressed in vintage, you probably shouldn't wait on customers. And you are in comfortable clothes, so why don't you bring a box up from the basement for sorting? Some of the racks are looking a little thin, and we should be well stocked before next week. You can grab anything that says 'Holiday' on it."

Camille looked momentarily aggrieved that she couldn't continue talking about turning Mimi's shop into a seething craptorium, but she just nodded. "Be right back!"

There was a blessed few minutes of quiet as Camille made her way into the basement. Dora finished picking out a new set of buttons for another dress and had threaded a needle before she realized Camille had been quiet far too long.

"Camille?" she called out. No answer.

Dora flipped the "Back in Five Minutes" sign on the door and locked it before rushing down the basement steps.

Camille was sitting in the middle of the concrete floor, two boxes splayed open around her. She was holding a pair of scissors.

"What the hell are you doing?" yelled Dora.

Camille jumped. "Dora! You scared me!"

"I thought I asked you to bring up a box for sorting?" Dora was scanning the pile of dresses Camille had dumped on the floor. Camille, scissors, and vintage dresses was a scary combination, but it didn't look as if anything had been damaged. Sprawled across the top of the pile was a gorgeous patterned-silk afternoon dress. Dora remembered Mimi buying it.

The woman selling it was one of Mimi's favorite pickers. She was retired, and she and her husband drove all over in their RV, visiting grandchildren and all her husband's old Army buddies. He'd hit the golf courses, and she'd hit the thrift stores and charity shops.

"I love this one," she'd said, picking it up out of a large rolling suitcase and handing it to Mimi. Mimi preferred it when pickers brought clothes in suitcases. She hated the mess of armfuls of hangers.

"I had a dress like this right after Arnie got out of the service. Wore it to darn near every party, until it got a cigarette burn in it—I just cried. That was when we all smoked," she said, glancing apologetically over at Dora, who was reading a book and trying to look like she wasn't trying to listen. "Glad that's gone out of fashion. It was all burns in the clothes and ashes everywhere and never having matches or a lighter when you wanted one. Such a hassle." Mimi had held the dress up to the light. Even Dora could see it was flawless. It didn't have tags but it looked as if it had never been worn.

"Judy, it's even still got the belt. You have such a good eye." Mimi hung it carefully on a rolling rack.

Judy laughed. "I'm just glad you're here to give me an excuse to buy these things, even if I just have them for a little while. I do love pretty clothes...and I've tried to give them to my daughters-in-law, but..." She shrugged. "Different strokes, I guess." She picked up one of Mimi's postcards from the counter and fanned herself with it. The air conditioning was on, but Judy looked hot and flushed.

"Dora, run down the street and get us a couple of iced teas, will you?" Mimi pulled a five from her pocket and dropped it onto Dora's book.

When Dora got back, Judy and her suitcase were gone. Mimi was hanging up the rest of the dresses Judy had brought. Dora put the iced teas in their styrofoam cups on the counter.

"Arnie came by early, and Judy had to go," Mimi explained. She turned back to the rack and straightened out a black jersey gown. "Look at this, Dora. I think it's

Halston, although there's no label, so I can't be sure. We'll have to put it on a mannequin; it looks like nothing on the hanger." Mimi fished a tissue from her pocket and blew her nose.

"Mimi…are you crying? What's wrong?" Dora had hardly ever seen Mimi cry.

"Oh, honey. It's Judy.…She's sick, and they're giving up the RV and going to live with their son in Ohio. I just don't think we're going to see her again."

Dora didn't know what to say, so she settled for giving Mimi a hug. Mimi hugged her back, then straightened up. "Waterworks don't get any work done." She blew her nose again, decisively. "People just get old, that's all there is to it." She pushed the rack away from the counter. "I'm going to go wash my hands.…Would you get me a packing box? I think I'll put these away for a little while."

"Sure." Dora had helped Mimi pack Judy's beautiful dresses. Somehow, it made Dora even angrier that it was Judy's box that Camille had messed up.

"Sweetie, those boxes were much too heavy for me and my back." Camille gestured with the scissors. "I thought I'd open the boxes down here and just take up a dress or two at a time."

"That would be fine, except that the floor is not so clean, and we don't want to have to dry-clean those dresses."

"Mimi had things dry-cleaned? A bunch of old clothes?"

"Camille, there's a difference between an old kitchen chair and a Chippendale, and these dresses are Chippendales, not Salvation Army fodder."

"Chippendales? The bachelorette-party guys?" Camille looked confused.

Dora sighed. "Never mind. Why don't you go upstairs? I'll bring these up."

Camille looked at her watch. "Oh, it's almost one-thirty—sorry, sugar, I have to run, it took me forever to get a manicure appointment at Hetty's. She said the new girl had to take me, and she only had this one time."

Hetty must have realized that none of her longtime staff would have Camille as a customer anymore; Dora felt bad for the new girl.

"That's fine, don't worry about coming back after—your nails will be wet, and I'd hate for you to get all smudged. Why don't we just meet back at the house for dinner?"

"If you're sure I can't help..." Camille didn't look too discouraged at being told to take the afternoon off.

"No, no, go! You don't want to miss your appointment. Say hi to Hetty for me."

Camille lumbered up the stairs, and Dora bent to gather the spilled dresses. They didn't look too dusty, and it seemed Camille hadn't nicked any of them opening the boxes with scissors.

Dora heard the bell jangle as Camille went out. She was almost at the top of the stairs when she heard the bell jangle again.

"Dora? Where are you?"

Dora's cousin Tyffanee was standing by the register, toying with a mood ring from the basket on the counter. Her overblond hair was stick-straight, hanging stiffly to her shoulders. She was wearing three layered tank tops, in different colors, with the topmost one bearing a logo in gold paint that Dora didn't recognize. Her denim mini was so artfully aged that it must have been brand-new, and so short that the bag of the pocket was peeking out from below the hem. A hot-pink hoodie with the Greek letters of her sorority topped off the whole look, with the fuzzy raised epsilon split exactly in half by the zipper.

"Where's my mom?" she asked, sulkily.

"She's gone for a manicure at Hetty's," Dora answered, moving around Tyffanee to lay her armful of dresses on the worktable behind the counter.

"Dammit," said Tyffanee, without much heat. "I told her to make an appointment for me, too. I totally need a wax."

Dora looked at Tyffanee's smooth, deeply spray-tanned legs, emerging like tree trunks from her short pink Ugg boots, and decided not to think about what Tyffanee wanted waxed.

"Do you know when she's coming back?" Tyffanee dropped the mood ring and started fidgeting with the hanging logo tag on her oversized handbag instead.

"She's not coming back here this afternoon," Dora said, trying to keep the relief out of her voice. "I told her I'd meet her back at the house for dinner. Are you...are you staying?"

"As if!" Tyffanee snorted. "There's no way I'm staying under the same roof as Mom if I can help it. I'm staying at the Kap Ep house over at Trinity—soooo much more fun."

Dora felt as if she should say something, express some sort of parental-restriction eye-roll sympathy, but she didn't have the heart for it. Tyffanee, though two years younger, had always made Dora feel as if she were the younger cousin. Tyffanee had, after all, been the one to show Dora the "good parts" of Camille's romance novels, had regaled Dora with stories of drunken high-school partying before Dora had even had her first beer, and had a serious boyfriend while Dora had still been reading Nancy Drew.

Tyffanee, thank goodness, looked disinclined to hang around the shop. "Tell Mom I came by like she asked, okay? And that I'm staying with Sheryn?"

"Would you like to come over for dinner tonight?" Dora felt she had to ask, although she couldn't think of anything she wanted less than having dinner with Camille and Tyffanee.

"Dora, no offense, but I so totally do not want to have dinner with you guys tonight. Anyway, there's a party."

"Oh, no problem, I understand." Dora tried not to look as relieved as she felt.

"Mom said you were interested in making this place sparkle a bit, and since I did really well in my Fashion Merchandising class last semester, she wanted me to take a look today, but I guess I missed her."

"Fashion Merchandising?" They didn't offer that at Lymond.

"Totally! I got a B-minus in that class, and everyone knows that professor only gives A's to anorexics! It's nice of you to want to help Mimi out, although I don't know what on earth we could really do here, you know? I mean, *Celebrity Style* totally declared vintage *out* last month. What people want now is labels they know. Anyway, I'll probably see you tomorrow. But if Mom asks, tell her we had a long talk about what changes we could make, 'kay?"

Dora felt a black rage settle over her shoulders like a heavy coat. A scathing remark was rising in her throat, but Tyffanee was halfway out the door, already on her cell phone, her voice trickling after her, sickly sweet and sing-songy. "Hey, bitch! Wassup? Let's grab some mochas and head over to the..."

Dora turned back to the dress she'd laid aside, pulling her threaded needle from Mimi's pincushion. Sewing the buttons on, she imagined all the things she could say to Camille that night. Souvenirs of Forsyth! T-shirts! B-minuses in Fashion Merchandising!

The rest of the afternoon was quiet. With no customers, Dora spent her time alternately sewing and fuming.

Right after four, the phone rang. It was Maux.

"I'm just calling to check in with you—not up on you, I promise." Dora could hear a loud clanging noise in the background. Maux raised her voice to be heard over it. "How's it going?" The noise stopped.

"It's going okay. I sold a suit. Camille came by and raised a fuss, but I warded her off with some garlic and a cross."

"I missed Camille?" Dora could hear Maux's eye roll even over the phone. "Were there any other visitors?"

"Tyffanee. Did you know she got a B-minus in her fashion class last semester?"

"I can believe it, but, then, I've been reading a lot about grade inflation at our leading universities...."

"Con said he might come by, but I haven't seen him." Dora regretted mentioning Con before it was even out of her mouth.

"Con? Oh, Mimi's architect friend?" Maux sniggered. "I just call him Beefcake, myself. That's one high-quality exhibit of a man, right there. Not my type, of course." The clanging noise started again, even louder. Maux paused, and it subsided again. "So when did you see him that he said he was going to stop by?"

"Well, I forgot the book Barbara Ann brought for Mimi in his truck on Saturday, after the movie, and so he brought it by the house yesterday...."

"Hold on, there, girlie. Movie? Truck? And Beefcake came by the house? Sounds like you learned more at college than you let on!"

Dora was about to protest when the clanging resumed. It was deafening now; Dora had to hold the phone away from her ear. "Goddamn it! I'll talk to you later, Dora," Maux shouted, and then there was a dial tone.

It was just like Maux to call Con Beefcake. Sure, he was tall, and he did have nice eyes that crinkled at the corners when he smiled, and he had excellent hands.... Dora shivered, thinking of him tying her apron strings. Con was so nice, Dora just wished being around him didn't make her think about one thing: Gary.

CHAPTER FIVE

DORA HAD FIRST REALIZED THAT SHE had a crush on Gary the third day they worked together. She wasn't sure what had triggered it: A bad joke? His puppy-dog look? Or was her resistance to flirting so low that one of his single entendres burst through her meager defenses? One minute he was her goofy boss, and the next minute he was her goofy boss and a crush of heroic proportions.

After that, Dora's summer fell into a kind of swoon. She'd get up every day, fortify herself with some Grape-Nuts, and think about Gary. What he would say. What she would say about what he said. Whether he'd wear that one particular pair of jeans that made something—she deliberately was not going to call it desire—rise in her chest. Then she'd head to the coffee shop, where she'd spend all day, every day, with him. It was like there was no one else in the world. Her friends were all elsewhere. Dora tried to convince herself that it was just a job, Gary just a co-worker, that she didn't think about him all the time, didn't replay their conversations over and over in her head, didn't wonder what, if anything, he thought about her.

Sometimes after a long day at work, Gary would hug her goodbye. Was that significant? Or, if Dora had the momentary upper hand in their banter, he'd squirt her with the sink sprayer. What did that mean, if anything? And what about the one time Dora had caught him peering down the V-neck of her T-shirt as she stooped to move a box of napkins in the storeroom? She had pretended she hadn't noticed, but had she really seen him blush? Everything was part of the absorbing puzzle that was Gary, but none of it added up to the actual relationship she craved.

Today they were painting. Dora had almost finished the first coat on her wall. She stepped back.

"Nice job, Rembrandt." Gary grinned. "Hold still—you've got a bit of paint on your cheek." He wiped it off with the wet rag he held. His hand was gentle. Dora held very still.

Gary grinned. "Hard to get that paint off, if you let it dry. I bet I'll have to take a scrub brush into the shower before my date tonight."

Dora dropped her roller in the tray. "You have a date?"

"Try not to sound so surprised, please. It wreaks havoc on my fragile male ego. Yeah, I met this woman in the library, she's amazing, she plays the cello and is studying the role of music in French novels of the nineteenth century. Really interesting stuff. And she's a grad student! There are so few of us at Lymond, it really narrows the dating options. I may have to turn to the law school soon." He gave a mock shudder.

"I suppose undergrads just don't meet your impossibly high standards?"

"Undergrads are off limits, one hundred percent. Best possible way to get yourself in a heap of flaming trouble: date an undergrad. You can get in trouble just looking sidewise at an undergrad." Gary mimed looking sidewise at Dora.

"Stop that, you'll get in trouble." Dora didn't remember pulling a muscle while painting, but suddenly she ached all over. "What are you going to do? On your date."

"We're going to have coffee, and maybe see that movie later."

"Oh, the one we talked about?"

"Yeah. If it's good, I'll tell you, okay?"

"Great." Dora picked up the trays and took them to the sink. She started washing out the rollers. The water was too hot, but the scalding felt appropriate.

"Hey, you okay?" Gary was putting the lids back on the paint cans.

"Yeah. Yeah, just tired. I think I'll go home and go to sleep."

Dora turned off the water and dried her hands on the completely ineffectual Chix towel before wiping them on her pants. Gary had gone to switch off the back lights.

"I'm going to get going," she called out.

"Hey, wait up, I'll walk with you...."

Dora wanted to flee but stood rooted by the door as Gary approached; they both reached for the handle at the same time.

"No, after you." Gary pulled the door open with a flourish.

"Do that tonight and you'll do well," Dora said brightly.

"No, really, do girls—I mean, *women*, of course—your age still like the doors-opening stuff?"

"You mean, do we appreciate gestures of courtesy, in this benighted age? Occasionally."

"So it's not insulting?"

"Not unless you preface it by stating, 'I know you are

too dumb to open a door; therefore, let me demonstrate to you the correct procedure.' "

"I thought chivalry was dead."

"Only the parts where women were property. The parts about performing little kindnesses for fellow human beings…Okay, that's mostly dead, too. But anyone who gets huffy about having the door opened for her should probably take herself less seriously."

"What about splitting the check?"

"The person who asks, pays, is the rule. If the decision to do something occurred to both of you simultaneously, split it. And if you're being the kind of jerkwad who thinks that paying for a pizza and a couple beers entails the automatic delivery of sexual favors, then you probably should expect her to offer to split the check. Or leave to use the bathroom and never come back."

"Pizza and beer entails sexual favors?"

"No. And if you think they do, you're an asshole."

"Okay. No sexual favors."

"No, it's 'no sexual favors as creepy weird "payment" for a dinner out.' "

"So there might be sexual favors?"

Dora looked away. "That's not up to me, now, is it?"

Gary looked as if he might be on the verge of saying something clueful, but his attention wavered. "Hey!" he shouted.

Dora looked. The quad was nearly empty, just a lone woman cutting across the grass in front of the library.

"Hey! Allison!" Gary shouted.

The woman turned and paused, then waved.

Gary started walking towards her. "That's her!" he whispered to Dora.

"Unless you think she has super-hearing, you don't have to whisper. She barely heard you shout."

"I want you to meet her." Gary's stride lengthened. Dora thought he might even break into a run. She half trotted to catch up, hating herself for doing so.

"Allison!"

"Hey, Gary." Allison was wearing a jean miniskirt and a black tank top. Despite being so casual, they were obviously expensive. Her flip-flops were thin leather, not rubber, and she wore a diamond pendant on a thin silver chain, large enough that Mimi would have pronounced it vulgar. Dora was sure she'd seen Allison's slouchy black leather shoulder bag in *Vogue*, maybe even in the editorial. Her dark-blond hair was pushed back on top of her head by her sunglasses.

"Allison, this is Dora."

"Hi," said Dora. She extended her hand. Allison shook it as if shaking hands was a quaint custom, something on the order of the curtsy.

"Dora is working with me to get the coffee shop ready."

"Oh." A faint flicker of recognition played across Allison's face. Gary chased it.

"We got a lot of painting done today.... I'm on my way to get cleaned up before we go out tonight."

"Oh." Allison put her hand on Gary's arm. "Oh, I'm so sorry. I was about to call you; I can't do tonight." She didn't offer any explanation.

Gary's face dropped. "That's okay," he said, unconvincingly. "I'm pretty wiped out—probably wouldn't be very good company."

"Another time?" Allison said. She didn't even try to sound as if she meant it. "Call me, okay?" She walked away toward the library.

Gary waited until she was out of earshot.

"Fuckity, fuckity, fuck, *fuck*," he muttered. He looked at Dora. "Sorry."

"Okay," Dora said. "But was it just me, or was she being a total bitch?"

"Total bitch," Gary said. "One-hundred-percent Grade A USDA Prime bitch."

"Why on earth would she agree to go out with you tonight and then bail?"

"Two words: 'ex-' and 'boyfriend.' I am an ex-boyfriend activator. I merely need to speak to an attractive woman and all her ex-boyfriends, every jerk and cad she's ever known, they just *feel* my vibrations or something and come out of the woodwork to try to date her again. Or at least sleep with her again."

"Really? That always happens?"

"Totally. Constantly. Infuriatingly. I bet she's going to meet some jerk right now. I bet he even owes her money."

Dora laughed. Gary looked angry; then he laughed, too.

"You're a lot of fun, you know that, Dora?" He looked at her, consideringly. "Too bad *you're* not a grad student."

"Give me time," Dora said. Surely Gary wasn't suggesting...

"Hurry up, why don't you?" Gary paused. Dora hesitated, holding her breath. "All right. Time to go home and listen to my housemate make fun of me for being stood up. See you tomorrow."

"See you," Dora said. Gary strode off, not noticeably downcast. Dora's heart lifted, too. "Hurry up and be a grad student, Dora," she said to herself.

The next morning, Dora felt her usual anticipation as she locked her bike to the rack outside the shop and headed for the door. But the door was locked, the shop was dark. Gary wasn't there.

One of the tasks on Gary's list was to get Dora her own set of keys, but he hadn't done it yet. The university changed the locks at the end of every year—much easier than trying to get all the keys back from the student workers, and cheaper in the long run, Gary had explained.

Dora decided to go outside and sit in the sunshine, instead of sitting in the musty hall. She was scrounging for a leftover student newspaper that she hadn't already read when she heard the heavy door at the end of the hall open.

"Gary?"

"Hey, Dora—am I late?"

He came through the door, but held it for a moment—long enough for Allison to pass through.

She was dressed just as casually and just as expensively as she had been the night before; this morning her miniskirt was white, and her tank a deep cobalt blue. She had the same sandals and bag, and her hair was pushed back with the same sunglasses, which had probably cost more than all the clothes in Dora's closet put together. Her white leather watchband looked like a stripe of paint against her tanned wrist. The diamond pendant, if anything, was more vulgar in the morning.

"You remember Allison, right? I met her on my way in and we stopped for coffee—ironic, I know, considering that I run a coffee shop, but we're a little understocked right now, as we undergo renovations...."

Allison's gaze flicked over Dora. Dora flushed, thinking of her raggedy painting clothes, contrasted with Allison's boutiquey elegance.

He tossed Dora the keys. "Why don't you open up

and we can give Allison a tour?" He took Allison's arm ostentatiously and swept through the door as Dora held it open, dumbly.

"This," he said, gesturing to the stacked tables and chairs, all pushed against the wall, "is our seating area. Arena. And this," as he gestured to the counter, "is our gastronomic coliseum."

Allison was obviously bored. "Nice," she said. She pulled her arm from Gary's and swapped her shoulder bag to the other side, letting it hang between them. She didn't look at Dora.

Gary seemed to realize he was losing his audience. He looked over at Dora, still standing by the door. "Hey, Dora, could you start pulling out the paint?" Dora trudged over to the storeroom, almost tripping over the drop cloth on the floor. She carefully closed the storeroom door behind her. She didn't want to hear their conversation.

She had a can open and the paint mixed, and was just about to pour it into the roller tray when Gary opened the storeroom door.

"Hey, sorry I was late this morning—I ran into Allison on my way in, and she apologized for blowing me off last night. It seems her sister came into town, and they don't really get along, but they had to get together. So that's why she was so bitchy about it."

"That's goo—"

Gary cut her off.

"She said she'd make it up to me. So we're going to that movie tonight. Maybe my ex-boyfriend karma is all worked off, what do you think?"

Dora said nothing. She concentrated on pouring the paint into the roller tray.

"I'm going to go grab the rollers. You want to bring out the trays?" Gary left the storeroom without waiting for her answer.

Dora stared at the wall, all scarred cinder block, marred with the sticky-tape marks where the previous manager's signs had once hung. A flyblown piece of paper with "FANTA AND ROOT BEER" written on it in careful capitals lay on the floor by Dora's feet; she picked it up and crumpled it carefully, then threw it full force against the wall. It was unsatisfying. *I. Will. Not. Cry,* Dora thought. She imagined her tear ducts turning to concrete, like the walls, or filling with sand. Her eyes felt hot, and she imagined her eyeballs freezing solid. She took eleven deep breaths, one for every letter of her name. It almost worked. One tear escaped. Dora wiped it angrily away, and went to set up the roller trays on the scaffolding.

She spent the rest of the day painting next to Gary. His iPod was jacked into the store's stereo, and she tried to hate every song it played. She didn't even complain about the weird dissonant modern pieces he liked, the way she had last week. She tried to hate his sloppy painting; she tried to concentrate on the fact that his hair was *definitely* thinning a bit on top. She tried to convince herself that his shoes were dorky and his gut was a bit flabby and that he made funny wheezing, whistling sounds as he stretched to reach the top of the wall.

It didn't work. She was all too aware of him, how he moved, how he smelled, how he hummed under his breath. Dora felt lightheaded, and told herself that it was just because she had skipped breakfast.

Gary, for his part, seemed to have soaked himself in oblivious before coming into the shop—or maybe it was the high of having had coffee with cool, elegant Allison. He chatted away, telling stories: crazy undergraduates he'd taught, like the student who brought in a note from a psychic excusing her from a midterm on the grounds that bad luck would befall her if she touched wood on that particular date, which the student had broadly interpreted to mean "pencils"; the guys who wanted to know if playing a kazoo would count as instrumental performance for their performance requirement; the mother who called him every day for a week after he'd given her son a B. "And it really should have a been a C, when you come right down to it, but it's hard to give a C these days. Grade inflation."

"You're quiet today," he said, when they stopped to get drinks out of the one cooler they'd left plugged in.

"I guess I just didn't get enough sleep last night."

He yawned. "Yeah, me, too. Maybe we should break off early? We've painted nearly everything we can reach to paint. We should really let some of this dry before we move the furniture around to get at the other wall."

"Sure." It was a sensible suggestion.

"And I could really use a nap before I go out tonight." Gary turned to rub the last of the paint on his roller off onto the wall.

Dora shrugged. It looked like a shrug from the outside, but inside it felt like a shiver. "Whatever you say, boss." She took the rollers and trays back to the sink to wash them out.

"All right, then," she said. "Tomorrow? Regular time?"

"Regular time," Gary said. He opened the door with a flourish. "You taking the library route?"

"I actually rode my bike today," Dora said. She turned towards the bike rack.

"Okay, see you tomorrow...."

"See you tomorrow—have fun!" Dora answered. She immediately wished she hadn't, but Gary answered her only with a vague wave. He already had his cell phone out of his pocket, and was looking at the screen disconsolately. She felt a little stab of glee that at least Allison had been too bored to even text him.

Dora made it all of two blocks away before starting to cry.

The next day was pure horror. Dora started by hitting the "snooze" button a few more times than usual; after dragging herself out of bed, she found no milk for her Grape-Nuts or bread for toast. She looked at her store of renovation-appropriate clothes before pulling out a banana-yellow T-shirt that did her no favors, and, what was worse, Dora knew it.

And yet she was still at the coffee shop before Gary. By twenty minutes. She'd almost made up her mind to call in sick, call in scorned, set something on fire, quit, or all of the above, when Gary strolled up. Allison wasn't with him—not physically, that is—but Dora could tell that their date last night had been a successful one. Gary looked smugly confident. Dora wanted to hit him.

"Hey," he said. "Look, I know I'm late, so I brought us some breakfast—those almond croissants from the new bakery, for us to try out. Want one? I know you like them...."

Dora's heart rose unaccountably, even as she tried to push it down. Gary had remembered she liked almond croissants. She forced herself to shrug. "Sure, I'll have one. Thanks."

They sat, in what Gary probably took for companionable silence, outside the shop, on a bench. Dora's croissant was gummy, or maybe her mouth was dry. Gary hadn't thought of coffee.

The rest of the day would have been normal if Dora hadn't felt like someone had removed all her skin, carefully, invisibly, and then dumped her into a swimming pool full of sand and rubbing alcohol. Everything was painful. Hearing about Allison. Not hearing about Allison. Gary's jokes, Gary's silence. Gary's grunting as they moved the furniture from one end of the shop to the other. Gary commenting on how she'd put on muscle, what with all the furniture-moving, and mock testing her biceps. Gary's blithe "Good night!" as they closed up, and his whistling as he walked away.

Dora rode her bike home, ate ice cream for dinner, and tried to top off her self-pity party with *The Princess Bride,* but had to turn it off when Buttercup realized the Dread Pirate Roberts was really Westley. Dora stared at the blank screen, and then called Gabby. "I need your advice," she said.

"You got it, honey." Dora heard Gabby sit down with a sigh. Dora pictured Gabby on the overstuffed chair in what she liked to call her "booo-dwar." "What's his name?"

"Who said it was a him?" Dora asked.

"Dorabelle, I am an expert on two things, and two things only: interior design and M-E-N. And your little apartment up there is as cute as can be. So if you want my advice it must be about a boy."

"His name is Gary."

"I don't like that name," Gabby said. She sounded serious.

"Really?" Dora tried not to sound surprised.

"He sounds older than you. I don't think any boys in your classes at school were named Gary. It's an older man's name."

"Gabby, sometimes you're scary. He's thirty."

"Thirty? And still in college?"

"Grad school."

"And you know him how?" Gabby didn't wait for Dora to answer. "Oh, no. He's that boy at the coffee shop, isn't he? Your boss?"

"I think I know what you're going to say," Dora said. "I've said it all to myself already, I think I just need to hear it from you."

"Oh, honey, it's that bad, is it?" Gabby's sympathy put a lump in Dora's throat. "I knew when you finally got hit you'd get hit hard."

"Well…" Dora pulled the afghan off the back of the couch and curled up under it.

"Tell me about him. What's he like?"

"He's funny. And he's a bit clueless. I know more about running a coffee shop than he does."

"Well, that's not a surprise. You know more than a lot of people." Gabby paused. "How does he speak to you?"

"He tells me all the time how great I am and how he'd be lost without me, and flirts constantly." Dora twisted the afghan around her feet. "And nothing else. I don't know what to think."

"Have you asked him to go do anything? Movies, or whatever you kids do? You can always do the 'I have an extra ticket' thing, although I know girls today ask boys out without a qualm, right?"

Dora snorted. "I can't. He says he can't date undergraduates."

"Well, honey, then you should look elsewhere. No sense knocking on a locked door. There are plenty of boys at Lymond, I understand it's a coed institution.…"

"Here's the thing. I could be a graduate student in January."

Gabby sounded confused. "How's that work? Don't you graduate in the spring?"

"Well, I have enough credits to graduate at the end of the fall semester, and if I do that, then I just squeak in under the wire for the deadline to apply for this Master's in Liberal Arts Program here. It starts in January, so you have to have your bachelor's degree by the end of the previous calendar year to qualify. So I lose one semester of undergraduate work, but I can start grad school earlier."

"Have you mentioned this to Mimi?"

"Not yet."

"Well, you had been talking about going to grad school. I think Mimi had hoped you'd work for a while before you did, though."

"Doing what, is the problem." Dora sighed.

"Okay, let's get back to this boy problem. If you're a grad student, you think he'd be interested?"

"I don't know...."

"Have you mentioned this plan to him?"

"I don't want him to think that I'm, well, hinting. So no."

"Well, it sounds like a complicated plan, but I'll cross my fingers for you, Dora."

"Could you cross your fingers on something else for me, too?"

"Sure, I got plenty of fingers. What is it?"

Dora took a deep breath. "When I go home for Christmas I'm going to ask Mimi to tell me about my folks. My dad and my mom."

"I don't think that's stupid. I think that's brave, and long overdue."

"I know they had a fight because my dad didn't want to work in the department store, but I don't know what it was that my dad wanted to do more."

"I don't know, either, honey. It was before my time." Gabby sounded sad.

"I wish he wanted to be a CIA agent, or swallow swords, or something, but he probably just wanted to do something normal and boring."

"Nobody Mimi raised could be boring."

"I'm taking a stab at it." Dora could hear the doorbell ringing on Gabby's end. "Do you need to get that?"

"Oh, honey, yes—Mimi's out." Gabby giggled. "I'll see you home for Thanksgiving, we can plot out how to approach Mimi then. Love you. And…good for you!"

"Love you, too.…"

Dora had settled back and let herself daydream about Gary. Once she'd graduated, she told herself, of course they'd be together.

Home in Mimi's store, though, it was harder to picture Gary in a boyfriend role. Mimi wouldn't have had any patience for Gary. Mimi found incompetence annoying, not endearing. Con, with his clipboard and truck—he was much more Mimi's style. Dora thought if Mimi could stock her closet with men as well as dresses, there would be a rack of Cons: Con in a hard hat, Con in a business suit, Con in a tuxedo. Dora lingered on the mental image of Con in a tuxedo. Just then the doorbell jangled again, and Dora jumped guiltily. No tuxedo, but it was Con.

CHAPTER SIX

CON HAD SEEN HER JUMP, BUT HE COULDN'T possibly know what she had been thinking of, Dora reassured herself. She blushed anyway.

He laughed. "Sorry, I didn't mean to startle you! Quiet day, huh?"

Dora grimaced. "*Parts* of it were quiet."

"Parts? What happened in the other parts?"

"My aunt Camille happened."

"Ah. I see."

"You know Camille?"

"Only from what Mimi's told me. And from reading between the lines of what Mimi *didn't* tell me. As in, she never told me anything nice about Camille."

"Well, there isn't anything nice about Camille. And, for extra bonus not-nice, she hauled in Tyffanee, too."

"Tyffanee?"

"Her daughter. Who got a *B-minus* in Fashion Merchandising last semester, so Camille thinks she might be able to help make this place 'sparkle.'"

"Why do I think that when someone like Camille says the word 'sparkle' she means it literally?"

"Because you're obviously a very perceptive guy." Dora blushed again. Did she really just compliment Con? She pretended to be looking for a paper clip for the day's credit-card receipts. All two of them.

"Bingo. I *am* a very perceptive guy. I am *so* perceptive, in fact, that I realized you were probably alone in the store today, and ergo you might be hungry. So, seeing as how it's nearly Southern Standard Suppertime, I thought I'd come by and see if you wanted to grab something to eat."

"I told Camille we would meet up at dinner tonight, after I go see Mimi...."

"Dinner? With the woman who, according to Mimi, won't eat any food that doesn't come in a shallow plastic tub?"

"I could call her...." Dora almost smiled.

"You could. It is entirely within the realm of possibility that you could call her."

"Actually, it's even better than that—I could call her *now,* when I know she's just had a manicure, and that way I won't even have to talk with her. I can just leave a voicemail."

"Voicemail. The last refuge of the scoundrel. But justified, in this case."

Dora already had her hand on the phone when it rang.

It was Gabby.

"Is...is everything all right?" Dora held her breath.

"Oh, baby. Yes, yes, everything's okay. I was just over at Baptist, and I thought I'd call you. The doctors said it would be better if you waited until tomorrow to visit. Mimi had a lot of tests today and she needs to rest."

Dora felt a curious mixture of relief and disappointment. She hadn't realized that she'd been dreading the trip back to the hospital all day, dreading seeing Mimi so reduced and drained.

"Oh, okay. Thanks, Gabby." Her voice was flat. "Oh—I told Camille I'd meet her for dinner back at the house, but she was just awful today, even worse than usual, and I think I'm going to cry off. I just want to warn you, in case you want to avoid seeing her, too."

"That woman!" Gabby was indignant. "Thanks for letting me know, honey. I'll find somewhere else to be, don't you worry. Don't stay out too late, though."

Con had drifted off politely to another corner of the store while Dora was on the phone.

"It sounds like today is not getting better. Everything okay?" His eyes were kind, and the tilt of his head as he looked down at her was somehow reassuring.

"That was Gabby—everything's okay. I mean, not much worse than yesterday, but Mimi's doctor wants her to get some rest tonight, so I'm not going over there."

"I hardly think you're unrestful, but listening to the doctors is usually a good idea." Con's forehead crinkled with concern. "Do you still feel up for getting something to eat?"

"Well, I feel even less up to dealing with Camille, so yes, please." Dora looked at the clock. Just past five. "Let me call Camille and close up."

Dora left a quick voicemail for Camille, explaining that she wouldn't be home for dinner.

Grabbing her bag from the back room, she caught sight of herself in the broken cheval mirror, the one Mimi had been meaning to get fixed since Dora was about twelve. The jagged reflection showed a pale and tired Dora in each shard. *If Mimi were here, she would nag me to put on lipstick.* A quick rummage in the little medicine cabinet in the bathroom turned up an old tube of Elizabeth Arden; Dora put it on carefully. She wasn't good with real, grown-up makeup like eyeliner and lipstick. She had always been more of a tinted-moisturizer and lip-balm kind of person, but tinted moisturizer and lip balm didn't really seem to go with her new-old wardrobe. The lipstick, according to a faded sticker on the end of the tube, was a color called Charming. It must have looked great on Mimi, Dora decided. It didn't feel as odd as lipstick normally felt, which Dora attributed to the aura of her dress. She smoothed the skirt and picked a stray thread off her hem.

Out on the sidewalk the night was warm and almost muggy. Dora was dusty and stiff from being in the shop. Suddenly she felt awkward. "Thanks for being—for being so kind to me," she said.

"I'm glad you're letting me help," Con said. Dora looked up at him. He looked serious. "Lots of folks did nice things for me when my dad was sick, and I was beginning to worry about all the karmic debt."

"Karmic debt—do they have a payment plan for that?" Dora felt at ease again.

"The terms are very reasonable. What you want to avoid is karmic bankruptcy. That's a killer. You can't get any good karma for seven years afterwards."

"Good to know."

Con grinned. "Where do you want to eat? Monday in Forsyth...so our choices are fast food, fast food, and the K&W Cafeteria. Or fast food." He stopped for a minute. "Huh. I didn't really think this through." He looked at his watch. "When do you have to get back? There's a great Mexican place I know, but it's in Greensboro."

"I don't have a curfew....Would you mind? I mean, driving to Greensboro?" Usually Dora loved the K&W, but it would be full of folks who would ask her about Mimi. "I know it's cowardly, but I think the sympathy is

almost the worst part. Far fewer people in a Mexican restaurant in Greensboro will ambush me with any."

"I understand." Con swapped his clipboard to his other
hand, and offered Dora his arm. "Greensboro it is. Your
chariot awaits."

Dora took his arm. She waited for the awkwardness to
hit, but it didn't feel dorky or awkward at all. "Must be the
dress," she muttered.

"What?"

"Nothing—Greensboro, please."

They hit a little traffic outside the airport. Con looked
over at her. "This is where real Forsythians complain
about how built up we're getting, just so you know."

"I suppose it's nothing to someone who's lived in New
York, huh?"

"Well, I didn't drive much in New York. Or at all. Sub-
way all the way, baby."

"Did you live in Manhattan?" Dora was trying to imagine Con in Manhattan. She could only picture the New
York of *Breakfast at Tiffany's*. George Peppard sitting up in
bed...She shook her head.

"Busted," Con laughed. "I couldn't afford Manhattan.
I lived in Brooklyn. Park Slope. Which is very, very, very
nice, as I explained to my mother about one hundred
thousand times."

"Didn't she go visit you?"

"She was going to—they were going to—then my dad
got sick." Con braked as a minivan swerved into their
lane. "One of my few regrets."

"I'm sorry." Dora wondered if she should reach over
and take Con's hand. Before she could make up her mind,

Con had reached for the radio. "Maybe we can get a traffic report."

While he fiddled with the dials, Dora looked out the window, and tried not to think about her own regrets.

By the time Con found a traffic report, the slowdown had passed. "Go figure," he said. "Gotta remember that trick—listening to the traffic report makes the traffic disappear."

"Now if only there was a parking report, you'd have everything Forsythians complain about solved...." Dora suddenly remembered her bike.

"I left my bike—Mimi's bike—at the shop."

"How about I pick you up, then, tomorrow, on my way into the Feathertons'? I have to warn you, construction starts early. Could you be ready at seven?"

"I could just drive...."

"There's a parking crisis, remember? I don't mind picking you up."

The restaurant was small—only ten booths. Loud Tejano music was playing, but the cook turned it down when they walked in.

"What do you want?" The choices were on a board above the counter.

"Um, just a burrito, I guess. Chicken?"

"I gotta warn you: they are as big as your head." Con cocked his head to one side and looked at Dora. "Possibly bigger. We could get one, and measure them both...."

"Three chicken tacos, with everything. And a Coke," Dora said firmly.

"Good choice." Con ordered for her, and got a burrito and a Coke himself.

They sat down, and the waitress brought their food, plus a giant basket of chips and guacamole and salsa.

Con dipped a chip in salsa and took a big bite. "Hot pepper," he gasped, and reached for his Coke. His eyes were streaming. Dora reached into her pocket and gave him her handkerchief. Con mopped his eyes, then raised his eyebrows at the knot in it.

"Nervous habit?"

"It's for luck." Dora took a more cautious bite of a chip laden with guacamole. "It's something Mimi does," she explained.

"Does it work?"

"We'll have to see," she said. She didn't look at him.

Con applied himself to his burrito. "Tell me something you hate," he said.

"Um, why?" Dora looked at him mock suspiciously. "Are you recruiting for something?"

"I just think you get a better idea of a person by asking them about what they dislike than about what they like— I mean, everyone likes puppies."

"I hate puppies," Dora said. Con's eyes widened. "Just kidding."

"Whew." Con used Dora's handkerchief to mop imaginary sweat from his brow. "You had me worried."

"What do I hate? I hate Velcro." Dora took a bite of her taco for emphasis. "It's too easy. And it makes noise. It's an accomplishment to be able to tie your own shoes. And tying your shoes is silent. Those are both good things. There is nothing good about Velcro."

"What about for astronauts?"

"What about for astronauts?"

"Like when there's no gravity, and they put Velcro on

the walls and their shoes so they can hang in one place and not float around." Con dared another chip, carefully avoiding the jalapeños in the salsa.

"I thought they did that with magnets."

"I'm pretty sure it's Velcro. Would you want giant shoe-magnets near the computer that runs the space station?"

"Well, I'm sure that if they can send a computer to space, they can shield it from cosmic rays and magnets and probably spilled coffee, too." Dora stuck her tongue out at Con.

"Velcro would be easier. I'm just saying."

"Well, what do you hate, Mr. Velcro Apologist?"

"Nothing. I am a man without animus." Dora threw a chip at him.

"Now we've escalated to physical violence, I see," Con intoned. "The reaction of the rabble to the man without hate is always instructive."

"Seriously." Dora looked at Con.

"Okay, don't out me to the other members of the He-Man Woman Haters Club, but I despise baseball."

" 'Despise' is a strong word." Dora looked down at her plate. All she had left were shreds of lettuce and cheese. She snagged another chip.

"If you know a stronger one, I'll use that. It's just a bunch of fat guys trotting around. And they use *tools*. That's not a sport, that's a job. A sport is bodies and a ball and that's it. Basketball is sport. Baseball is . . . interpretive dance."

"Interpretive dance where they keep score?"

"People always keep score, Dora," Con said, in a cynical voice.

The waitress came over and refilled their water glasses. They were the only diners left.

"For instance," Con went on, "I bet you're keeping score on me right now. Right? What do I score?"

Dora smiled weakly. "Um, on what scale?"

"Any scale. Every scale. Pick a scale."

"I know one where you're off the charts." Dora looked Con straight in the eye. "Kindness."

Now Con looked down...and did Dora see a blush? Or was it the aftereffects of the hot peppers?

"Aw, that just means I'm picking up the check." He got up before Dora could stop him and paid at the register. Dora dug around in her bag and dumped a handful of singles and a five on the table. She went to stand beside Con at the register. "I left the tip," she said.

He glanced back at the table. "You left two tips," he said. "You'll have to eat at my brother's restaurant sometime; his staff would love you."

They played "What do you hate?" all the way back to Forsyth. Dora hated ankle-high socks ("especially on men"), cigar smoke, the noise a pepper grinder makes, and Con hated chocolates with "wet insides," any show where people burst into song for no reason ("But what if the reason is that they're *in a musical*?" asked Dora, which Con ignored), and some kind of hammer that Dora immediately forgot the name of. "It's a terrible hammer, let's leave it at that. And imagine how bad at hammering something has to be to be a bad hammer," said Con. "Your turn."

"Camille."

"Okay, okay. I understand she's pretty bad, as family goes, but she's still family."

"No—there's Camille, waiting on the front porch."

Con peered through the windshield.

"She looks terrifying. You want me to talk to her?" She was sitting on the front porch in the same grubby bathrobe. Dora felt mortified.

"No, no—that's okay. She's probably waiting for Tyffanee," she said, with a conviction she didn't feel. *If anything has happened with Mimi . . .*

"If you're sure . . ." Con reached out and squeezed Dora's hand. "I'll see you in the morning. Seven sharp."

Dora didn't want to move her hand, or to open the door and leave the safety of Con's truck, either, but she could see Camille gathering herself to come off the porch and across the lawn to the street.

"Thank you again, Con . . . for everything. Good night."

"Good night."

Dora hurried over to Camille. "Camille, what on earth?"

"Do you *know* what time it is?" Camille made a big show of looking at her watch.

Dora cut her off. "Camille, whatever time it is, it's too late for you to be sitting outside in your robe."

"And who was that?"

"A friend of Mimi's," Dora said. "Conrad Murphy."

"Mimi has young man friends?"

"He's a contractor doing work in the building, and Mimi was helping him with some other project, I think. He took me to dinner to cheer me up."

"What do you know about this person? How do you know he really knows Mimi? And he bought you dinner, of all things? I don't like it," said Camille, in rising tones. "I've seen stories about stuff like this. People are vultures when someone is sick."

The irony of the statement was clearly lost on Camille; Dora swallowed the urge to point it out.

"It is late, Camille, and I'm really tired. I'm sorry you were worried. We can talk in the morning."

"That we will." Camille looked smug. She stomped back through the front door.

Dora left her bag on the hall table. Gabby's bag wasn't in its usual place, and her keys weren't on the hook where she kept them (when she remembered). Dora called out to Camille, who had settled herself back in front of the television.

"Camille, did Gabby call?"

Camille actually muted the television to reply. "I haven't seen her all evening. If she's here, she flew up the stairs."

Dora wished she could fly up the stairs. She trudged up them instead.

Dora was hunting around for her phone charger when she saw the power light of her laptop winking at her. The only problem with Con's "distractions," she thought, was that they almost made the nondistracted time more difficult. Email. She should check her email.

ANT UPDATE
Dear Dora,

The ant-o-cide was today; the exterminator came immediately and was very efficient. He assured us everything was food-safe but now we blow the sugar off the powdered doughnuts before we eat them just to be sure.

We've missed you, is everything okay? When are you coming back?

G.

ARE YOU THE KEYMASTER?

Dora-ble,

If not, who is? Sheila lost her key and we should probably get the locks changed.

Still miss you.

G.

WHAT WAS LOST HAS BEEN FOUND

Yo, D.:

Sheila's key fell in the coffee beans. Key fine, grinder dislocated. Coffee machine repair number not answering. Ideas?

Really miss you.

G.

PS Yes we threw out all the beans that were in the grinder when we found the key.

ODD QUESTION

Dooooooooooora,

What would you do if a full can of soda fell behind the biggest cooler and exploded? Would it involve ignoring it and hoping it goes away? Please say yes.

And by "fell" I mean "was thrown."

Words cannot express how much we all miss you.

XOXO

G.

AND ANOTHER THING

Dora,

Actually, everything else is fine. Just wanted to drive home the point that we miss you and want you to come back asap.

XOXO
Gary
PS I lied. I can't find the bakery order sheet.
PPS Amy found another grinder repairman. His name is Jacques, and he's what Amy calls "a hottie." I hate him.

Gary's emails made Dora feel oddly impatient. He was a grown man, wasn't he? It was one thing to be needed, another thing to be the object of infantile dependence. Besides, Dora had a pretty good idea of who had thrown that soda. She started to hit "reply" to the last email, then sighed and closed the laptop.

She emptied her pockets out onto the dresser. Con had kept her handkerchief.

CHAPTER SEVEN

DORA WAS UP IN PLENTY OF TIME TO shower and take a little extra time choosing a dress from the closet. Today's was a deep-plum mandarin-collared shirtdress with gray piping along the placket. Dora dropped her lip balm into one pocket, and a clean handkerchief into the other, and grabbed a gray cardigan before going downstairs to make coffee. She tiptoed past Camille's door, but heard nothing but deep, resonant snores coming from within.

Con was there, right on time, at seven. He didn't honk, but he didn't have to, because Dora was watching at the window for his truck. She carried out two travel mugs of coffee.

"You like it black, right?" she said, as she climbed into the truck. The seat didn't seem so high today.

"I do, and I thank you. I'll have to call my regular coffee place and let them know I'm not dead, though. They worry if I don't come in."

"No rule against drinking two cups of coffee, you know."

In the quiet of the early morning Dora and Con were quiet, too. Forsyth's glorious fall was almost over. The leaves left on the trees were flaming red and orange, the gutters full of fallen leaves.

They were nearly at the shop before Con spoke. "I like your dress," he said. "It suits you."

"Thank you. Mimi picked it out for me."

"She has a good eye."

Dora didn't know what to say, but luckily they were already at Mimi's shop. "Here we are," he said, as his phone rang.

"Yes, Mrs. Featherston, I'm right downstairs now.... Be right up...." He waved as Dora hopped out. She waved back, a bit limply, as he drove around the corner.

●   ●   ●

Tuesday was busy. Dora spent the time before opening setting out new stock and refilling the racks, and she was glad she had. She sold four dresses, a suit, a handbag, and a pair of 1950s stilettos before they'd been open an hour. None had had a secret life. Dora had been so sure that one of the dresses (a wool sheath with a complicated, fussy neckline, in a strident royal blue) would have one, but there was nothing in the file. It was a dress for a bossy woman, but the customer who had tried it on had been hesitant, asking Dora question after question. Did it fit quite right in the shoulders? Could she really wear something this bright? Would she have the right shoes? What kind of jewelry would you wear with that neckline? Dora answered all the questions truthfully, as best she could, but she knew there was some underlying unarticulated question that Mimi would have known how to elicit. Even though the woman bought the dress, Dora felt like they were both left vaguely dissatisfied with the sale.

Dora even started jotting down a few notes about the dress and its secret life on the back of one of the store postcards ("Bossy woman?—Meeting debacle?—never worn again?") before a gaggle of high-school girls came in and swallowed her attention. Things stayed busy until Maux showed up at lunchtime, and by then Dora had to run out to the bank for change.

"Usually bank robbers go for larger bills," a deep voice from over her shoulder interjected as Dora juggled three rolls of quarters and tried to jam a stack of singles into her pocket.

Startled, Dora dropped a roll of quarters, and it landed on the terrazzo with a thud. Stooping to pick it up, Dora found herself facing Con.

"It's not a dropped handkerchief, but at least allow me the trivial courtesy of retrieving your...laundry money?"

"It's for the shop—we've had a crazy morning. Mimi used to say Tuesdays were good days, but I had no idea it would be this busy. Thanks again for the ride, by the way."

"Not a problem, happy to do it." Con gestured to the ATM line. "I'd better take my place—if I don't get cash I can't buy the boys lunch, and I like to do that if they're going to spend the afternoon taking out the cabinets they installed yesterday. Do you need a ride to the hospital tonight?"

"Gabby's going to take me, actually, on her way to some meeting or other." Dora looked down at the bank floor. "I should just drive down here, but Mimi always went to ridiculous lengths for car-pooling....She hated driving more than absolutely necessary. I mean, I don't think she hated the driving, as much as the parking. Every time I drove to the store I could see her thinking that it was one less parking space for a paying customer."

Con laughed. "I can see that. The Featherstons are rabid on the subject of parking around here. They're always complaining that the building doesn't have enough spaces."

"What, they can't just buy them?"

"They've tried. Nobody's selling. Everyone in the building has figured out that if they sell their parking space separately, they'll never resell their condo. And even the Featherstons aren't rich enough to buy a whole apartment just for the parking space. Yet." Con shrugged. "Anyway I might stop by at the hospital tonight, if you don't mind. I thought I was going to have to work late, but Mrs. Featherston still hasn't decided on her molding, so we should be done by six, at the latest." Con gave her a questioning look.

"And for tonight's distraction—what do you think of bowling? We could grab pizza there, or something, unless you owe Camille a dinner to make up for yesterday." He smiled at her. "Evenings after the hospital were always the worst for me. I'd eat a frozen burrito and watch reruns of *SportsCenter*, and that's not a fate I'd wish on anyone."

"Did you thaw them first?" Dora smiled. "The burritos?"

"Mostly. Sometimes they were a little cold in the middle. So tonight? Bowling?" He paused. "Unless you'd rather watch *SportsCenter*?"

"No, no *SportsCenter* for me."

"Okay. I'll meet you at the hospital. See you then—and, look"—Con nodded towards the security guard, who was busy flirting with one of the tellers—"I think you can still make a clean getaway."

"Got it. Don't rat me out, now, you hear?"

"Wouldn't dream of it."

Dora turned to let a shuffling man, who must have been creeping up on eighty, rearrange his cane and adjust his hat before graciously accepting his offer of an opened door. Her skirts swished as she walked by, and the heels of her loafers clacked pleasantly on the floor of the lobby.

Maux was swamped at the register and sent Dora a look of exasperation as she came in the door. "What took you so long?"

"Ran into someone at the bank. You know, people asking about Mimi."

"People?"

"Con."

"Oh, you mean *Beefcake*. He's dreeeeamy." Maux's singsong made Dora laugh.

"We're going bowling tonight, after the hospital. He has this distraction karma to pay off, or something."

"Really?"

"Are you surprised at the bowling? Or that I'm going with Con?"

"Well, a little of both. You're a terrible bowler. And aren't you supposed to be alternately moping and scheming about that boss of yours?"

"Gary?" Now Dora sounded surprised. "I didn't even think about Gary."

"Now, that's surprising."

Dora was about to protest, but then she saw a girl heading for the dressing room with a fragile thirties silk dress that, conservatively, was three sizes smaller than she was. Dora ran to go talk her out of trying it on.

"That was well done," Maux said later, when the rush had finally died down. "I hate to discourage people from trying things on, but she was going to demolish that dress."

"I told her it was mislabeled as a ten when it was really a six, and that I'd been meaning to re-mark it all day. Then I showed her that red ruffle dress."

"The 1970s one that looks like nothing on the hanger but great when you have it on?"

"Yep, that one. She bought it." Dora tried not to look too pleased with herself.

"Did it have a secret life? I always thought that one would."

"Wait, did everyone but me know about the secret lives?" Dora tried to sound like she was joking.

Maux looked uncomfortable. "Um, I didn't know Mimi hadn't told you. She'd just started giving them away—she called it her new project. Honestly, Mimi didn't really make a big deal out of them. It was like the auto-body shop giving out calendars, or something. Just a business thing."

"Right. Short stories about dresses, refrigerator magnets, totally the same thing. Did Mimi write them?"

"I think so, but she's never come out and said it. You know Mimi, she wouldn't take the credit even if she'd brought about world peace."

"Hmmm." Dora was still trying to figure out what she thought about the secret lives. "I forgot to look." Dora turned to the spindle that held the completed receipts. "It was number nine oh five—want to check?"

"Oh, yeah." Maux sounded satisfied. "It's got one, I knew it!"

I'm a dress that's built for dancing. It's very simple to say, but it's complicated to explain. There are all kinds of dancing, pink tulle dancing and black leotard dancing, dancing with those dresses that stick way out, dancing with bells and ribbons. There's dancing you do with partners, of course, and I've done some of that. And every kind of dancing has a different kind of dress.

I didn't really know that I was a dress built for dancing, though, until she started dancing by herself. She'd put me and the music on and just spin and spin. I don't know if there were steps, or if she was doing "a dance." All I know is that she'd move until the record sputtered out, and then collapse, laughing.

As far as I know, she never wore any other dress to dance in, and she never did anything in me other than dance. If something just does one thing, it's made for that thing, right? That's how it seems to me. A knife cuts and a hose waters and I help her dance. That's how it is.

Maux folded the secret life and put it carefully back in the envelope. There was something weird about her left hand. Dora was about to ask if Maux had hurt herself when she noticed that what she'd thought was an injury was Maux, admiring a large new ring.

"Maux?" Dora looked pointedly at Maux's hand.

"Ha, I won!" Maux almost shouted. Dora was confused.

"Harvey thought that, with everything going on—you know—you wouldn't notice the ring before closing today. I told him you were like Mimi, you notice everything… but I was starting to worry, Dora."

"You're…" Comprehension snuck in.

"Engaged!" Maux threw some of the desk postcards in the air like confetti.

"Congratulations! I mean, how wonderful!" Dora rushed to hug Maux, who accepted it with good grace.

"Don't worry, I won't tell Mimi you congratulated a bride," Maux smirked. "I must have heard her say a thousand times that you felicitate a bride and congratulate a groom, although I have no idea why there's a difference."

"Oh, she explained it to me once," Dora said. "You congratulate a groom because you congratulate someone for achievements, and he is supposed to achieve you. The other way around sounds like what Mimi called 'husband-hunting.'"

Maux snorted. "Then you can congratulate the hell out of me. I landed Harvey and I'm gonna keep him."

"So...how did he propose? Do his parents know?"

Maux sighed. "That whole rigamarole of going out to dinner with them two nights in a row was because Harvey dicked around and muffed the proposal before the first dinner. He was all set to propose to me at the fountain, you know the one downtown, and he forgot the ring! His parents had been in on it, and that dinner was supposed to be our let's-celebrate dinner, and then he had to take them aside and tell them that he hadn't proposed. So then we did it all over again the next night. Only this time, he remembered the ring!"

"So let me see it!" Dora grabbed for Maux's hand. The ring was a black piece of onyx, cut like a traditional diamond in a prong setting.

"Wow." The ring was disturbingly beautiful—like Maux. "Harvey did a good job."

"Yeah, we're not actually diamond people, you know. I think they generally look like shit. And Harvey has such strong goth connections—he had a friend make this for us." Maux held her hand out and regarded it. "Needless to say, I love it. And him. And I'm getting married!"

Dora and Maux talked wedding details the rest of the afternoon, in between customers. Maux even looked at Mimi's rack of wedding dresses, which she kept in the back room—strictly by appointment only.

"Too soon," she said, fingering a satin column. "I gotta get used to the idea first."

Maux insisted on helping Dora with the closing. "You've been doing too much," she said. "Harv and I are going out tonight to do a little engagement celebration with our friends, but it won't start until late. I've got plenty of time."

She tidied and cleaned and even hauled out the vacuum cleaner, while Dora did the register tally. It had been a good day.

Maux had just left when Gabby rushed in. It was only a few minutes after six, but Gabby apologized as if it had been midnight.

"I just don't know what's gotten into me lately, Dora," she said, shaking her head. "I swear, if my head wasn't attached I would leave it on the bus. Not that I take the bus. On the front seat of the car, maybe?"

Gabby looked at Dora, consideringly. "That's a good dress, Dora. Did you have a good day in it?"

That was so much like something Mimi would say that Dora couldn't answer. She only nodded. She took a few deep breaths. "It was a great day—I'll tell you all about it. What did you do today?"

"Oh, this and that," said Gabby, airily. "Errands. You know." She seemed disinclined to elaborate.

Dora locked up and pocketed the keys. "Well, here's the big news; Maux and Harvey are engaged!"

"Don't that beat all!" Gabby looked genuinely pleased.

She sniffled a little. Gabby almost always got a bit teary at just the mention of a wedding.

"Here's the funny thing: Maux has this huge ring, of course, but it's an onyx cut to look like a diamond, in a Tiffany-style setting, and everything. It's amazing. I'm sure she can't wait for you to see it." Dora smiled. "But that's not the funny part—it took me until way late in the day before I even noticed it!"

Dora glanced down at her own ring fingers. She never wore rings. Gabby usually did—big cocktail rings, mostly, cheerfully fake. But her rings today were smaller than her usual rings. They looked almost real.

"Gabby, did you get some new rings?"

"Oh, no, just some old things I hadn't worn in a while; I thought I'd take them out for a spin...." Gabby quickly put her hands in her pockets.

"Well, anyway, good for Maux and Harvey!" Gabby said, then changed the subject. "Did you see that they're putting an addition on the Gallaghers' house? I don't think it's your Con Murphy that's doing it, though."

"He's not my Con Murphy," Dora protested.

"He could be if you wanted, I bet," Gabby teased.

"I don't know where you and Mimi get the idea that I'm some sort of femme fatale, you know. It's not like I've paraded a string of men past you two."

"And don't think Mimi wasn't grateful. When you think of all the trouble you could have gotten into, like that girl in the class ahead of yours, Missy what's-her-face..."

"I think she's in law school now, so it couldn't have been that much trouble, Gabby." Dora didn't remember Missy; she just wanted to get Gabby off the subject of her and Con Murphy.

Gabby drove to the hospital by a different route; instead of going on the parkway, she took the more scenic route, past the golf course and the campus. Dora didn't mind; she wanted to see Mimi, of course, but at the same time she didn't want to be in the hospital. Dora longed for Gabby to drive her home, and to see Mimi come to the door, and have it all be an elaborate practical joke.

Gabby pulled up in the hospital's ambulance-loading circle.

"I don't want you walking through that garage at night, Gabby. I know it's only Forsyth, but…"

"It's okay, honey. I'm just going to drop you off, and then I'll come back for you whenever you call. I went in earlier today, and you should have some time with your grandmother without everyone crowding you."

"You don't crowd me, Gabby," Dora protested.

"That's as it may be, but I'm dropping you off. When do you think you'd like me to come back and get you?"

It felt like junior high again, with Gabby dropping her off at a dance, considerably out of sight of the other kids, so as not to "embarrass" her.

"Con's actually going to stop by.… He asked if I wanted to do something afterwards." Dora didn't want to say bowling; it seemed absurd. First go visit your ill grandmother, then go bowling.

"Oh, would that be he's-not-my-Con-Murphy Con Murphy?" Gabby teased. "Okay, okay. But call me if you need me."

Dora kissed Gabby goodbye and went in.

CHAPTER EIGHT

TUESDAY NIGHT AT THE HOSPITAL WAS weird. Mimi's hall was quiet, deserted, a few nurses moving silently between the rooms, until the PA punctuated the silence with demands for various doctors to come to the ER, stat.

Dora sat next to Mimi's bed, and held her hand. Talk to her, she told herself.

"I was at the store today," she said. "Con Murphy gave me a ride this morning."

Dora felt that if this was all she could manage, Mimi would never recover.

"Maux has some news! She's engaged. To Harvey, of course. Maux and I did a little more inventory. There's a fantastic bridal gown we found in one of the boxes, I can't believe you didn't have it on the rack. Very Grace Kelly princessy, but Maux looked at it for a really long time.... No matter what she wears she'll make a gorgeous bride."

In a normal conversation Mimi would have had a thousand questions already. Instead there was just her breathing, which sounded far too loud in the quiet room, interrupted by the clueless and insensitive noises the machines made. Dora felt her eyes fill up.

"Mimi, I'm sorry I bothered you about my parents. I know you had good reasons for not talking about them.

I know what it feels like to have something hurt too much to talk about."

Dora stood up. She leaned over and kissed Mimi's forehead.

"I'll be back tomorrow, Mimi. I love you."

A nurse came in, intent on checking charts. Dora fled.

When Con arrived he found her sitting on the bench in the hall, tying knots in another handkerchief.

"Everything okay? Is the doctor in there with her? Did they say no visitors?"

"She's able to have visitors. I'm just not able to be a visitor right now."

Con sat down next to her and put his hand over hers. Dora marveled at how much it helped. His hand was warm, and a bit rough. "It's okay, I know."

"I don't think it's going to be okay." Dora concentrated, hard, on not sniffling.

"Maybe not in the short term, but in the long term, it will be."

"How long term is long term?" Dora kept her hand very still, afraid Con would take his away, although he was giving no indication that he would.

"We can start on the geologic scale and work down from there."

Dora tried to smile, but a few traitorous tears ran down her cheeks. Con took his hand away from hers... and put his arm around her shoulder instead.

"Hey, hey, it's really gonna be okay." Dora let her head rest on his shoulder. His shirt was cool and smooth.

They stayed that way for a minute, and then the nurse came out of the room.

"Miz Winston? You can go back in now." As if she had been the reason for Dora's flight. Dora sat up.

"You don't have to, you know," Con said, as the nurse padded down the hall in her plastic shoes. "You can sit right here. I'll go in for a minute, if you don't mind, and then we'll go bowling. Have you eaten today?"

Dora tried to think. "It was so busy.... I had coffee. And a red-hot from Mimi's candy dish."

"Part of a balanced breakfast, sure." Con gave her a squeeze. "Then we'll definitely eat. Maybe some starlight mints, then we can move on to butterscotch discs."

He moved easily into Mimi's room, like it wasn't a hospital room at all—like it was Mimi's house, and he was invited for dinner. All he was missing was a bottle of wine.

Dora was still sitting on the bench when Con came out. Her handkerchief was one big knot.

Con didn't say anything. He just offered Dora his arm again. Gratefully, she took it.

CHAPTER NINE

CON'S TRUCK WAS AS CLOSE TO THE DOOR of the parking garage as it could be without being in a handicapped space. Dora was slightly disappointed. Walking with Con—even in a parking garage—was nice.

They were in the car and out of the garage before Dora spoke.

"Would you mind if we didn't go bowling? I just—the noise—"

Con stopped her. "Dora, it's okay. We'll wear ridiculous shoes another time, I'm sure. But you really should get something to eat. How about Lud's—that okay with you?"

"Lud's, oh, absolutely." Dora looked out the window for a minute, until she was sure she wasn't going to cry. Con seemed to understand.

"So did you hang out at Lud's? In high school?"

"Not really," Dora's voice was slightly thick. "It was more of a guy place. You'd go with a guy after a movie, or with a group of girls who were all dressed up to be looked at but pretending not to be."

"Ah, I remember that. Giggling and hair-tossing?"

"Well, those that could toss, did. Some of us were less gifted in the tossing department."

Con reached over and pulled one of Dora's curls, gently.

He let it sproing back into place. "Hmm. I see. I never liked the hair-tossing myself. Seemed unsanitary."

Something about the gesture made Dora smile. Con didn't notice; he was concentrating on finding a parking spot.

Inside, Lud's was crowded, even for a Tuesday night. Con looked dismayed.

"Hey, there's a booth opening up over there," Dora said. "If you go stand by it and look menacing, I can order."

"I'll order—you go menace. What do you want?"

"Italian, light on the peppers, and a Diet Coke." Dora fumbled with her bag, but Con waved her off.

"I got it. Go grab us a seat. Go light on the menace, too, we don't want to get kicked out."

Dora got to the booth just as the previous occupants were picking up their last napkins and heading to the trash. She sat down quickly, and smiled at the busboy who wiped off the table.

Con sat down with the tray, and slid a sandwich across the booth to Dora.

"Italian, light on the hot peppers. Diet Coke. Plus chips."

"Oh, perfect. I forgot chips." Dora unwrapped the sandwich and took a bite. "What'd you get?"

"Roast beef and cheddar with peppers." Con pulled a napkin from the dispenser.

"That's Mimi's favorite," Dora said. She hoped she said it matter-of-factly, the same way you'd say, "It's Tuesday," but she wasn't sure she'd pulled it off.

"Really? I would have pegged her as a tuna-fish-and-sprouts."

"No—Mimi hates tuna fish. Any fish in a can, actually.

No sardines. No canned salmon." Dora took a careful sip of her soda.

"Huh. That never came up." Con smiled at Dora. Not a fakey "It's okay" smile; a real one. "I know exactly how Mimi feels about the new traffic light at First and Cedar, but not her favorite sandwich. Or any of her favorite foods, actually."

"Do you want to know her all-time favorite thing to eat?"

"You know I do."

"Pigs in blankets."

"You mean those little hors d'oeuvre things?"

"Exactly. When I was little we'd have 'parties,' just me and her, and she'd heat up a package of those frozen ones and we'd drink ginger ale on the rocks and I'd feel terribly, terribly sophisticated."

Con laughed.

"I know, I know—I think she did it just to get out of cooking. And of course I loved it—what kid wouldn't?"

"Mimi should meet my brother," Con said. "He'd give her hors d'oeuvres until her head spun."

"Where does he work?"

"At a a very, very fancy restaurant—some of his plates are more 'architectural' than anything I ever made. It's in Savannah."

"Does he come back here much?"

"Once or twice a year. If we're lucky." Con smiled. "Do I sound bitter? I hope not."

"Is he older, or younger?"

"Oh, he's older. A couple years. Just enough to give him an advantage in every fight we had as kids... and for him to already be an established chef when my dad died."

"Now you sound bitter."

"I'm sorry." Con tried for a smile. "Kevin worked every summer with my dad, and spent the winters training as a chef. I don't think my dad ever took the chef thing seriously, but Kevin did. So, when he decided to leave construction and be a chef full-time, my dad was pretty mad. I was just finishing up architecture school, so my dad was left to run the whole business himself."

"And then he got sick." Dora's voice was flat.

"And then he got sick, and I came home."

"Do you mind it—living here again? Especially after living in New York?"

Now Con really smiled. "The funny thing is, I love it. I love the work—even for Mrs. Featherston. I like making real places for real people, instead of making imaginary places for imaginary people, like I did before. And I like being near my mom, even if she does spend half her time down in Savannah with my niece and nephew, and the other half nagging me about why I'm not married."

Con's eyes dropped to his sandwich. Dora felt awkward.

"So—why aren't you married?" Dora tried to sound jokey, but it didn't quite work.

"No bride price saved up. You know how long it takes to amass a herd of cows?"

"Couldn't you hang out for a big dowry instead?"

"Hmm, hadn't thought of that."

"Not very romantic." Dora carefully adjusted the bendy angle of her straw.

"If anything, an arranged marriage would be good for me—but please don't tell my mom that! I tend to fall in love with ideals and then be heartbroken when they turn out to be just plain real."

"Oh?" Dora took another bite.

"Yeah…I once spent a semester in school in love with the sister of my roommate, based only on his description of her. Then, when she came for a visit…it was terrible."

"How terrible?"

"Well, I found out later that he had two sisters, but I had mixed them into one person. Who obviously fell short of my expectations. But in my defense, their names were Bella and Della. How was I expected to keep that straight?"

Dora laughed.

"Names aside, I should have figured that it would be hard for the same person to be a symphony oboist and training to be a doctor to help sick kids in Africa."

"People surprise you," Dora said.

"They do, at that." Con's voice was considering. He paused, and grinned at Dora. "So that's me. Family business and nagging mom. I could be a sitcom. Tell me more about your childhood." Con was mopping up the melted cheese from his sandwich with a potato chip.

"Well, I used to have to read Mimi bedtime stories."

"Huh?"

"After I learned to read, she said that reading stories out loud was so much fun that she didn't think it was fair to hog them all herself, so every other night it was my turn to read to her."

"That sounds like a very sneaky way to get you to read."

"Mimi's very sneaky," Dora laughed. "Gabby and I used to say that if she went to college she would have majored in reverse psychology."

"Mimi didn't go to college?"

"No—her parents couldn't afford it—and they spent their money on her half-brother, my uncle John, since he was a boy. They thought college would be wasted on a girl who only needed an 'M-R-S degree,' anyway." Dora sighed. "Which is probably why she was so flat-out insane about me going to Lymond."

"Lymond's a good school," Con said.

"Yeah, but it's kind of overkill for me. You can be just as aimless and undirected at a mediocre school, and you have to write fewer papers."

"I don't think of you as aimless." Con inspected the bag for any hidden potato chips. "You seem pretty precisely aimed to me."

"Oh, did Mimi tell you I was thinking about grad school? That's me hitting the snooze button on the 'What do I do with my life?' alarm clock."

"She does talk about you a lot—but I was thinking about the store. Not a lot of people could step right in and keep all the plates spinning the way you have."

Dora sighed. "It's just to keep busy, and keep Camille and Tyffanee away, really. I'd burn the place down for the insurance money before I'd let them sell their tacky crap in Mimi's place. She'd never forgive me."

"Don't look now, but I think Mimi's insurance guy is over there by the door, so perhaps you want to keep your voice down?"

Dora giggled.

"Mimi's insurance guy is Mr. Bannell, and he would love it if I burned the place down. He seems to think Mimi's been cheated because she's never had to make a claim. He might go in and smash a few windows himself. I've never seen a guy so eager to pay out money...."

"Bannell? He's, like, ninety, wears bow ties?"

"That's him."

Con looked stern. "I've seen him hanging around Mimi. I bet he has a crush."

"What he has is five remaining clients and retirement-induced boredom. He's so bored he's itching for paper-work to file." Dora pushed her half-finished potato chips over to Con, who started eating them absentmindedly.

"Didn't Mimi ever think of remarrying? After your grandfather died? What was he like?"

"I don't really remember my grandfather—he wasn't in good health when I was born, and he died when I was about three. But Mimi really loved him.... There's this *warmth* in her voice whenever she talks about him. Like she has a private joke she doesn't want to share. I don't think anybody else could ever measure up. Plus she had me—I don't think there are many retired guys who want to spend their golden years raising someone else's grandbaby."

"And there's Gabby."

"Can't forget Gabby. She has had enough husbands for both of them."

"How many? Four?"

"Just three."

"*Just* three? How many are you planning to have?" Con looked stern.

"Oh, I thought I'd start with one, see how that works out," said Dora, airily.

"Right. Sounds like a plan. Got any applicants?" Con crunched a chip with what seemed like unnecessary force.

"Not at the present time." Dora felt a little stab, a little twinge, in the sore place that was thinking about Gary, but she ignored it.

Con looked as if he were going to say something else, but a loud, singsongy *"Dorrrr-uhhhhh"* interrupted them, followed at slightly less than the speed of sound by Tyffanee, who clomped up to their booth in her pink sheepskin boots.

"Dor-a, I went to the shop and it was closed!" Tyffanee made an exaggerated sad-face.

Dora didn't let herself be drawn. "Mimi closes at six on Tuesday, Tyff. I thought you knew."

"The mall stays open until eight p.m., so I totally thought she, I mean, you would, too." Tyffanee's pout was layered in lip gloss so wet and shiny that Dora felt embarrassed to look at it, as if it were somehow obscene. She supposed that was the point.

"Not enough foot traffic in that neighborhood to justify staying open until nine," Con broke in. He extended his hand to Tyffanee. "Hi, I'm Con, you must be Tyffanee. Nice to meet you."

Tyffanee stopped whining for Con, Dora noticed. Her voice dropped, and she flicked her hair back over her shoulder like a shampoo commercial. "Nice to meet you, too, Con." She drew out his name and looked up through her lashes at him. "How do you know Dora?"

"Con's a friend of Mimi's," Dora said, a little too abruptly.

"Well, any friend of Mimi's..." Tyffanee trailed off with a little giggle, and cocked her head to the side for good measure.

"Tyff! Tyff! *Tyff!*" The gaggle of girls that had accompanied Tyffanee into Lud's had grown restive. "Gotta go!

See you 'round?" And with a final hair-toss, Tyffanee was absorbed back into the group.

"Ah. So that's Tyffanee?" Con sounded amused.

"That's her. In the aggressively tanned flesh."

"She has a, um, different aesthetic than you and Mimi, doesn't she?"

Dora looked down at that day's dress. All of a sudden, she felt self-conscious, costumey. "I still don't feel like I have the Mimi aesthetic down, but Tyffanee...Let's just say she'd rather shave her head than wear a dress from Mimi's."

Con's eyes had drifted back to Tyffanee, who was vying with her friends to be the one to proclaim the loudest about how bad they were being by eating an actual sandwich. "I can see that."

Dora felt awkward; Con had made his way through the rest of the chips, and another couple was standing nearby, eyeing them hopefully.

"We should let someone else sit down," she said.

"I guess..." Con agreed reluctantly. At least, Dora thought Con was showing reluctance, but what did she know? Con looked at her quizzically. She must have been staring. But "Can I give you a ride home?" was all he said.

"Actually, could you drop me at the store? I should ride my bike back—it's not far."

"Are you sure? It's pretty late."

"I'm sure—I probably shouldn't leave it locked up there two nights in a row. Nobody would steal it, but they might cart it off as abandoned."

Con nodded and gathered up their trash. "Okay, one ride to the store, coming up."

"Thank you—and thank you for dinner—it was really nice of you!"

"Anytime," Con said. He smiled.

It took a few minutes to get out of the parking lot. The whole time, Dora felt like she had forgotten something in Lud's, but she had everything. Her bag, her keys, her phone, her wallet. They stopped in front of Mimi's store. Con seemed to be tilting in her direction, almost as if he was planning on a good-night kiss. Had this been a date? Dora didn't know.

"Okay, then, have a good night," said Dora, as she fumbled hurriedly with the door handle. "Are you working tomorrow? Come by the store when you have your lunch break. I mean, if you want. If you have time. Okay?" She was babbling.

"Will do." Con looked a bit bemused.

Dora hopped out, and instantly felt as if she'd done the wrong thing. For all she knew, Con kissed everyone goodbye. Even Mrs. Featherston.

●   ●   ●

Dora rode home, put the bike in the garage, went inside, sorted through the mail, put on pajamas, and made herself a cup of tea. Camille was mysteriously absent, and Dora didn't feel any need to track her down. She was halfway through half watching a rerun of *Buffy* when Gabby called.

"My meeting tonight is taking a little longer than I thought, sweetie. Don't wait up—you get some rest."

"The flower-show committee reach an impasse?" Dora joked.

"Something like that. I'll see you tomorrow. Sleep well, baby."

"I will. Good night, Gabby."

Dora plugged her cell phone into the charger and set the phone to vibrate. Her tea was cold. She thought about seeing if Camille had bought any Chubby Hubby, but even ice cream didn't sound appealing.

Dora got halfway up the stairs before she realized she'd left the front light on, just as she used to do when she was expecting Mimi home late. Defiantly, she continued to the top. Another thirty cents' worth of electricity wouldn't tip the environment into global-warming catastrophe, she thought. And she should really leave it on for Gabby. Gabby really never was out this late, though. Something was definitely going on. Dora dropped another coin of worry into that particular piggy bank.

She was asleep almost immediately, but not before she heard Gabby's voice at the front door. There seemed to be a long pause between the door's opening and closing, but Dora was too drowsy to wonder about it.

CHAPTER TEN

THE STORE OPENED LATE ON WEDNESDAYS, but Dora went in early. The more time she spent in the store, the more time she wanted to spend in the store. This morning she planned to redo the mannequins.

It'll be a surprise for Mimi, she told herself, but really it was a self-indulgence. When Dora was little, when she was very good, she'd been allowed to add something to a new window display when Mimi put it up. Mimi had been very particular about her windows, so Dora would spend an afternoon trawling through the store, winnowing through the possibilities. She'd always restricted herself to accessories, though: jewelry, hats, scarves, shoes—once or twice a jacket or two, usually thrown over the mannequins' shoulders, as their arms were even more unyielding than their akimbo postures would suggest.

She'd never ventured a dress. Until now.

The whole process was complicated by the mannequins themselves—not their fragility and rigidity, but their personalities. Because they did have personalities. Nedra, in the north window, was tough, confident, maybe, just maybe, a tad brassy or vulgar; Nellie, in the south window, was fragile, retiring, highly refined, and a bit of a hypochondriac (that's why she had the south window). Nellie was always threatening to lose a limb.

Mimi's windows had always had stories, Dora realized.

She had already undressed the mannequins and drawn the curtains to hide the empty stands. They weren't stories like the big department-store Christmas windows, like "Cinderella," or "The Nutcracker"; but they were stories nevertheless.

Nedra had swaggering stories. "This window is Nedra becoming vice-president of a corporation," Mimi would say, and there Nedra would be in the window, obviously an executive in a trim suit (but still Nedra, with one too many buttons on the blouse left undone), a hat at a rakish angle, a flashy brooch on the jacket. "This window is Nellie writing letters to her soldier," and Nellie would be in a housedress, a basket of folded linens at her feet, a gold necklace with a little pen on it around her neck, half of a friendship-token bracelet dangling from her wrist. (That last had been Dora's one addition.)

Dora thought that in her windows Nedra would be living a life of intrigue—sexy spy, she decided, wrap dress or pussy-cat bow under a long trench, maybe leather, definitely sunglasses—and Nellie would be her pop-culture counterpoint, the sexy librarian, solving a problem in her prim dress and elegant cardigan, glasses perched for effect on the top of Nellie's head. (One of Nellie's many disappointments was that her extremely flat ears—in fact, they were painted on—did not allow for sunglasses.)

Dora wrestled Nedra into a deep-green wrap dress (more subtle than red) and draped her leather trench over her shoulders. Her sunglasses were aviators, and Dora adjusted a binoculars bag to rest on her hip just so. Fedora, or no fedora? Dora left it on the counter to get Maux's opinion later.

Nellie was harder to get into her cotton shirtdress, her loose arm always threatening auto-amputation, but soon her cardigan was nicely draped and a string of colored beads was balanced right where Nellie's collarbone would be, if Nellie had been endowed with one.

Dora finished just before opening time. She unlocked the door, pulled open the window curtains, and went outside to gauge the effect.

Con was on the sidewalk, talking into his phone. "Can I put a rush on this delivery? How much of a rush? Well, do you have a time machine? Yeah, yeah, same client, Larry." Con waved at Dora, making "in a minute"–type faces at her.

Dora looked into her windows. Nellie looked off-center. She'd have to fix that. Nedra looked pretty good, though. Not up to Mimi's standard, of course, but better than most of the windows on the block (the hardware-store display of sun-bleached plumbing snakes being a particularly low point).

Con hung up. "Hey, good morning, Dora! How's it going?" He paused. "You changed the windows—they look good."

"Thanks. I know they're not as good as Mimi's...." Dora stopped. The phone was ringing inside the store.

"We're not open quite yet—I'll let the answering machine pick it up." Mimi always used to yell at her, when she was little, for running for the phone. "Don't answer it all out of breath, it makes people wonder what you've been doing," she said.

The answering machine clicked on. "Miss Winston, this is Dr. Czerny at Forsyth, could you..."

Dora ran inside. She knocked the waiting fedora to the floor as she lunged for the phone.

"Hello?" Dora paused to catch her breath, willing Dr. Czerny to talk.

"Dora? This is Dr. Czerny. I think you should come to the hospital."

Dora barely managed to choke out an "Okay. I'll be right there." She looked up. Con had already picked up the hat. "I'll drive," he said.

●   ●   ●

Dora sat in the hallway. Nurses walked back and forth and didn't look at her; people walked in and out of the other rooms, and Dora didn't look at them.

Dr. Czerny stopped in front of her. "Dora. I'm glad you came so quickly."

Dora didn't think she had been called in for good news. But she felt she had to leave the possibility open. "There's been a change?"

"We managed to stop the bleeding in her brain, but her heart couldn't take the strain. I'm afraid she's failing."

"I did find her living will, but I keep forgetting to bring it." Dora unreasonably felt as if Dr. Czerny was her teacher, and that Dora was trying to explain why she didn't have her homework.

"That's okay. We got a copy of her DNR from her internist."

"DNR?" Dora felt that at one point she had known what those initials meant. She was a terrible student today.

"It's a do-not-resuscitate order. If Mrs. Winston's

heart stops, she doesn't want us to restart it by artificial means."

"And her heart is going to stop."

"It's not certain, but it's likely."

"How soon?"

"We don't know. It could be in an hour, or it could be a day."

Dora looked up. "A day?" A day seemed like forever.

"Not longer than a day, I'm afraid." Dr. Czerny held open the door to Mimi's room.

* * *

Dora sat by the bed and held Mimi's hand. Dr. Czerny had mentioned that it was unlikely that Mimi would wake up, but that it wasn't unheard of. Dora didn't ask Dr. Czerny what she'd heard.

Con had disappeared after dropping her off; Dora had left a message on the home answering machine, then dialed Gabby's cell phone frantically the entire trip, getting no answer, and he promised to keep calling until he tracked her down, and to let Maux know, too. Dora listened for the clack-clack of Gabby's shoes in the hall, but there was nothing but the beep of the machines.

A nurse swept in and performed a dozen small tasks, each one executed in precise and careful ways. Dora envied her. She wanted something concrete to do: a blanket to smooth, a temperature to take, something to write and check off on a chart.

Before she left the room, the nurse came over and put her hand on Dora's shoulder. "Let me know if you need anything," she said, and her voice was soft.

Mimi stirred briefly as the nurse left but did not wake. Her hair had lost its set and was greasy at the temples. Dora felt uncomfortable and embarrassed watching Mimi this way. It was so hard to see Mimi's face slack, without the usual look of puzzled love that animated it whenever she looked at Dora.

Dora had just opened her mouth to say something—anything—to Mimi—"I love you," or "I invited Con to come by for lunch today," or "I think we should sell reproduction shoes in the store, like Maux wants"—when all the machines exploded in an arcade's worth of beeps.

The nurse came back in, and moved quickly along the other side of the bed. "I just have to check this," she said as she disconnected the machine.

Dora held Mimi's hand tighter. She counted three breaths, and then the last one was held until Dora couldn't imagine that it was just being held anymore.

Then the kind nurse led her away.

Dora sat in the room with the soothing green furniture and the soothing blue walls, where there was a machine in the corner playing soothing ocean sounds, if you needed more soothing. Dora needed more soothing but she didn't think ocean sounds were going to do it. The ratio of boxes of tissues to chairs was two to one, which was a good thing, because when Con found her there she had shredded nearly an entire box, twisting them in her hands, before dropping them back on the table.

He sat down next to her and put his arm around her shoulders. She leaned in against him, dropping the last tissue in her lap.

Con didn't say anything, which was one thing for which Dora could be thankful.

* * *

Gabby rushed into the room and all but tackled Dora in her need to hug her. Gabby's makeup was smeared from crying, and her hair mussed.

"Honey, honey." Gabby's beringed hand was smoothing Dora's hair. "I'm so sorry."

Dora let the tears run down her face, silently.

Con stood, awkwardly. Bits of Dora's torn Kleenex stuck to his jeans.

"You call me right away if you think of anything. I'll call tonight, Gabby, and see if there's anything I can do." He patted Dora's shoulder, gently. Dora put her face back into Gabby's shoulder, and didn't watch him leave.

* * *

Somehow they got all the paperwork done, made the right arrangements. Dora wanted to wait until they had gone home and brought back Mimi's funeral folder, but Gabby insisted they make a start. "I know what Mimi wanted, we talked about it often enough. Don't look so surprised, Dora, that's what old ladies do. Girls plan weddings, and old ladies plan funerals."

So they filled out forms and left things blank if they had to, and Gabby pushed it all through with a combination of bereavement and pure charm. Dora wrote things mechanically, checking boxes, answering things as Mimi would have wanted. Yes to "organ donation." "Name of funeral home." Signed next to "next of kin," and then remembered: Camille.

"Camille's going to make a fuss about Uncle John not being next of kin, isn't she?"

"Maybe she will and maybe she won't," Gabby said. "I don't care. I'll sweep her out of the house with a broom if I have to. And that sniffy John, too. Mimi always said he was an adorable little boy once, but I can't see it."

Dora tried to smile, but she didn't think her face responded.

•   ●   •

In the car, Gabby tried to be soothing. "We're going to head right home, and get you into a hot bath. And I'll make you a cup of hot tea. And soup."

Dora realized that Gabby was treating her as if she'd been caught out in the rain.

"It's okay, Gabby. Don't fuss." That was what being an orphan really meant, Dora decided. No one to fuss over you.

The best thing about growing up with Mimi had been that Mimi never fussed. Mimi didn't fuss if you only ate carrot cake for three days straight. "It'll all balance out," she'd say, eating a piece herself. Mimi didn't give Dora a curfew: "Come home when you're tired," she'd say. But if Dora stayed out so late that she overslept the next day, Mimi wouldn't wake her up. "Your choice, your consequence," she'd say, when Dora tore downstairs, her ride waiting impatiently in the driveway. Dora didn't stay out too late much. Mimi didn't care if Dora saw an R-rated movie. "Talk to me if it makes you feel upset," she'd say, or even plop down on the couch and deliver a running commentary, which Gabby called "MBO," for "Mimi's Box Office."

Dora knew that Mimi's lack of fuss was because her father had died. Mimi had done everything right with him, Dora knew. And he died anyway.

And so Mimi had turned her back on careful mothering, and had taken to a kind of detached grandmothering. Not that she didn't love Dora; Dora's first memory was of sitting in Mimi's lap, playing a game of "I can hug you harder." Mimi loved Dora, but Mimi also gave her up to the gods. Mimi knew a child could die before his mother, and thus a grandchild could die before her grandmother. No amount of nagging about eating vegetables was going to change that.

If Dora had come home soaking wet, from being caught in the rain, Mimi would have greeted her with a raised eyebrow, and let Dora draw her own bath. Maybe she'd make Dora a cup of tea, but only if she was making one for herself anyway.

The only thing Mimi ever fussed about was clothes, in a resigned way ("There are girls all over the world who would shoot somebody for a dress like that one, and you're wearing cargo shorts and plastic shoes," she once groaned, after Dora refused to wear yet another vintage gem), and school—"That's your work," she'd tell Dora. And, of course, what Dora was going to do after graduation.

●　　●　　●

They saw Camille from a block away, sitting on the front porch, and looking livid. She walked into the driveway to meet them.

"I've been calling and calling," she started, and then stopped when she saw Dora's face.

"Oh. Oh, honey. I'm so sorry." Camille's voice softened. Her whole posture changed. Even her hair seemed less brassy.

She took the keys from Gabby's hand and opened the door. "You all sit right down. I'll make tea." Gabby led Dora to the couch.

"I've put the kettle on," Camille came in and announced, minutes later. Or maybe it was hours. Dora wasn't sure. "There's plenty to eat," Camille went on, talking slowly and loudly, as she would to a foreigner. "There's a ham, and someone made biscuits—they look as good as yours, Dora. I'll just make up some plates and put them in the fridge for later." She looked at Dora, her face kinder than Dora had ever seen it.

"I spoke with John. He sends his condolences and says he will come tomorrow; he doesn't think he should drive tonight. His eyes aren't so good after that surgery he had last year. I'm just going to run out for some ice cream." She looked stern. "We'll want it later. Believe me."

Dora managed a weak "Thank you," but Camille just waved. "Back in a bit."

Dora stumbled over to the couch. "I'm just going to lie down here for a minute," she mumbled. Gabby covered her with the afghan, and she was out.

Sometime later, she barely registered Camille coming in with eight flavors of Ben & Jerry's; Gabby offering her some ham; and several phone calls, none of which she answered. Eventually Gabby helped her upstairs to her bed, and undressed her like a baby.

CHAPTER ELEVEN

DORA SLEPT LATE, LATER THAN SHE HAD for days. Weeks, even. Although it didn't feel like sleep, real sleep; she felt semiconscious, like at the dentist's. She heard the doorbell ring, people come in and out. She heard quiet conversations, peppered with her name, and Gabby's voice, answering questions.

It was well after noon when she made it downstairs. She had hesitated in front of the closet—a black dress seemed so self-important, but she didn't want to wear anything bright and seem disrespectful. She settled on navy blue. Dora hated navy blue.

Gabby was just closing the front door as she came down the stairs.

"Did we wake you, honey?" Gabby hugged Dora. "How are you feeling?"

Dora couldn't answer. She managed a weak smile.

"You must be starving. Let me make you some eggs."

Gabby made her a huge breakfast of eggs and ham. Dora spread strawberry jam on a leftover biscuit mechanically, and ate it without tasting it. She broke her yolks and drew her fork through them in circles on her plate. She cut up the ham and pushed it back and forth. Gabby kept her cup full of hot tea, and Dora dropped in sugar lump after sugar lump.

Gabby sat at the table across from Dora. She had found

the folder marked "Funeral" from Mimi's desk drawer. Dora looked away from it.

Gabby opened it up. "I've called everyone on Mimi's list, and we're all set for the chapel on Saturday."

Dora just nodded.

"The man from Riffett's is coming by today to get Mimi's clothes. She had them all set aside, we don't have to do anything."

Dora nodded again.

"The store's closed today, and it will be closed on Saturday, of course, but Maux called and she'll go in tomorrow after her class. I can go in to open up tomorrow, if you want me to."

Dora found her voice. "I want to do it. I want to be in the store."

"We'll have to figure out what to do when you go back to school, but I can pitch in for a while, and Maux said she'd take extra shifts until we sort things out."

"I'm going to stay and run the store." Until the words dropped out of her mouth, Dora hadn't known she was going to say them. She didn't feel any need to take them back. It felt like the right choice.

Gabby patted her hand. "You don't have to decide now, you know. It's okay. Mimi would have wanted you to take your time. Mimi wouldn't expect you to give up on what you want to do...." Gabby trailed off.

"Gabby, if I had something special I wanted to do, I'd do it. But I don't. I just have things I don't want to do, and the store isn't one of them." Dora took a breath. "I like the store. I like the dresses and the people and Maux calling people jackasses."

Gabby smiled. "They usually are, at that. But you

shouldn't decide this based on a few cuss words and missing Mimi."

"Mimi wanted my father to come into the store, right? I mean, not this store, the old department store."

"Yes, but, honey, that was years ago. Decades. It's not something you have to do, any more than it was what your father had to do. Even Mimi knew that, eventually."

"It's not just that," Dora said. She swirled her tea around in the bottom of the mug. "I don't know why, but I know I want to do it. I can always change my mind, right?"

"That's true." Gabby looked relieved. "Honey, you want another biscuit?"

The back door rattled, then opened. It was Maux.

"I don't know if you want me, but I'm here. Just tell me what the hell I can do." Maux swallowed Dora in a hug. Her face showed signs of crying.

"I'm glad you're here." Dora didn't want to let Maux go.

"Anyway. I'm here. What can I do? I bet there's a metric fuckload of stuff that has to get done, and none of it is anything anybody wants to do."

Dora looked lost, but Gabby pulled out a list. "I was just trying to think of all the food we should have on hand for after the service," she said. "Nothing makes people hungrier than funerals. Of course they'll all bring things, but we'll need drinks and some cold cuts and so on."

Maux grabbed the list. "We'll go to Costco. I know just what we need. C'mon, Dora, we'll get you out of the house."

Maux was driving a white Toyota. "Excuse the car. Harvey's pissant Mustang is in the freaking shop again; this is the loaner."

Dora smiled. "He can't drive this, can he? So uncool. I bet he has your scooter."

"Got it in one."

The warehouse store was almost empty. Maux wrangled a huge cart out of the tangle in the parking lot, and Dora trailed behind. The door checker waved Dora through. "I'm so sorry about your grandma, honey," she said.

"I forgot how small Forsyth is," Maux said. "I don't even know that lady!"

"It's someone Mimi knows from the library, I think. She helps with the book sale, maybe?"

Maux shoved the cart to the deli. "Cheese, cold cuts, bread. Giant jar of mustard?"

They passed a ten-foot stack of Lorna Doones. "Those were Mimi's favorite," Dora said. She put her hand on a box.

"Sure, let's get some. But doesn't Gabby hate them? Don't get too many, or they'll just get stale when you go back to school."

"I'm not going back," Dora said.

Maux looked smug.

"Don't look like that," Dora said. "I'm not dropping out. I can finish up and graduate from here. I'm just not going to grad school. Not right away, anyway."

"I don't think you should make any decisions this week," Maux said. "Even the ones I agree with. It's going to be a hard week."

"I know, I know. It's just...when I think about staying in Forsyth, and running the store, that seems right. Grad school just seems like a band-aid."

"Band-aids do keep you from bleeding all over your clothes." Maux put a box of cookies in the cart.

Dora didn't want to let it go. "I thought you didn't think grad school was a good idea," she said.

"I don't think it's a good idea. I just want you to decide when you're not grieving and missing Mimi." Maux grabbed a package of napkins and some paper plates. "And what about Gary?"

"What about Gary?" Dora said. "There's not any 'about Gary.'"

"I thought you said there might be, if you only got rid of your inconvenient undergraduateness."

"Yeah, well, it's a long shot. At best. He's emailed all week to say that he misses me...in the context of running out of Snickers bars and needing the number of the exterminator."

"Two weeks ago, Gary just saying your name out loud would have had you over the moon."

"Two weeks ago seems like forever ago."

"Look out, friend of Mimi's at two o'clock. I'll run interference if you want me to."

"No, it's okay." Dora managed to smile at the woman, whose name she once knew. She didn't have to do anything other than nod a lot and look appropriately sad, and eventually the woman went away, with promises to come to the service on Saturday.

Maux had been quietly stocking the cart while Dora accepted condolences. "Let's get the hell out of here before we run into anyone else," she said.

In the car, Maux brought up school again. "Have you heard back from the admissions office yet? I mean, you might not even have a choice you have to make. Not that I think you would have any trouble getting in, of course."

"Not yet. I should hear by next week, I think. So it's not

even certain that I have a grad school to go to, and I really think I'd rather be here. Grad school isn't going anywhere, but once I give up the store, it's gone."

"And you'll just live with Gabby?" Maux braked a little too hard. "Think you can keep her out of trouble? That's a big job."

"She has been more scattered than usual," Dora said. "She didn't answer her phone for hours on Saturday, and when she did show up she was missing an earring. I think she might have even forgot to put it on."

"Gabby forgetting jewelry? That's like the sun forgetting to rise. It's probably just the stress...But you should think about what other commitments you'll be taking on if you come home, Dora."

Dora just looked out the window. She didn't want to think about that right now.

Camille was there when they got back to the house. "Oh, hi," she said to Maux. She made no move to help bring in the groceries from the car. Camille was done with sympathy, it seemed.

Gabby looked cornered. "I've just been letting Camille know about Mimi's wishes for the service."

"I don't know why she wanted to be cremated," Camille said. "It's just unnatural. All burnt up."

"Camille...," Gabby began.

"I know, I know. It's what she wanted, blah, blah. I just think it's strange, is all. There's a space for her in the Winston plot and everything, and now she won't even fill it up."

Dora almost laughed, but knew Camille would take it the wrong way.

"John called a while ago; he'll be here late this

afternoon. We'll stay at the golf club; John likes it there. He doesn't want to impose." Gabby did an elaborate eye-roll. Dora's uncle John hadn't stayed in Mimi's house since Gabby had moved in.

Maux pulled Gabby aside. "Gabby, I need your help. I know it's not the best time, but could I ask you some wedding questions?"

"Oh, honey, of course. And Mimi wouldn't have minded—except for not being here for your big day. Have you looked at any of the dresses at the store?" Gabby let Maux draw her aside.

Dinner was ham again. Maux stayed, and they told Mimi stories. After dinner they each had two bowls of ice cream.

Dora went to bed, if not with a light heart, then with a restful mind. She could do it. She could stay in Forsyth, and live with Gabby (and take care of her, if it came to that, better than she had managed to take care of Mimi), and run the store. Bicycling to the store in a June Cleaver dress every morning suddenly seemed like the most normal thing in the world. She'd read through all the secret lives tomorrow, Dora decided, and learn all about the dresses as Mimi had seen them....

And then there was Con....Dora didn't let herself think too much about Con, but he was there as she drifted off to sleep.

CHAPTER TWELVE

DORA WOKE WITH A GUMMY MOUTH, A lingering bad dream, and a complete absence of NPR. The gummy mouth and the bad dream weren't unusual, lately, but the lack of somebody's soothing tones explaining the geopolitical situation or something about baseball was puzzling, until Dora saw that the switch on her alarm clock was firmly at OFF. She also saw that it was nearly eleven o'clock.

"Hell," she said, to no one in particular, and jumped out of bed. Mimi might be gone, but she wasn't letting the store go, too.

She'd have to drive, parking be damned. Her car had that musty undriven smell, and the steering was stiff. She finally found a space four blocks away, crammed between an SUV and the yellow curb of a tow zone. She slammed the door shut and ran for the store.

At the shop, Dora fumbled with her keys, but as she leaned against the door, it opened. The lights were off inside; had she forgotten to lock up on Wednesday? It seemed like a million years ago.

Dora pushed the door all the way open. Camille was behind the counter, with the register drawer out. She shrieked and dropped a roll of quarters.

"Dora! You gave me a turn! I thought you were breaking

in." Camille sniffed. "This store isn't in the nicest part of town, you know."

"What are you doing here, Camille?"

"You looked so worn out last night, I just decided to let you sleep, and come in early and open the store myself."

Camille was wearing denim capri pants, hems liberally encrusted with rhinestones, blinding white sneaker-slides with no socks, and a fuchsia tunic top with a bejeweled neckline. Dora's eyes hurt looking at her.

"Camille, it's okay, I'd really rather be working."

Camille heaved a heavy, dramatic sigh. "Dora," she said, shaking her head, "you really need *time* to *pro*-cess. You're young, why would you want to be around all these dusty old things, especially now?"

Dora stiffened. "I love this store, I love these things...." She suddenly noticed that Camille had cleared a rack right at the front of the store. "Where did..." The empty rack was as ugly as a missing front tooth.

Camille interrupted. "I know you feel you owe it to Mimi, but she wouldn't have wanted you to waste yourself here."

"Mimi would have wanted me to be happy." She was *not* going to cry again, not in front of Camille.

"See? Exactly my point. You wouldn't be happy here, not for long."

Dora was steeling herself for another assault against Camille's certainty when the door opened again. It was Tyffanee, dragging in a large cardboard box. She looked up at Dora.

"Little help here?"

Dora automatically turned to help Tyffanee with the door. Tyffanee up and active before noon was a bad sign.

"What's in the box?"

"Just some stuff for the store." Tyffanee straightened up and turned to Camille. "Ma, where do you want all this?"

"Oh, anywhere's fine, honey." Camille looked slightly nervous.

"What is in the box, Tyffanee?" Dora ignored Camille.

Tyffanee shoved her gum to the side of her mouth, and cocked her hip. She looked at Camille. "Well, you see," she said, flicking her hair back over her shoulder, "a girl in my Fashion Merchandising class said she could get us some great new stuff, and Ma and I thought it would go well in the store as we transition to more of a contemporary boutique—'cause it's vintage-y but, like, new."

Dora opened the box and pulled out a mess of random garments, some on hangers, some not. What they all had were tags from an upscale chain store.

"Tyffanee, these can't be sold here."

"Why not?" Camille interrupted. Camille's petulant face had reappeared.

"Because they fell off the back of a truck, is why. Look at this. These are new, with new tags, from another store."

"Are you saying that my friend is a thief?" Tyffanee reddened under her makeup.

Dora was furious. "That's exactly what I'm saying. Your friend is a thief, and you two should have known it."

Camille sputtered. "I'm sure we had no idea....We were just trying to *help*....Some people are so ungrateful...."

"You're not trying to help. You're trying to take over. Mimi would hate this, and you know it!" Dora's face was crimson.

"What-*ever*," said Tyffanee. She grabbed her handbag from beside the counter, and pulled on Camille's sleeve. "You heard her, Ma. Let's go."

"And take this with you." Dora pointed to the box. "Or I'm going to call the cops and ask them to come pick it up."

Camille said nothing, but glared at Dora while she and Tyffanee struggled with the heavy box. Dora pointedly held the door open for them. She could hear them whining to each other as they stuffed it in Camille's car.

"That better not end up back at the house," she yelled after them. Dora went over to the counter, to close the register. The roll of quarters that Camille had dropped was the only thing in it. They must have used the opening money to pay for the hot merchandise. Dora fumed.

Dora had made it back from the bank with change for the day just as the first customers arrived. The empty rack looked terrible. Mimi would no more have opened the store with an empty rack than she would have worked naked.

Camille had unceremoniously dumped the dresses on the floor of the back room, and Dora worked furiously to refill the rack.

As she smoothed the disrespected dresses with the steamer and lint brush and rehung them, Dora couldn't help speculating about their secret lives. This brocade cocktail dress must have been owned by the wife of a university professor, with its label from a shop in Ann Arbor, Michigan. And this sundress was a young wife's, in a honeymoon summer after a June wedding. This shirtdress—Dora couldn't think of where it had been. She checked the tag, looked at the number: 124.

"Let's see what Mimi thought your life was like," she said. She was talking to dresses; she must be truly losing it.

The file drawer was stuck, and Dora really had to pull to open it. But there it was, an envelope for number 124. Dora remembered her resolve to read all the secret lives. She'd start with this one, take the rest home tonight. Dora pulled the drawer all the way open, dumped all the envelopes into her bag, and read.

I didn't think that I'd ever be a witness to this kind of thing. If it were going to be anyone, wouldn't you bet on the red sheath, or the black chiffon? Not me. Wash 'n' wear isn't really what you wear for an affair, is it?

I think it was a Monday when I got the first inkling. She was halfway down the stairs with a basket of dirty laundry when the phone rang, and she nearly killed us both running back up to the extension in the bedroom, even though the kitchen was probably closer.

I only heard her side of the conversation, of course. But it was enough.

"Oh, it's you." Her voice was darker and thicker than usual, and there was a purr in it. I don't know if I'd ever heard that purr before.

"Tuesday? No, no, I couldn't possibly. Thursday? My, you are eager, aren't you?" She was coquettish. It didn't sound like she was planning a bridge foursome.

"All right, all right—Thursday. Afternoon? Oneish?" She paused. I could feel her heart beating hard. She must have still been breathing hard from the dash up the stairs.

"You're terrible. Simply terrible. But Thursday. Just for old times' sake, mind you!"

She practically skipped down the stairs.

He was waiting at the foot.

"Who was that, honey?"

"Oh, just Keith. He wanted to know where he could go to get his car serviced. I told him to go to Andy's; I wouldn't trust Booth's for a foreign car. But if you think he should go to Booth's..."

"Oh, no—I would have said Andy's, too."

She leaned over the banister and kissed the top of his head. "I'm glad, it would be just too embarrassing to call him back and say I made a mistake!" Then she pushed past him, headed down to the laundry room.

She wore me again on Thursday, as they sat companionably across from each other at the breakfast table.

"What about I play hooky today, eh, and we go do something fun? A picnic? Drive up to the lake?"

"Oh, darling, that would be wonderful! But I've got so many errands to run—I have to go to the butcher today, and I promised to stop by Mrs. Torini and check up on her. I could call her, though, and tell her I'll come over tomorrow, and we could have the butcher deliver...." *She looked up at him. "Do you really think Charles wouldn't mind if you took the day off? You haven't in a while...."*

"He probably would mind, the old ogre. It wouldn't do to get him riled up, with the Benton account about to close... and I know how Mrs. Torini relies on you. How about this: I'll tell him today that right after that account closes I'm going to take a long weekend and take you to the city. We'll see a show. You can even do some shopping, if you keep it reasonable."

"Shopping is not an activity that can be qualified with

the word 'reasonable,' dear." She gave him a big smile. "I'll give your love to Mrs. Torini."

"No, don't! Keep it all for yourself. Mrs. Torini got plenty from Mr. Torini, in her day."

"You're terrible."

"You like it."

"I'm not going to admit it, though."

He got up then, and grabbed his briefcase. She turned her face up for a kiss.

After she did the breakfast dishes (with an apron over me, which she usually didn't bother with), she spent a long time over her hair and makeup. She must have put on the red lipstick and wiped it off three times. She finally left it off. I agreed; red lipstick looked silly with me.

We took nearly no time at the butcher's; she must have called in the order early. And then Mrs. Torino wasn't home.

But there was a man waiting by the gate that led from Mrs. Torino's house to the house next door. We'd been here quite a bit, but I'd never noticed this man before.

"Keith," she said. That was the first time I saw him. She cut across the lawn and met him at the gate. He opened it and she stepped through.

"Barbara." He kissed her on the cheek, an urbane kiss. She blushed.

"You're the only one who calls me Barbara," she said. "I'm Babs to everyone here."

"Babs, then." He smiled.

"Oh, no, please call me Barbara. I miss it."

"Do you want to see the house?"

I could feel her stiffen a bit, but she didn't sound reluctant. "Of course I do. Every woman in town wants to see *what the notorious bachelor Keith Rickert has done with the old Townsend place."*

"You're hardly every woman in town."

"I still want to see it."

All houses look pretty much the same to me. I'm interested in sinks, and laundries, and closets, and things like that, but he showed her his library, with a bar (which had, I must admit, a tiny sink) and books and heavy leather furniture.

"Drink?"

"Keith, in the middle of the day?"

"It's five o'clock somewhere. And when we were working together we had many a drink at this hour."

"That was when I was a career girl. In the city. With a big lunch!"

"Want me to make you a sandwich?"

"That's okay, I'll just take the drink."

I'd never seen her drink a real drink before. Coffee, sure, and iced tea, and orange juice, but not something with a slice of lime in it. She shivered after she took a sip.

"I see you still make 'em strong."

"All the better to eat you with, my dear." He waggled his eyebrows at her. She laughed.

"So what brings you back here? Surely you're not ready to settle down and live in suburbia, Keith?" She had kicked off her shoes, and tucked her feet up under my skirt on the big leather sofa. Her drink was already nearly empty.

"Well, suburbia does have its attractions. And when this house came on the market—it's an excellent investment."

"You always did talk about real estate."

"What else did I always talk about? Or have you forgotten?"

"Keith..."

"Don't 'Keith' me, Barbara."

"You went to Hong Kong!"

"You could have come, too."

"Not the way you wanted me to."

"Oh, I forgot." He looked at her with a sardonic smile. "You weren't that kind of girl."

I could feel her blush. She swirled the last lonesome ice cube around her glass, and put the glass on the wide arm of the sofa. I suspected it was going to leave a mark, but neither of them seemed to care.

"Barbara, I'm sorry."

She didn't reply.

"Barbara..." He reached over and took her hand. He pulled her, gently, and she unwound towards him like a piece of string.

I'm not entirely sure what happened next. To tell you the truth, I tried not to pay attention. I knew it was wrong, I guess. I did get very wrinkled and mussed, though, and one of my buttons actually came off. She didn't seem to care; she hummed all the way home.

She barely had time to get in the door and start dinner before he came home.

"And how was your day?" he said, as he came up behind her at the stove. His arms went around her waist. She wasn't wearing the apron.

"Oh, the usual. The butcher's...I went to see Mrs. Torini, but she wasn't home! I'm wondering if she had a doctor's appointment she had forgotten about. But—oh, Keith was home, you know he took that Townsend place next door, right?"

"Yeah, I heard he had. What's he done with the place?"

"I didn't see much of it—I saw him in the yard and said hello, and he asked me where he should put the toaster in the kitchen. Poor man, he hadn't unpacked the kitchen at all! He's been eating off paper plates for two weeks!"

"Sounds good to me, no dishes to wash. . . ." She wriggled out of his embrace, and turned to set the table.

"You would say that! Anyway, I helped him unpack some, then I came home. Hand me those napkins, will you, dear?"

"You two used to work pretty closely together, didn't you, back at the agency?"

"Ah, well, as closely as a very junior girl copywriter and the head of the account ever worked. Mostly I got him coffee and sharpened pencils."

"And he was lucky to get that, I think."

"I am considered an excellent pencil-sharpener." She grinned up at him. I don't know how she managed it.

"I'll have to put you to the test sometime. . . . Do you want a drink?"

"No, dear—I'm just going to change into a fresh dress before dinner, okay?"

We went upstairs and she tossed me into the laundry. And after the laundry, I went into the mending pile for that missing button, and I've been there ever since. And I don't know what's happened. I'm not sure I want to. She can leave me here forever, for all I care.

Dora looked up from the story, startled by a rapping on the counter. From the impatient sound of it, whoever it was had been there for some time.

"Dora." Uncle John always said things as if he dared you to contradict him.

"Oh, Uncle John." Dora hardly ever thought of Camille as her aunt, but Uncle John never lost the "Uncle" in front of his name.

"I understand the service is tomorrow, and that Mimi chose cremation." Uncle John managed to cram both his disapproval of Dora and Mimi and his obvious displeasure in not being consulted into one sentence, accompanied by a disdainful look.

"Yes, that's what Mimi wanted." Dora wasn't going to add that it was what she wanted, too—Uncle John wouldn't have taken that into account at all. Uncle John looked as if whatever Mimi wanted didn't matter, but he let it pass.

"I brought some documents with me." Uncle John carried an old-fashioned leather briefcase, meticulously maintained. Dora imagined him saddle-soaping it on Saturday afternoons, listening to college football on the radio.

He seemed to expect Dora to do something. She hurriedly cleared off the counter. Uncle John looked around as if he expected a chair to miraculously materialize, then sniffed a little when he realized he'd have to stand.

"I didn't draw up Mimi's will," he said. "Since I'm a beneficiary, that would be improper. A colleague of mine did it."

Dora hadn't thought about Mimi's will. Of course she would have one, just as she had had a living will, and flood insurance, and a warranty on the hot-water heater: all the trappings of responsibility.

Uncle John waited patiently. Dora let him wait, not wanting to give him the satisfaction of thinking her curious.

"It's very straightforward, but I wanted to talk with you about it before the service, when...emotions will be heightened." Uncle John couldn't have heightened emotions if he suspended his from a crane, but Dora let it pass.

"The house was left to you in my care as your guardian, although, since you are of age, guardianship is now not necessary. There's life insurance, as well. The insurance should keep you comfortable while you complete your education." Uncle John looked as if he wanted to add the words "such as it is," but he didn't. "Camille mentioned you were applying to grad school—and the house can be sold, although it won't fetch much in this market, and of course it's a bit small."

Uncle John and Camille lived in a six-bedroom McMansion, with an exercise room, mudroom, gift-wrapping room (never used), and a separate sauna.

"There are some other bequests, mostly small sums to charity. Her jewelry, silver, and china goes to you, of course. We can arrange for storage when the house is sold. The store has been left to me."

Dora couldn't believe it. Mimi left the store to Uncle John? Suddenly she felt completely adrift.

"Camille has expressed an interest in taking it over— with Tyffee's help, of course—and I'm sure they'll make something of it." He looked around, and sniffed again. "I did not agree with Margaret when she decided to turn it into a secondhand store."

Secondhand store? Dora flared to anger, and resisted the urge to throw the stapler at Uncle John's head.

"Was there any...provision...made for Gabby?"

Uncle John coughed a dry little cough. "This will was made before Mimi's...association...with Gabby."

Dora counted back. "That means it was made when I was thirteen! Or even earlier."

Uncle John nodded, a movement he made so slow and so ponderous Dora wondered if his head might break right off his neck and fall to the floor.

"A good bit earlier. It was when the store carried more...contemporary merchandise."

"She couldn't have meant for Camille to run the store now, then," Dora said, almost to herself.

Uncle John was offended. "Your aunt Camille is a known tastemaker in Fayre. Certainly she is more suited for running the kind of trendsetting boutique this store could blossom into than someone not even out of college." He sniffed again. "You couldn't have expected that Margaret would leave her business to a young girl. You don't even have a business degree."

"Fine." Dora took her keys out of her pocket, pulling the store keys off the ring. She dropped them on the counter. "It's all yours. Call Camille, and tell her to come back." She calmly picked up the secret life and put it in her pocket. Shouldering the bag crammed with the others, she headed for the door.

"I didn't expect you to be so grasping, Dora," Uncle John said in a more-in-sorrow-than-in-anger voice. Dora assumed he practiced it every day, the better to bamboozle juries with. "I think this conduct is very unbecoming, given the circumstances."

Dora turned to face him. "Oh, you mean more unbecoming than Camille swooping in this morning and turning the place upside down? Before we've even had the service? You might want to ask her—strictly to assess liability, of course—where she found the 'contemporary merchandise' she tried to bring in here this morning."

Dora let the door jangle shut behind her, satisfied by the puzzled look on Uncle John's face. Camille was not going to enjoy explaining to her husband what Dora had meant.

She drove recklessly all the way home, not caring if she was honked at or not. *Camille had better not be here,* she thought, as she opened the door. She slammed it behind her like a warning, knocking the mail off the hall table.

Dora bent and picked it up. A circular, the water bill, and an official-looking letter forwarded from Lymond, the last addressed to Dora.

She opened it. "We're happy to inform you that you have been selected for the Master's Program in Liberal Arts at Lymond, pending your completion of your undergraduate degree. Please come in for a placement interview...."

The interview was scheduled for the following Monday. Dora tried to feel happy. She tried to feel anything, even anger at Camille and Uncle John, or sadness at missing Mimi, but she only felt tired.

Dora dropped the letter on the table and headed upstairs. Maybe she should just lie down for a minute.

It was hours later that she woke up, in the dark gloom of the late afternoon, to the sound of the doorbell chiming. Dora waited to see if Gabby was home to greet whoever was coming by to drop off another casserole—but there were no footsteps, no voices. Just the insistent chime of the doorbell.

Dora stumbled down the stairs, her dress crumpled from her nap, her hair beyond fixing. She opened the door.

It was Con.

"I went by the store to check on you, and you weren't there. Just Camille, and Tyffanee, and some really stern-looking guy who was yelling at them." Con looked at her with concern. "Are you okay?"

Dora didn't know what to say.

"Wait, sorry, that's a stupid question."

Dora almost smiled. "Come in."

Con looked uncertain. "I don't want to intrude," he started.

"You're not, really. Come in."

Dora led Con into the kitchen, and put the kettle on.

"Does it feel this way for a long time?" she asked, as she got down the mugs and found the sugar bowl.

Con looked serious. "Like you're in a fog? Slightly numb? Nothing seems real?"

"Exactly."

"It lasts a while. I can't say how long. It gets easier, eventually, but it's never gone."

"I figured. I mean, I didn't think you were going to say, 'You'll be fine by next Tuesday at three o'clock, four at the latest.'"

"I can say that if it makes you feel better."

"Not sure what would make me feel better." The kettle sang. Dora poured hot water over the tea bags.

"Trashing Camille might be a start. Why were they in the store? I know she's your aunt and all, but Camille looked like a hooker at the opera. And who was that guy? Was that your uncle? He looked like he thought he was the most important person in a thousand-mile radius." Con put four lumps of sugar into his tea.

"That's my uncle John. Mimi's brother. Well, half-brother. He's always thought he was the most impor-tant person in a five-thousand-mile radius, I'm pretty sure. Mimi didn't talk much about how it was when they were growing up, but I got the impression that he was the golden boy, and she was Cinderella. After her father died, I'm pretty sure her stepmother spent her share of the insurance sending John to college, and then on to law school."

"Wow. And she still talks to him?"

"She said it wasn't his fault—he was probably too young to realize what his mother was doing. Anyway, she must have forgiven him, because she left him the store."

Dora stared into her mug. "Which means it's Camille's new toy now."

"Wait—Mimi actually left the store to that stuffy guy?"

"Her will was made a long time ago. I don't think he was such a jerk back then. I think he probably wasn't doing very well, at the time. He kept moving to smaller and smaller towns, I remember, until he found the right-sized pond to be a big frog in. I was just a kid when she drew it up, so it probably made sense."

"It doesn't make sense now."

Dora shrugged. "I don't know. It doesn't matter, any-way. I'll just go back to school."

"You could take an incomplete, you know. Graduate in the spring, like normal people." Con tried to smile, but it didn't reach his eyes.

"I can still graduate now...and I should. I got a letter

today. I got into that master's program I applied to—if I graduate. And if I don't mess up the final interview."

"Oh." Con looked at her. "They'll cut you some slack, what with everything. When's the interview?"

"Monday. And I don't want to tell them. I couldn't bear the fussing and all that sympathy." Dora shuddered.

Con nodded. "Monday is soon." He took a deep breath. "I know you haven't asked me, but I don't think you should go to grad school. I think you should try to keep the store."

"Uncle John was right. What do I know about running a store? I've got no experience. I'm a liberal-arts major who can make industrial-sized pots of coffee and sell doughnuts."

"Experience is just paying attention as time passes. You have something more than that—you love that place, don't you?"

Dora shrugged. "People love things they can't have all the time."

Con looked angry. "It just doesn't seem fair to me. You could fight—I bet your uncle John wouldn't like the fuss, and people talking."

"He might back down, except that it's something Camille wants. He's never said no to Camille—or Tyffanee, either."

"There's always a first time," Con offered. "You won't know unless you try."

Dora frowned. "Do you have any other clichés you'd like to hand me? Like maybe 'It's always darkest before the dawn'?" Her voice rose. "If Mimi thought I was capable of running the store, she would have changed her will. She didn't. And Mimi was always right."

"She wasn't always right," Con said mildly. "Nobody's always right. Maybe she didn't have time. You haven't even graduated yet. She knew you were thinking about grad school. Maybe she didn't want to burden you."

"Mimi didn't believe in burdens. She always thought people were capable of more than they thought they were—and that nothing was worse than whining. 'You walk the road in front of you,' she always said."

"How did she feel about giving up?"

"I don't think going to grad school is giving up."

"Maybe not for some people. But for you? That's the road in front of you?" Con's voice was soft, sympathetic. Dora couldn't stand it.

"I'm really grateful for all your help this past week, Con," Dora said flatly. It was a dismissal. She'd known this guy for a week; who did he think he was? "You've been very kind." Dora stood up and took her mug to the sink.

Con looked as if he wanted to say something else. "I'm glad to do it," he said. "For Mimi." He stood up. Dora walked him to the door.

"I'll check in tomorrow. See if you or Gabby need any help." Con hesitated. Dora did not.

"Good night."

Dora closed the door and leaned against it. She felt like crying again, only not about Mimi this time. She called Maux instead.

"So—change of plan," she said when Maux answered.

"You need me to come over before the service tomorrow?"

"No," Dora said. "Change of life plan. I'm not going to take over the store."

"Oh." Maux stopped. "I thought ... What changed your mind?"

"I didn't. Mimi did. She left the store to my uncle John." Dora stopped.

"That jackhole. He's a lawyer! What the fuck does he want with a vintage store?"

"He doesn't. But Camille does. With Tyffanee's help, they can ruin it in just under twenty-four hours. They brought in stolen clothes today, by the way. I went in and caught them at it."

"Oh my God. Dora, I'm so sorry."

"I'm sorry, too, Maux—this probably means you don't have a job, either."

"Like I'd work on the same block as Camille. That woman makes my fucking teeth hurt." Maux sighed. "I'm just sorry for you, kiddo. Are you going to go back to school?"

"Well, I got into that grad program today." Dora tried to make her voice sound hopeful, but it stayed relentlessly flat. "If I don't screw up the interview on Monday."

"You won't. You couldn't. They will love you."

"Yeah, I suppose it's for the best. I mean, if Mimi thought I could run the store she would have left it to me, right?"

"I don't think Mimi deliberately left it away from you— I think she just wanted to give you space to be who you wanted to be."

"Too bad it turns out that who I want to be is Mimi," Dora said.

"Who wouldn't want to be Mimi?" Maux tried to make a joke out of it.

"You never told me how your wedding talk with Gabby went." Dora changed the subject. Maux let her.

"She seemed okay. Maybe a little daydreamy, but that could have been just fatigue. It's hard to tell, given everything that's gone on this week. She was hell-bent on getting you into a sea-foam-green bridesmaid's dress, so watch out."

"I'm okay with sea-foam green. Did she have any opinion on the diameter of the butt bow?"

"No, but you should sound her out tonight.... I'll expect a report ASAP."

Gabby still wasn't home. Dora could call, but what would she say? "Come home, the house is too big without Mimi in it"? Dora wasn't a baby anymore. Mimi might not have thought so, but Dora was feeling depressingly adult.

She locked the front door but left the porch and hall lights on, and went upstairs.

Her laptop was on the bedside table, the power-cycle light glowing and dimming like a slow wink, or a buoy beacon.

There was only one email from Gary this time. The subject line was GOOD NEWS. Dora opened it, braced for another ant update.

Hey Dor-belle,

I heard from a friend of mine in the MA-LA program that you were accepted (pending graduation and the interview, which, between you and me and my friend there, no one has ever failed except a guy who had a horrible halitosis problem). Why didn't you tell me you were thinking about graduating early? That is super-fantastic good news, in more ways than one....

We all miss you here, some of us more than

others. Paul is totally slacking off, you need
to crack the whip over him when you get back
(…and let me watch, mmm, Dora with a whip).
   XOXO
   G.
   PS An entire box of butter pats from the dairy
melted together and we had to throw them out.
I got a new order sheet but they don't carry that
brand anymore (because of the melting). There are
ten other brands/styles/models/flavors of butter.
How to choose? What to do?

Dora felt ill, like she'd bitten into a chocolate from a
fancy box only to find it full of grit. She deleted the email,
closed the laptop, and opened the closet doors.

There were three black dresses in Dora's closet. One was
a long black sheath, which practically came with a pocket
for some *Breakfast at Tiffany's* cigarette holder. That wouldn't
do. One was black chiffon with ruffles around the neck—
a look Gabby would call "flirty widow." The last was the
dress Dora knew she would have to wear: black crêpe,
probably late 1930s, with a round collar edged in soutache.
It buttoned from just below the waist to the neck, and had
bracelet-length dolman sleeves, two drapey flapped pockets, and a thin patent-leather belt. It wasn't what Dora would
have chosen, but it was what Mimi had chosen for her.

Dora dug out the right underwear and a pair of black
calf pumps, and steeled herself to try it on. If it didn't
fit, she could wear something else. There were some
gray dresses in the closet, and a few dark brown. Mimi
wouldn't fault her if the black dress didn't fit.

Of course it fit. The combination of the high collar and

the long skirt made Dora look as much like an orphan as she felt. She shuddered and turned away from the mirror. As she took it off, she felt a crackle in the pocket—another secret life.

When she put me on, I almost pulled away. I'd never felt such strong emotion. And it wasn't sorrow—I'd been prepared for sorrow, when you're a black dress you learn pretty early that no one wears you to ride the Ferris wheel at the state fair. It wasn't despair, or depression, or hopelessness— all those would have seemed, if not desirable, understandable. No, what I felt was anger.

It was a deep anger, and yet she felt hollow, light, like a reed. The angrier she got, the hollower she felt, until I thought she would lift right up into the sky, a zeppelin of pure rage. But I'm ahead of myself here.

She put me on and buttoned each button like she was thrusting a knife into someone. She ran a comb through her hair like a scythe; her lipstick (not too red, she was so pale) put on like battle paint. A handkerchief, a key, a folded bill—that was all she asked my pockets to hold. As she stood at the mirror, she plucked another handkerchief off the dresser. One for each pocket. She wore no hat, although there was one on the bed (bad luck!), with a black veil. Her shoes clicked in march time down the hall.

In the car she held herself so stiffly that every turn and stop made her lurch. Her shoulders were pushed back; her back was straight and tall. She kept her hands folded in her lap. No one spoke to her, and she spoke to no one.

Clumps of people clustered around the door to the church; some nodded, some looked as if they would speak, until they met her eyes. Then they turned away. An usher came and took her by the arm, led her down the aisle to the front pew. There was an older woman there, on her knees already, saying a rosary. She didn't genuflect or kneel as we entered the pew, but sat right back.

To tell you the truth, I didn't follow the service. She didn't, either. She was focused on breathing, on sitting still. I could feel how much she wanted to get up and walk out— run out, if she could. She looked at the rose window above the altar; I thought I could feel her eyes resting on each color of glass in turn, that's how attuned I was to her. It wasn't as if she was wearing me, it was as if she was being me. A harsh black dress for a harsh black day.

At one point everything stopped. There was a pause, and I realized it was directed at her. She stood up slowly, like a black rose blooming. She moved towards the pulpit smoothly, like a shadow passing.

The hush that fell in the congregation was absolute.

"The best thing about Jimmy was that he loved everybody. The worst thing about Jimmy was that he loved me, too. Jimmy shouldn't have loved anyone in particular; he knew better than anyone what his life was like, and the dangers he ran, and that the odds were five out of seven that he wasn't going to come home one Saturday morning.

"Well, one Saturday morning came, and Jimmy didn't. He's never coming home again, and, please, for the love of God, no one tell me that he's in the best home he's ever known, or I will strike you down on the spot with one blow. Mine was the best home he'd ever known, with hot meals and good talk and his chair always before the fire.

"He shouldn't have had that home, and he shouldn't have had me, and he knew that, every minute he had both, grinning. And he stole all the pleasure he could out of *everything he shouldn't have had, just like he stole smiles from each of you, even at his worst.*

"I know some'll say Jimmy was taken before his time, but that's not true. Jimmy had all his time, and some of mine. But if there were years left to Jimmy that he should have had, I hope they come to me as his widow, because I need all my threescore and ten and then some to work on forgiving James Bartholomew O'Loughlin before I see him again."

She stepped down then and walked straight out of the church. No one followed. The heavy doors boomed shut behind her.

Dora suddenly felt that same anger. How could Mimi leave when Dora still needed her? How could Mimi take the chance of knowing about her parents away from Dora, take the store away, take herself away? She knew she was being irrational, but she couldn't help it.

Dora ransacked the closet. She turned every pocket inside out, looked inside every bag. She didn't find any more secret lives.

She grabbed an empty hanger and threw it across the room. It bounced off the old dress form and landed with an unsatisfying dull thud on the floor.

She heard Gabby calling from downstairs. She must have just come home. "Everything okay, honey?"

"Yes—fine—I just dropped a hanger—" Dora called back. Dora hurried to the bathroom and turned on the shower. Gabby would leave her alone in the shower.

She took the black dress off and hung it up on a padded hanger. She left the one she had thrown where it lay on the floor. She stayed in the shower until the hot water ran out.

CHAPTER THIRTEEN

THE SERVICE WAS TERRIBLE.

It was lovely, of course. Mimi had planned it years ago—preplanned, as the funeral director said, to which Dora had wanted to retort that Mimi couldn't very well have post-planned it.

Mimi had chosen the music, the flowers, and the readings. Uncle John had read a short passage, which he managed to make sound like a letter to the editor about a proposed waste-treatment center. Camille sat next to Dora, in a print dress. Gabby was appalled, but Dora just shrugged her own black-clad shoulders. She'd given up feeling anything about Camille, even the pleasure of indignation. The minister said nice things about Mimi, gesturing vaguely to a large floral display. Then they sang another hymn, and it was over. "Such a tasteful service," Dora overheard, as she made her way out of the pew and down the aisle.

But for Dora, the service was terrible. Everyone claimed their moment with her: Mimi's friends, shuffling up, looking as if they had barely made it out of the chapel themselves; the neighbors, to whom Dora was still a teenager, if that; businessmen who came because Mimi was a good customer; people from the library committee and the park committee and the Downtown Chamber of Commerce. Dora spent so much time saying hello to everyone else that she felt she'd had no time to say good-bye to Mimi.

Afterwards, everyone came back to the house, and then it was even worse. Camille loudly explained Tyffanee and Lionel's absence as being school-related, to anyone who would listen. Gabby snorted. "One's too hung over and the other flat-out refused to come," she said to Dora in the kitchen. Dora gave her a look. "What?" Gabby said. "The rule is, don't speak ill of the dead, not don't speak ill of the dead's terrible relatives."

And at the house they all had drinks, and with the drinks came advice. All of the advice started with "You're young, Dora," and went downhill from there. Nobody mentioned the store; it was just assumed she wouldn't run it, Dora thought. Or maybe Camille had gotten there first. "Oh," Dora imagined her saying, "now that the kids are in college, John just thinks I need a new *creative outlet*. For all my *creativity*. I'm a very *creative person*."

Dora just accepted hugs, nodded at all the advice, and put out more cheese and cold cuts.

Con had been at the service, but Dora hadn't seen him come back to the house. She didn't expect him. The service had been for him to say goodbye to Mimi, not to Dora. But when she went into the kitchen to cut up more lemons, there he was.

"I'm sorry—I came in the back door. I brought ice."

They *had* been almost out of ice. Dora stood still for a minute, then remembered what to say. "Thank you."

Just then Gabby bustled in. "Conrad, darling. How wonderful of you. I was just about to send someone out for ice, but they're all one hundred and seven years old, and we'd be in another ice age ourselves before any of them made it back." She neatly relieved Con of the two bags. "I'll just go sort these out."

"Dora," Con started.

"If you say 'you're young,' to me, I will cut out your tongue with this paring knife."

"You're old," he said, smiling. "How's that?"

"I feel old." Dora put the knife down. "I feel older than Agnes Troutman, and that's saying something."

"Don't let her hear you say that, she's very protective of her status as the oldest citizen of Forsyth." Con looked nervous. "Is she here?"

"No. She only came to the service."

"Oh, good. She always tells me about the time my grandfather kissed her. I never know what to say to that."

"I wouldn't know what to say, either."

Camille backed in through the door, carrying an empty pitcher.

"Dora, honey, how are you holding up?" Camille was sickly sweet—she could afford to be, now that she had her way.

Con did not look pleased by the interruption, but Dora grasped at it. "Oh, Camille," Dora said, "did Uncle John have a chance to talk with you? He wanted to ask you about the, um, *merchandise* that Tyffanee brought into the store yesterday."

Camille looked at Dora as if she had suddenly turned into a snake. "Oh, that's all fine," she said, airily. "I hate to bother you, honey, but we're out of lemonade." She gestured with the pitcher.

"In the fridge, Camille." It hadn't made her feel any better to be mean to Camille. She had really hoped that it would.

Camille put the empty, sticky pitcher in the sink and grabbed the new one.

"Thanks, Dora. And just so you know, there's a man out there that I swear is Gabby's first husband, Jerry something. I know he knew Mimi way back, long before my time, but he's trailing Gabby like a puppy, and that's just awkward, don't you think?"

"I'd better go out and see if Gabby needs me, then." Dora fled the kitchen, leaving Con to Camille.

Dora saw Gabby with a man who could have been Jerry, but she didn't look harassed, so she left her alone, and spent the rest of the afternoon managing to avoid Camille, Uncle John, and Con. It wasn't hard; there were old friends of Mimi's to listen to, and plenty of drinks to refresh.

At the end, Dora hid in the garage for twenty minutes, while Gabby shooed people out the door, murmuring things like "overwhelmed" and "lying down." She came back in when she heard the door shut and she and Gabby stood in the middle of the kitchen, surrounded by casserole dishes.

"I hope you like lasagna, honey," Gabby said. "I don't think Olive Garden has as much lasagna in their freezers as we will have in ours."

"We also now have ninety percent of the tuna casserole cooked in Forsyth over the past week. I guess they all remembered that Mimi hated it and thought, *Aha, now it's safe to bring some over,*" Dora snorted.

Gabby made a halfhearted effort to fit another dish into the refrigerator.

"We should triage," Dora said. "Tell me who the best cooks are, and we'll save those. The rest we'll just throw away, and wait a month before we send home the dishes."

"Let me do that," Gabby said. "It's easier. Marnie Wood, definitely keep; Jill Forrester, no; no name on this dish, no..."

Dora leaned back against the doorframe and closed her eyes, half listening to the freezer door open and close while Gabby murmured and fussed. She felt Gabby's hand on her shoulder.

"Honey, go on up to bed. We can clean up in the morning."

"I have to drive back to Lymond in the morning—I'm going to leave early to avoid the traffic. I'll probably be gone before you are awake."

"Right. Good luck with that interview, honey. Mimi would have been so excited, I just know it."

Dora just smiled weakly, and hugged Gabby good night.

CHAPTER FOURTEEN

SUNDAY MORNING, DORA HESITATED, looking at the ratty T-shirt and cargo pants she'd worn on that horrible trip down from Lymond. It felt like they belonged to a different person. She chose a dress from the closet instead, a brown floral-print dress with a full skirt. Dora thought it would be comfortable for driving. An Aran sweater, wool socks, and a pair of suede desert boots—Dora felt like she was dressing Nellie, for another window.

Dora checked the pockets twice—no secret life.

Packing for the interview was harder. The closet was full of possible candidates. Dora discarded anything too bright: she wasn't sure just when she'd feel like wearing pink or grass green again. Next she excluded anything too fussy; she didn't want to be fiddling with bows or belts during her interview. One dress, an olive crepe, was almost perfect, but when she tried it on it was just slightly too big. In the end she took four possibilities, wrapped up in a garment bag, packing the right underwear and shoes automatically, as if she'd been dressing in vintage for grad-school interviews her whole life.

It felt odd to head out of Forsyth, away from the center of town and Mimi's store. Dora tried not to think about the store.

At the last minute she'd thrown the bag of secret lives

into the trunk, and she could feel them there, like the comforting weight of a heavy blanket. Dora tried to imagine Uncle John demanding their return, as part of the "store and its inventory," and failed. They were hers, by right if not by law, because there was no one else in the world who needed them more.

Dora's tiny apartment was just as she left it. The milk had gone off and the bread had gone moldy in the fridge, but other than that nothing was out of order. Dora bought a couple of cans of soup and just enough milk for her morning coffee from the corner store. She didn't have the energy to restock the larder. At the last minute she added a box of Lorna Doones.

Dora puttered around, hanging up the dresses she'd brought, looking for an overdue library book she needed to return. It wasn't until nearly five that she made herself soup and curled up on her couch with the bag of stories, the box of cookies, and a box of tissues within easy reach.

She gobbled the first few stories, opening one envelope in such a rush that she tore it. After that she was more careful. She tried to imagine which of the dresses from the store had belonged to each story, and penciled her guesses on the back. The dresses may have been lost to her, but she could keep their stories.

It was midnight before she reached the last story. She was cold, even under the afghan, and her legs were stiff. Her eyes were itchy from crying, and there were Lorna Doone crumbs everywhere. She felt sick, and not just from too many cookies. She opened the last envelope.

When he walked in, I thought it was her. Which was impossible, since she never wore trousers. And of course she was wearing me at the time. But it was uncanny. If anything, he was more beautiful, with that transparent, painful beauty that fair-skinned people sometimes have. You think if they catch the light just right it will burn right through them.

"Diana" was all he said, but he didn't have to say anything. She knew he was there before she even looked up.

"Go away, David. Back to wherever it is you've been."

"I wanted to be here, Diana," he said. "I'm sorry."

"Sorry butters no parsnips," she said. "It also attends no funerals."

"I couldn't." He didn't force his case. He just stood there. There was something about the way he stood, and the fit of his suit, that made me think: prison.

"What do you want now?" She was cold. She still hadn't looked up.

"I want to help. I want to come home."

"There isn't any home. Not anymore. I had to sell the house."

I heard his intake of breath, and so did she. It infuriated her.

"That's what you have to do, you know, when someone dies and there are debts and a business to run. You sell what you can sell."

"Where are you living now?"

Her eyes went involuntarily to the back room. He couldn't see the cot, and the hot plate, and the cold-water sink, but he knew they were there, I think.

"Diana," he began again. She was not encouraging. "Jeff?" he asked.

"He married Annabel Hough. It was in all the papers."

I could see he was angry; his fist clenched for a moment.

"He let me keep the ring. I sold that, too." She sounded

amused, almost. "It wasn't as expensive as he had let on, of course. Big and flashy, but second-rate quality."

Suddenly he laughed. She tensed, but then she laughed, too. Before I knew it, they were both laughing so hard they couldn't stop, bent over opposite sides of the counter, holding their sides. I thought she was going to pop a button right off me, but I didn't care. I had never heard her laugh, and I was enjoying it.

Eventually she caught her breath, and looked right up at him. "Are you really home?"

"I'm really home." He looked her straight in the eye. When I saw his face, up close, in the light, I could see that he looked older than she did. "Home to stay. Home for good."

"I can call Mrs. Moran; she'd find a place for you in her house. Remember when she used to 'do' for Mother?"

"Oh, yes—and I could just go over there."

"You'd better let me call first." She didn't press it, but I think that's when he realized what it would be like, coming back. He must have known it would be hard, but I think he was concentrating on the big hills, and not all the small bumps he'd have to go over, too.

She called, and he idled in the front of the store for a moment, before grabbing a broom and doing a quick sweep around. He handled the broom with grace, much better than she did, and I wondered how he had come by that particular talent. When he went through the shaft of sunlight that pierced the window, I could see how gray and shabby his shirt collar was.

On the telephone to Mrs. Moran, she was all business. She had to be now. No time for social calls or pity. But there was a tiny hint of something in her voice that hadn't been there before.

After she put down the phone she went into the little lav-
atory closet, and opened the medicine case. She took out the
bottle of brandy inside of it, and looked at it for a minute. I
thought she was going to pour it down the sink, but she hid
it behind the radiator instead.

"Mrs. Moran will have you," she said. "It's the attic
room, and it will be terribly stuffy." She waited for him to
protest.

"I don't mind," he said. "Thank you."

"Thank Mrs. Moran. I don't know how we'll pay her,
but we'll think of something."

"I have a little money," he said. "Enough for a week at a
boardinghouse."

"Her handyman O'Malley went back to the old
country—you could offer to help."

"That I could. Better than O'Malley, I bet. He drank,
anyway. . . ." His face colored. "Diana, that's done with."

"It better be." Her face had closed up.

"I can spend mornings here, and then go back to Moran's
in the afternoon, when her boarders are out."

"What can you do here?" She sounded dismissive, and
resigned.

"I can clean the front and repaint it, repair the awning,
make deliveries—anything you want."

"It's not fun, you know." She stared at him. "This is not
a game, we're not playing store, like we did when we were
children. This is all we have."

"I owe it to you. And to Father, I think. And a lot more."

She looked terribly sad when he mentioned Father. "I
miss him, you know," she half whispered. "When I'm not
cursing him for being so reckless and irresponsible . . ."

"Like me."

"Like you." She paused. "You know, I can tell just by looking that you've grown out of it. Father never did. His personality always carried him through, all red blood, backslapping, and beefsteak. We're too much like Mother for that to work for us."

"Luckily she didn't have to see the end."

"Of any of us." Diana gestured down at me, which wasn't quite fair, but I took it calmly. I knew I was only a shop dress, bought at a place that pinned the price tag on the sleeve. I knew what her other dresses had been like before; there were still a few in the closet.

"We've got a long way to go until the end, Diana." It wasn't until then that they touched. He reached his hand out and she grasped it, and then I was pressed tight against his shabby suit. I thought I felt her sob, but I was probably wrong. She never cried.

"Go see Mrs. Moran." Her hand in my pocket tightened around her handkerchief.

"Thank you, Diana." He looked like he wanted to say more, but he didn't.

"And be back here tomorrow at eight. That awning will take a lot of work."

It was only after he left that she did cry. She turned the sign on the door to "Closed" and sat right down on her cot and bawled. Then she got up, washed her face in the battered sink, and ran a comb through her hair.

But when she had opened the store door again (to a few waiting children eager for penny candy), her face was all smiles. I even saw her give the littlest one an extra bull's-eye.

Dora turned out the light and lay staring at the dark for a long time before she fell asleep.

●   ●   ●

Dora was wearing a charcoal-gray dress, narrow-skirted, with long sleeves ending in pointed cuffs and a matching sharply pointed collar. Dora was wearing the dress, although it had been a close call—when she first put it on, the dress had been wearing her. It had taken several minutes of walking around her apartment this morning (how small it seemed, and how remote from being hers now!) before the dress had been forced into submission and Dora could practice saying, "Thank you for the opportunity to come in and talk with you, Dr. Santin," in front of the mirror.

Dr. Santin, of course, hadn't noticed the dress at all. Dr. Santin had a pencil tucked in her hair, wore "comfort walkers" worn down at the heel, and the kind of denim jumper that might have been worn for gardening the previous Saturday and haphazardly washed.

"Thank you for the opportunity to come in and talk with you, Dr. Santin," ventured Dora, in as confident a voice as she could manage. Dr. Santin gestured to a chair, and Dora perched at the edge of it. The professor sank back into hers.

"Please, call me Emily," said Dr. Santin. Dora thought she'd rather cut off her own thumbs, but what she said was "Thank you."

Dr. Santin—Dora couldn't even think of her as Emily—opened her application folder. Dora could see the green paper clip she'd used and suddenly regretted it as not sufficiently serious.

"This interview is just a formality, of course. Your transcript is excellent—you've managed to get a very broad and well-rounded education here at Lymond."

"Thank you," said Dora again.

"You're graduating early?" Dr. Santin looked over her glasses at Dora.

"I had completed my degree requirements, and by graduating early I could apply for this program," Dora explained.

"The program. Can you tell me what drew you to further liberal-arts studies?"

Dora felt blank. "I...I really felt that my undergraduate work only skimmed the surface of the subject...subjects. And it really interests me." Dora took a breath. "I mean, um, how things are connected. The different disciplines."

"Hmm" was all she got back from Dr. Santin. "And you've held down a campus job as well?"

"Only for the past few months," said Dora. "In the coffee shop." Without realizing it, she smiled her first real smile since walking in the door.

"I know the one. Excellent pound cake." Dr. Santin smiled back. "I've never stopped to think about how the coffee shop is run. Tell me a little bit about your work there."

"It's really not very difficult—it's just a coffee shop. You sell coffee and baked goods and candy, and then pizza and sandwiches and sodas at lunchtime, and then clean it all up by five and get it ready to do all over again the next day."

"But how do you know what will sell?" Dr. Santin looked puzzled. "I don't think you had that pound cake last year, for instance."

"It's not what you would call a science—I just sat in a few other coffee shops around town and watched what people bought, and then figured out if we could offer similar things, or the same thing cheaper—college students never have any money, of course—and I asked our best customers what they would like to see, and once I spent a few hours watching what kinds of candy sold best at the bookstore." Dora smiled, remembering feeling like a grown-up Harriet the Spy.

"Didn't they wonder why you were standing by the register at the bookstore for hours?"

"I sat in a nearby chair with a big book, and made little check marks on a piece of paper hidden in it. Very industrial-espionage."

"Sounds like social-science research to me." Dr. Santin looked thoughtful. "What about your co-workers? How do you manage them?"

"I'm not the head manager—the head manager is a grad student in the Music Department." Dora didn't want to say Gary's name out loud, to an intimidating and much-too-perceptive stranger. "I'm just the student manager. I am there most of the time, though, since I only have an independent study this semester. But, really, it's generally considered a pretty good job to have, so people mostly manage themselves. I just make sure everyone has enough of what they need."

"Like coffee?"

"Oh, definitely coffee. And stirrers—people get really upset when there are no stirrers! And the rest of the stock. And the right shifts, so they're not rushing in or out or late for classes, and the right people to work with, so they don't spend the whole time either chatting and ignoring the customers or arguing and ignoring the customers." Dora was suddenly aware she'd been gesticulating wildly. Embarrassed, she sat straighter in her chair, and put her hands back in her lap.

"What made you take the job in the first place?" Dr. Santin had unclipped a pen from the file folder, but Dora could see she hadn't written anything down.

"I had been guaranteed a summer job through my scholarship, but that fell through. They probably could have found some kind of make-work for me, but that same day I ran into the head manager, and he was desperate. So I took the job."

"The manager must have been very persuasive."

"Very pitiful, is more like it," Dora said. "But I'm glad I took the job."

"Meaningful work is a gift. If you can find some, it doesn't matter what it is, only that it engages you. The coffee shop sounds very engaging."

Dora's face flushed. "I know it's just coffee, but little luxuries are really important to people, especially things like coffee that they look forward to, and plan their day around. Sometimes it seems to me that, the smaller the thing is that people want, the bigger the disappointment when they don't get it, or it's not exactly right."

"And the simpler someone believes something to be, the harder it is to do it to their satisfaction, too." Dr. Santin looked thoughtful.

"Exactly." Dora smoothed her skirt over her lap. "My grandmother," and she went on, carefully keeping her voice even, without a catch, "had a vintage-clothing store, and so many people thought it was just selling 'old clothes.' But it's not. It's selling history and glamour and...*experience*...and all sorts of things that can't be put on a hanger. You don't just stick a pretty dress in the window and be done with it."

"Hmm," said Dr. Santin again, although it was a confirming "hmm."

"People sometimes think clothes are superficial and shallow—I know I used to—but for my grandmother they were very deep. She wasn't selling something to wear, she was selling something to *be.* We think of things as belonging to us, but we don't realize that we belong to our things, too. She wanted to give people things worth belonging to. Especially vintage clothing, things with history and patina and provenance. She was finding people a place in the history of an object, like she was gathering people into a family, almost."

Dr. Santin looked interested. "Your grandmother sounds like a fascinating person," she said.

"She just knows—knew people," Dora said. "And she was *interested* in people. She used to say that only boring people got bored, so I guess that means that interested people are interesting. She was interested in people and things, and how they fit together. She was like a museum curator and a therapist wrapped up in one."

"Did you work in her store?" Dr. Santin made a quick note with her pen.

"Only for a little while," Dora said. She swallowed the lump that had appeared in her throat. "But I grew up there." She didn't add "this week."

"Dora, have you given any thought to the kinds of topics you'd like to explore in the program?" she asked.

Suddenly Dora was unsure again. "I'm interested in…problems of information gathering and decision-making," she said. "I don't have anything more specific." Her hands fell to her lap again, and she realized that she'd spent most of her time talking about cake and clothes. Dr. Santin must think…She didn't want to know what Dr. Santin must think.

Dr. Santin walked her to the door, and there was another student there, a boy Dora vaguely knew from a Russian-literature class. She remembered him as overly ingratiating, and dreaded a year's worth of classes with him.

She suddenly dreaded a year's worth of classes with anyone, even the kind and understanding Dr. Santin. She stopped on the threshold and blurted, "Dr. Santin, I'm really, terribly, terribly sorry, but I don't think this program is for me."

Unexpectedly, Dr. Santin smiled. "You know what? I'm delighted to hear you say so. Not that I don't think you'd do well, it's just—well, it sounds like you've found something else you'd like to do better. I think your grandmother was a better teacher than any of our faculty for what you want to do."

"I'm so sorry to waste your time."

"Oh, no, you've given me quite a bit to think about." She looked down at her shapeless jumper. "I'm not sure I want to belong to this dress, for one thing." She smiled again. "I know you'll do well, Dora. Good luck!"

●　　●　　●

The Liberal Arts program office was just across the quad from the coffee shop. Dora could stop by, straighten out the butter ordering and check on the ant situation, and tell Gary she wasn't going to do the M.A. program. What that meant she *was* going to do, she wasn't sure. There was no law against living and working near Lymond and not being a student, right? There were plenty of little shops near the college she could work at, while not being an undergraduate. Plus, Gary never said he couldn't date townies.

This late in the day, the coffee shop would be closed, but there was sure to be someone there, cleaning up or just hanging out. Sure enough, the back-room lights were on. She tapped at the door before hauling out her key from the bottom of her bag. Someone had left the stereo on, and, wonder of wonders, her iPod was still next to it.

Dora walked to the back room and stood still. Gary was there, leaning against the counter—well, not leaning against the counter, but leaning against a woman who was sitting on the counter, her legs wrapped around his waist. Her arms were around his neck, and he was kissing her thoroughly (and, Dora noted, a little sloppily).

"Oh." It was a stupid thing to say, but Dora said it.

Gary and the woman broke apart instantly. The woman was Amy. She reached up to adjust her headband.

"Sorry to interrupt, I came by to..." Dora thought she was going to say "order butter," but what came out of her mouth was "...quit."

She picked up her iPod, turned, and walked out, past the chairs overturned on the tables and the empty napkin holders lined up to be refilled. She saw they were out of Snickers again; not her problem. She heard hurried whispers from the back room, but she didn't stop to eavesdrop. She walked out the door and didn't bother to lock it behind her.

She was nearly to the library before Gary caught up with her.

"Dora, Dora, Dora"—he came running up to her—"you can't quit, please don't quit, I need you."

"That's your problem," she said. "I have different problems, and I'm afraid you aren't the solution to any of them."

"Is it about Amy? We're just having fun, it doesn't mean anything. . . ."

"I don't think any better of you for saying that."

Gary stood still, his mouth open. "I guess you wouldn't." He looked sheepish. "Well, um. I'm sorry. If I gave you the wrong idea, or anything. I know I flirt too much, and I guess sometimes I cross the line." He gave her what he obviously regarded as a winning smile. "And you look amazing in that dress, by the way."

Dora was surprised at how little pleasure Gary's saying that gave her.

"I came to quit because I'm moving back to Forsyth. My grandmother died and I'm taking over her store." Dora didn't know how she was going to do this, exactly, but Gary didn't need to know that.

"Oh." He shifted from one leg to the other. "Um, you won't report me, will you? For, um, dalliance with an undergrad?"

"No. It's not worth my time." Dora looked at her watch. "I really have to get going. I'll email you with the address for my final check." She turned and walked away. She didn't look back.

•   •   •

The drive back to Forsyth seemed more like flying. There was no traffic, the rush hour having rushed by, for once. Dora didn't even plug in her iPod. She spent the miles practicing her speech for Uncle John. "I feel Mimi would have. . ." "I know Mimi would have. . ." "Camille and Tyffanee could set up their own. . ." "Continuity in the community. . ." She didn't have the right words yet, but she knew she would get them. Her uncle John would appreciate a good argument; he would be swayed by logic, if she could find some. As long as she didn't stray into ad hominem attacks on those idiots who were, after all, his wife and daughter, she should be fine. He had to have been shaken by those telltale tags on the clothes Tyff's friend had "supplied," no matter how much hand-waving Camille had used to try to explain it away. He might be stuffy and overly fond, but he wasn't entirely stupid.

She tried calling Maux, but it rang through to voicemail. "I bailed on grad school, Maux. And I bailed on Gary, and how. I'm going to get Mimi's store back somehow. I'll call you in the morning."

Dora decided to swing by the store on the way home, just to look in the windows, and see how much havoc Camille and Tyffanee had managed to wreak in a day. She parked on the quiet, dark, deserted downtown street; all the lights were off, and it seemed as if even the sidewalks were rolled up for the night.

As she got closer, she saw a white paper in the window. Just like Camille and Tyffanee to put up some half-baked notice, Dora thought: "Camille's Craptorium & Tyffanee's Tacky Tackle & Bait Shop, coming soon," would fit the bill.

Instead, it said NOTICE TO VACATE in big letters, and LEASE REVOKED in smaller ones.

There was a smaller piece of paper, too, in the window next to the door. It said BUILDING PERMIT. It was dated Saturday. And "Intent to demolish storefront and construct 4 (four) parking spaces, garage-style, ground-level/closed. Overhead door. Street cut to be made 11/12." There were two numbers to call on that one. One was for the Forsyth

Planning Commission, and the other one was for Murphy Fine Construction.

Dora dialed it. She didn't care how late it was.

Con answered. "Murphy," he said.

"Parking spaces?" was all that Dora managed to say. "*Four* parking spaces?"

"Dora, I'm so sorry. I didn't know, I can explain. . . ."

"Your company's name is on the building permit, so, unless there's been a really convenient kind of identity theft, not to mention memory loss, you knew."

"No, really, let me explain. . . ." Con sounded pained. *Let him,* Dora thought.

"So that's why you were hanging around Mimi? So you could take her store for parking spaces? You never would have talked her into it, you know."

"Dora, Dora, I promise you, that's not it at all. . . ."

"I don't care what it is, now that I know what you are." Dora pressed the "end call" button with force.

●　　●　　●

Gabby, for a change, was at the house when she got back. "Oh Lord," she said, when Dora walked in. "I was afraid you were Camille come back."

"Camille?"

"She's been here all day, trying to find a copy of Mimi's lease for the store. I guess the building management came in this morning and told her and Tyffanee that Mimi only had a life lease, and that they weren't going to renew."

"'Oh Lord' is right."

Gabby shuddered. "You have no idea. The screeching

alone—that woman should not be allowed to talk on the phone."

"What about Uncle John?"

"He's washed his hands of it—said he doesn't have time for this foolishness, and if they want to run the store, they have to figure it out themselves."

"Did Camille tell you what they were being kicked out for?" Dora asked.

"No, I just thought they wanted more rent than Mimi was paying, and had a more reliable tenant than Camille lined up. Which wouldn't be hard," Gabby pointed out.

"It's parking spaces. They're turning it into parking spaces. Like a garage."

"Makes sense," Gabby said. "It's at ground level, and there's no parking around there at all. Nearest garage is blocks away. I remember they made a big stink about it when they converted the old department store to condos."

"Makes sense? It's terrible! And what's worse, Con's doing it."

"Con's doing what?"

"He's the one turning the store into a garage. The permit was pulled Saturday. He came to Mimi's service after deciding to turn it into parking spaces."

"Well, that was a low thing to do, I'll give you that." Gabby considered. "But, honey, why are you so upset? I thought you were giving up the store and going back to Lymond? How did your interview go, by the way?"

Dora looked down. "I kind of quit grad school. I mean, I told them I wasn't going to enter the program. I quit the coffee shop, too...and Gary—I'll tell you more about that later." She looked up at Gabby and smiled a weak smile.

"I came back to talk Uncle John into giving me the store back."

"That I'd like to see," Gabby said. "Not that I don't think you could do it, sugar, I just think it would take some doing." She looked thoughtful. "But there's not much to give back now, is there? Without the space, what would you do?"

"I could find somewhere else. It's not the storefront—it's the stock that's special. What are they going to do with the stock?"

"I don't know, but they have to do it fast—they have to 'vacate' by the end of the month."

"That's *tomorrow.*"

"That's when the lease ends. They didn't even give thirty days' notice, can you believe? I wonder that Mimi signed that thing—I bet she had John review it for her, and I'm sure he's telling Camille he didn't know a thing about it. That man is oily."

"I'm going to go over there first thing tomorrow. Maybe I can straighten it out."

"I'll come with you, honey. Least I can do." Gabby gave her a hug, then yawned a huge, jaw-stretching yawn. "I'll see you in the morning, sweetheart. Wake me up when you get up."

Dora felt wide awake, a combination of indignation and adrenaline. It had felt so good, putting Gary in his place and popping that bubble. He was sure to have sent her an email, but she wasn't even going to check. No sense getting sucked back in, now that she was free; she had so many other, more important things to worry about. She turned the light back on and grabbed the notepad from the table by the bed. She should make a list....

The furnace clicked on, and Dora heard the old vents groan as the air flowed through them. She noticed a flutter in the corner of the room, by the vent. It looked like paper. She jumped out of bed and grabbed the folded sheets.

Sometimes now she'll take me out of the closet and look at me for a minute, but I never get worn. I never even make it off the hanger. I understand, I do, but it gets a bit lonely, and when you've only been worn once, you don't have a lot to fall back on.

The weather was heartbreaking, the day she wore me, because you knew it wouldn't last: one of those early-autumn days where the sun and the wind conspire to keep the temperature perfect, and where the sky is so blue and clear that you swear you can see the stars twinkling right behind it, just waiting for the lights to go down so they can shine.

She had an early dinner date, not really a date, more dinner with a friend. A male friend. The kind of male friend that occasions last-minute applications of lipstick in shop windows, and smiling at strangers, and a new dress, like me. Nothing too fancy, nothing that looked like she was trying too hard, but something that made her feel good, attractive, almost pretty. He met her on the right corner, not even late, and they walked through the park together. He talked; she nodded. She seemed used to his peevish tone. She listened, jollying him along. She'd crack a joke and he'd let out a sharp "Ha!," smile for a minute, a patch of still water in a rough current, then go back to his roster of complaints. Someone had underrated him; someone else, he was sure, was out to get him, had never liked him; yet another person had an undeserved triumph that should have been—was rightfully!—his. There was a woman; there were several women; none of them were the right woman. He didn't think there was a right woman, not for him. He was on the verge of giving up, he was. He didn't comment on the new dress.

I could feel her breaths get shallower; how she held herself tense, hoping for some kind of flattering comparison, between herself and the not-right women. It didn't come.

They were at the restaurant; it was nothing special. Not a date restaurant, a neighborhood restaurant, but it wasn't his neighborhood, and it wasn't her neighborhood. I thought I felt her stiffen again; was it the kind of restaurant where you took someone you didn't want to be seen with? He smiled at her as she sat down, and she relaxed a bit.

There was nothing on the menu he really wanted; he was concerned for his digestion. Finally, after much inquiry as to the exact composition of sauces and the amount of butter used on the vegetables, he decided on a chop and a potato. He wanted wine, but said it gave him a headache, so he didn't order it. Tap water for him, please. She had a club soda, although I thought she really wanted wine, too. He criticized her steak-frites order: "Aren't you girls always watching your weight?" She put down her half-buttered roll and barely touched the frites, when they arrived.

He kept talking, on and on, about how Rita was much too flighty, not serious enough for someone of his intellectual caliber; Laura was too boring—she didn't even like to go out to the cinema (he always said "cinema," never "movies"); and how Beth, though accomplished, clever, and undeniably striking, was just not his type—and besides, she was too fast. What was he to do?

Her stomach was a hard knot.

"I think you'd better start running open-call auditions, then," she said, and it came out in a bitter tone. She colored.

"Oh, Kitty... not this again, is it? You're a good friend, and a good girl, but..." He had a look of mock sorrow on his face, with a bit of smirkiness around the edges.

"I know. I didn't make it to first callbacks." She looked him full in the face, defiantly, and for a moment, she saw him as he was. Perpetually aggrieved and churlish, fighting a rearguard action against his failures, afraid to approach anything in a generous spirit, lest some unknown competitor take unfair advantage. What had there ever been, what had she read into him, that should lead to a new dress for a weeknight dinner in an unfashionable restaurant?

"Oh, Leonard, it's just too bad," she said, and now there was an air of finality to her non sequitur. He almost looked like he understood; he almost said something of consequence, but then the check came, and in their scrupulous splitting of the bill, the moment was lost.

Their goodbyes were quick. There was no setting of a future meeting, no *"When should we get together again?"* She didn't linger, but headed back downtown with her head up and her arms swinging. If her eyes were wet, a casual passerby would never know, and if she muttered *"Goddamn fool"* under her breath once, or even twice, no one could have heard.

"Kitty!"

Her head turned round.

"Kitty! What are you doing so far uptown?"

"Leonard." She made a face, a little moue of exasperation.

"Oh, sweetie..." Ruth looked sympathetic, but a bit wary.

"Why didn't you tell me he was one-hundred-percent pure wet blanket? I feel like such a fool!"

"I did! Well, I tried to. You weren't hearing it. You were all 'He's misunderstood!' and 'He's really funny if you give him a chance!' and all that nonsense."

"I'm so sorry, I really am. I just... I just woke up, I guess. I just feel a bit shaky. And so foolish."

"Honey, you've got nothing on the rest of us. Remember how I was about Greg? And that was worse, he was married! And such a bore. When I think of all the time I wasted, waiting for him in dark hotel bars, making a gin and tonic last forty-five minutes... only to have him show up and talk about model railroads, if you can believe it. And what about Julia and her cruise-ship dancer, and Anna, whose latest beau is seventy-five if he's a day?"

"I guess I'm in good company, at least. But, oh..."

They talked a bit more, dissecting their friends there on the corner, and started several times to go get a cup of coffee, or a dish of ice cream, but never moved from the spot. Dusk had turned to full dark when Ruth looked at her watch.

"I'm so sorry, sweetie, I have to run! I promised Doug I'd call him an hour ago!"

"It's all right, go, go. Call me later, and we will actually go have coffee...."

She walked the rest of the way back to her apartment, blocks and blocks. I could feel how tired she was as she climbed the last flight of steps. I came off right after her shoes, and was draped across a chair. "So goddamn foolish," she said, with a grimace. Ten minutes later, the lights were out, and the next day she hung me up without a word. I haven't been worn since.

Dora smoothed out the papers and put them carefully on top of the dresser with the other stories. She looked behind the door and on the floor of the closet, but nothing else came to light.

CHAPTER FIFTEEN

THE NEXT MORNING WAS CLEAR AND bright and crisp, a perfect fall day; Dora nearly bounded out of bed. Craftily, she waited until the coffee had brewed before going to wake up Gabby, and brought a cup along with her. Gabby was not a morning person.

"I'm up, I'm up," she said, rubbing her eyes. "Oh, bless you," she said, taking the mug.

Dora rushed Gabby out of the house, which Gabby took mostly good-naturedly. "I don't know why you're rushing," she said. "It's not like Camille is the earliest of early birds."

Dora had parked down the street before she remembered. "I gave my keys to Uncle John!"

"I didn't," said Gabby. "He didn't know I had keys, and it didn't occur to him to ask, the old windbag."

They didn't need the keys, anyway, because they found Camille and Tyffanee already in the store, in matching hot-pink T-shirts and bad moods.

"If you hadn't..." Camille was scolding Tyffanee, but stopped when she saw Dora and Gabby. "Come to help?" she trilled.

"Depends on what you're doing," Dora answered. Camille and Tyffanee had an open box of large black plastic yard bags, and were holding one each. Tyffanee's looked as if she had been shoving dresses randomly into it; Camille's was still flat and empty.

"The management company"—and Camille made "management company" sound like "child molester"—"says we have to be out by today at five p.m. And if there are any movable store fixtures or stock left then, they will fine us one month's rent."

"So we're getting ready to toss everything," said Tyffanee cheerfully. "Sucks, doesn't it?"

Seeing that Dora was about ready to explode, Gabby pulled her aside. "Give me one sec," she said cheerfully to Camille and Tyffanee, who went back to their argument. She pulled Dora outside.

"Let me make a call, okay?" Gabby pulled her cell phone out and hit a single button. Dora looked on in wonder—speed dial was not something she thought Gabby knew about, much less used.

"Honey? Do you think I could get a truck, and maybe some crates? When? Well, about now would be good." She listened for a moment. "Oh, you're a lovely, lovely man, and I knew you could do it if anyone could. I knew I was smart to marry you." Gabby made a kissy noise into the phone. Dora tried not to be shocked.

"Thirty minutes, he said, and I bet he does it in twenty, if he has to wake up half of Forsyth." Gabby looked satisfied.

"Um, who?" Dora asked. "A truck?"

"Well, honey, I've been meaning to tell you, it's just, with one thing and another, and of course Mimi and everything, and it's a bit embarrassing, but...Jerry and I are back together."

"Jolly Jerry?"

"Well, yes, I suppose that's what I used to call him. I just call him Jerry now. Or sugarbear." Gabby grinned. "We got married again. Last week. Down at the courthouse."

"Um, congratulations?" Dora didn't know what to say. "You look...happy."

"Well, don't look so surprised. You young people aren't the only ones who can get all moony and distracted. I swear, since Jerry came back, I can't find my own thumbs unless I write down where I left them." Gabby giggled. "So you can stop worrying about me, I'm not senile yet. And don't think I didn't know exactly what you and Maux were up to, with her asking me all those questions the other day. She's not what you would call subtle."

"Oh..." Dora felt enlightened. "But married?"

Gabby smiled again. "Well, we went and had coffee, and I don't think we'd even had the waitress offer to refill our cups before he asked me to marry him again. Turns out he'd never gotten over me. Or me him, I guess." Gabby held out her hand. "And I had kept the rings all this time, after all....He told me he wasn't going to wait one second longer than he had to, but with everything that was going on, we didn't feel like a wedding-wedding was appropriate. Anyway, we had one of those city-hall deals. I've had enough white-dress weddings."

Dora was having trouble following. "But...Jerry has a truck?"

"Jerry has a dispatch business he retired from. If he says he can have a short-haul truck here in thirty minutes, he can have one here in thirty minutes. Or less. Just like a pizza."

"But where are we going to take the stuff? We can't take it all back to the house—it won't all fit in the garage."

"Well, no, but we can figure that out once we have it on the truck."

"I can help." It was Con, carrying two cups of coffee. His habit of just appearing at all the right times was disconcerting. Dora started to tell him this, but remembered how angry she was, just in time. She bristled.

He handed a cup to Dora. "Peace offering?"

"I should throw it in your face," she said.

"Please don't," he said. "But I'll admit I let it cool down a bit just in case you did."

Dora laughed in spite of herself. She took the cup of coffee.

"This better be good. Your story and the coffee."

"I can only vouch for my story." Con suddenly looked as angry as Dora had been.

"So the Featherstons, my *ex*-clients, have been complaining to the management forever and a day about the lack of parking. They've been after Mimi's space for a long time, although I didn't know that. They'd finagled a copy of her lease, and when they heard that she died, they pressured the management company to enforce the life clause."

"Bastards," Dora said. "Go on, sorry, I'm listening."

"And Mr. Featherston has a crony on the planning commission. So he called him up and got the permit in about ten minutes flat. On a Saturday, even."

"But why is your name on it?"

"Because they needed a contractor's name for the permit, and since I was on all the other permits they pulled, they just used mine. Cronies are very understanding in that regard. This is why they are my ex-clients, by the way. I decide what permits I'll work on."

"Can we get the permit overturned, or unpulled, or whatever? Go to the mayor?"

"Notice I haven't said who Mr. Featherston's crony is." Con took a sip of his coffee. "Damn, cold."

"Oh." Dora's shoulders slumped.

"But...if you need a place for a store, I think I have one. At least short-term. Maybe longer. It depends on what you want."

Dora looked at him.

"I have an old Victorian down by the university, in that new commerce district. Remember, I told you that Mimi was helping me with advice on how to turn the ground floor into a boutique, or something. For the college kids. It's not done yet, or anywhere near, but the basement is finished, and dry. I bet most of the store would fit in there, and what doesn't, we can find a place for."

"Oh, Con." Dora didn't know what to say.

"I told you I'd do anything for Mimi," he said.

Gabby interrupted. "Dora, that truck will be here soon—you should tell Camille and Tyffanee what you want to do."

Dora squared her shoulders. Con was a reassuring presence behind her.

"Here's the deal." Camille and Tyffanee looked up. They had not gotten much further. In fact, Tyffanee's bag had already ripped from the hangers, leaving them worse off than when they had started. "I'll take care of clearing out the store, and guarantee you won't be fined, and in return you will sign over all the stock to me, and make no claim on the name 'Mimi's.' "

"Sounds good to me," Tyffanee said. "We were just going to throw all this old stuff out, anyway, and if you do it, I can do something *fun* with my weekend." She glared at her mother. "And besides, we were going to rename the place *Tyffanee's*."

"Or *Camille's*," Camille put in hastily. "We hadn't decided." She looked around at the store's full racks and shelves. "If that's what you want, Dora, I'll do you this favor."

"Great. You go on and call Uncle John, have him draw something up. He can fax it to the store's number—it's written on the machine. We'll go get some doughnuts while you sort that out."

Camille started flapping about how was that really *necessary*, and that they were *family*, and how John was *playing golf*, until Tyffanee interrupted. "Shut up, Ma, and call Daddy. Unless you want to explain how we have to pay that honking big fine, on top of everything else."

Camille glared at Tyffanee, but she dragged out her cell phone and put on her wheedling-wife voice. Dora and Con and Gabby escaped outside.

"We don't have much time—I'll see if Maux can help." Risking death in phoning Maux before noon, Dora filled her in. Maux was surprisingly chipper. "Hell yeah, I'll be there," she said. "I'll bring Harvey, too."

Maux and Harvey showed up in fifteen minutes, almost awake, Maux wearing men's jeans and a vintage football jersey that said WILCOSKI across the back; Harvey was wearing black jeans, a black T-shirt, a black sweater, and an equally black expression. He mumbled something to Dora that might have been "rat bastards." Dora hoped he meant the Featherstons and wasn't just mad to be outside in daylight hours.

The truck was there in twenty-seven minutes. Gabby

timed it. Jolly Jerry (just Jerry, Dora corrected herself) climbed out from the cab and kissed Gabby resoundingly. Blushing prettily, Gabby handed him a doughnut.

"I called a couple guys to help load and pack," he said, as they emerged from the cab after him. "I thought this pretty rattlebrain wife of mine might have forgotten that." He put an arm around Gabby and squeezed, making her giggle and jump.

Camille emerged from the store and handed Dora the fax, curling and flimsy from Mimi's old fax machine. "There you go," she said. "John said that would do." From her sour-pickle expression, Dora guessed John had said some other things that she hadn't wanted to hear.

Dora read through John's legalese, making sure he hadn't tried anything sneaky. Camille stood by and fumed, until Dora said, "Looks okay."

"Ma?" Tyffanee was calling from the doorway. "Let's go, before I break another nail, okay?"

•　　•　　•

It was a near thing, but they got everything into the truck before five. Jerry's helpers handled the heaviest of the fixtures, and Harvey wangled supervising the loading of the truck, and Maux, carrying the heaviest of the boxes, made some scathing comments about poets.

At ten minutes to five, Dora was sweeping out the storeroom, more than ready for the building agent, a guy she vaguely recognized from high school. "Sorry about this," he said, as Dora handed him the keys. He looked puzzled when Dora assured him with a smile that it was no trouble at all.

"Lord, I'm tired," Gabby said, leaning against Jerry. The truck and loaders had gone to a secure storage lot. He assured them that he himself had locked a padlock on the door, and handed the key to Dora. "You just call when you want it all back, and I'll have it over just as soon as you hang up the phone," he said. He gave her a crushing hug. "I feel almost like you're my own—I don't know—niece? Gabby talks about you so much." He grabbed Gabby's hand. "We had reservations for tonight, I better take her off to get cleaned up, and me, too." He leaned in toward Dora, and said in a stage whisper, "She cleans up better'n I do, but don't tell her I said that." Gabby laughed and smacked him on the arm.

Gabby leaned over and whispered to Dora: "I hope you don't mind if Jerry stays over with me tonight. That senior-living place smells too much like disinfectant." She wrinkled her nose. "We've been house-hunting, but we haven't found any place we both like yet."

Harvey and Maux peeled off, too. "We've got to go listen to a friend of Harvey's read his new work," Maux said.

Harvey scowled. "It's derivative, but Maux likes it."

"Ignore him," Maux said, and hugged Dora goodbye. "Call me early tomorrow, okay? Like, noon early."

That left just Con and Dora. "What do you want to do first?" he asked. "See the space, or eat?" Dora almost pointed out that he was taking it for granted that Dora would want to do both, but she found she didn't really mind.

"I want to grab sandwiches and eat in the space. Soak up the atmosphere."

"Soak up some dust, is more like it, but sure. Lud's to go?"

"Sure." Dora couldn't believe she'd been angry enough to run him over the night before.

They didn't talk on the way to Lud's. But as he pulled into the drive-through lane he asked, "Italian, easy on the hot peppers, Diet Coke?"

"I'm impressed you remembered." Dora grinned. "Roast beef and cheddar with peppers?"

"I'm impressed *you* remembered. Oh, wait, that was Mimi's favorite, too." Con looked over at Dora. "I think she would have been proud of you today."

"Gabby did all the heavy lifting. Well, all the metaphorical heavy lifting. You and Maux and Jerry's guys did all the literal heavy lifting."

"But she only called in a favor because you were willing to fight for it."

"And ready to serve Camille a wrong turn," Dora pointed out.

"That, too. But still."

Dora didn't answer, but she smiled at him, maybe her first real smile since she'd lost Mimi. It felt strange, but not terrible.

Dora was impressed by the Victorian. Con stumbled over himself trying to apologize for it. "It needs to be painted— Mimi was helping me with the painted-lady colors— and I have new windows on order, and the steps will be repaired…." He stopped short. "I'll have more time for this renovation, if not all that much money, now that I've quit the Featherstons." He sighed. "The plan was that I would use the money from their job to finish this renovation, and then sell this place." He unlocked the front door. "I'm really hoping I don't have to sell it before I can finish it—I'll barely make back my investment if I have to do that."

They ate their sandwiches sitting on overturned milk crates in the old parlor.

"Mimi said the two front parlors would make good boutique space, and we could turn the old pantry into a dressing room. The kitchen and dining room would be the storage space and back room. She thought this place had a lot of possibility."

Dora looked around. "I think the clothes would seem more at home here. The space downtown was pretty sterile. Too new, even though Mimi'd been there for years."

"This neighborhood's up and coming, too." Con sounded like he was trying to convince himself.

"Oh, totally," Dora said. "The students won't bother to go downtown if there's enough here for them." She looked around. "What's upstairs?"

"Oh, three apartments. One's mine."

"And the other ones?" Dora asked.

"Well, one's a two-bedroom. It's rented—a young couple with a baby." Con smiled. "They keep making noises about moving, needing more space, but they haven't yet. The other's a one-bedroom, but it's not finished yet."

"Sold."

"Huh? What do you mean, 'sold'?"

"I mean, sell it to me! Or at least part of it? I can sell Mimi's house, plus I can use the life-insurance money, since I won't need it for grad school. Or maybe I could lend you money to finish it? Don't some businesses pay their landlords to have space finished the way they want it?"

"Dora, you shouldn't make any big decisions now. Especially when you have mayonnaise on your face." He reached out and wiped the corner of her mouth with his napkin.

"I'm serious. Gabby loves that house, and she and Jerry need a place. I could sell it to them—Jerry's obviously loaded—and then I could still go back whenever I missed Mimi. Half the furniture is Gabby's anyway." Dora looked up at the ceiling. "I'd need a place to live. How long would it take you to finish that other one-bedroom apartment?"

"You have it all planned out." Con sounded impressed. "Well, if you're not too picky about fixtures...not long." He folded up the paper from his sandwich precisely into quarters and shoved it in the bag.

"I won't make you rip out perfectly good sinks, if that's what you mean," Dora said, and yawned in spite of herself. Con looked solicitous. "I saw that. I'm taking you home."

"I won't argue. I may fall asleep in the car." Dora yawned again.

"As long as you don't snore..."

Dora laughed and threw her balled-up sandwich wrapper at him.

Dora did almost fall asleep on the way home. Con tried to be quiet, but couldn't help asking her how she felt about wood floors versus linoleum, and where she thought the register ought to be.

"Mimi already answered these questions, didn't she?" Dora asked, as they pulled up to the house.

"She did, but I'm just double-checking with you."

"I want whatever Mimi wanted," Dora said.

"That's very good," said Con. He took a deep breath. "Because Mimi wanted me to ask you out. Although she might have said 'court you.' I thought I should tell you before we become business partners. Or landlord and tenant. In case you think I have ulterior motives."

He looked so painfully earnest that Dora almost laughed.

"Well, if Mimi wanted it…," Dora said. She smiled. Con leaned in for a kiss.

Not sloppy at all, Dora thought.

"I don't know if you noticed, but Gabby just flicked the porch light off and then on again," Dora said.

"I haven't noticed anything outside a two-foot radius for the last ten minutes," Con admitted.

"That was her signal in high school that I'd been in some boy's car long enough."

"Some boy's car?" Con looked dismayed.

"Well, usually I was spending the ten minutes talking nervously and at top speed, so very little kissing actually happened. But I was grateful to Gabby for thinking it was. And sometimes for getting me out of it."

"Are you happy to be 'getting out of it' now?"

"Not at all." Dora put her hand up to Con's face. "I say we make her flip that switch a couple more times."

"I'll call you tomorrow," Con said, when Dora finally opened the door to go.

"You'd better," Dora answered. "I'm your new tenant, and I expect a very responsive landlord."

"You got it." Con smiled.

CHAPTER SIXTEEN

 DORA'S PHONE RANG EARLY THE NEXT morning. It was Maux.

"I can't sleep for shit, so it's my turn to wake you up. What are you doing today? Besides thinking about Con," she added.

"How..."

"Oh, please, like it wasn't obvious. He's been, like, crazy in love with you for months."

"But we only met last week!" Dora was wide awake now.

"I guess Mimi talked you up so much he was intrigued. And then smitten. And then infatuated. And so on. I used to overhear their conversations in the store. Ninety percent about you, and ten percent about everything else." Maux sounded smug. "I was the one who suggested to Mimi that she should introduce you to Con, by the way."

"You can't start matchmaking before you even get married," Dora protested. "That's not how it works."

"Who died and made you the matchmaking referee? Anyway, what are you doing today? Let's go get sweet rolls."

Dora sat up in bed. "I have to go get Mimi's urn. Out of the safe-deposit box. And pick up her ashes from the crematorium."

"Oh." Maux paused. "I can go with you, if you want."

"It's okay, I can do it." Dora hesitated. "I'd rather do it alone, I think. But we can get sweet rolls first, if you come pick me up. Con drove me home last night, and my car's still downtown. I'd better get there before ten or I'm going to get a ticket."

"All right, I'll move my ass. See you in a few."

Dora stretched and looked at the racks of dresses across the room. *What do you wear to pick up your grandmother's ashes?* Dora wondered.

She settled on a hunter-green dress with brown buttons. Very autumnal, Dora thought, as she stood in front of the mirror.

Gabby was still asleep, and Dora didn't want to wake her—or Jerry. She scribbled a note—"Out to grab car"—which was part of the truth, if not the whole truth.

Maux gave Dora a mock-stern look as they sat at the counter. "Well, young lady. I have plenty of questions about Mr. Murphy."

"I don't know what to say about him," Dora admitted. "He's…very nice."

"I won't tell him you said that," Maux said. "It would fucking kill him. Seriously. 'Very nice'? What the hell is up with that?"

"It's just…it's been a long week, and I'm a bit off-balance right now." Dora smiled at Maux. "That's all."

"All right, all right," Maux growled. "You get a week's pass, but by next week I need details."

"Next week, check." Dora assumed an air of innocent inquiry. "I assume there's a form to fill out?"

"Fucking-A. In triplicate."

Then it was Maux's turn—she was bubbling over with wedding details. Dora was able to nod and express interest in all the right places, and was even drawn into a long defense of Jordan almonds, which Maux thought were projectiles, not candy.

"I should go," Dora said, when Maux had finished her last sweet roll. Maux looked sympathetic, but didn't argue. She patted Dora's hand. "Call me," she said. "And Sunday you should come help me look at places to hold the reception."

"Bowling alley," Dora responded. "I've always wanted to be a bridesmaid and bowl a three-hundred game in the same night."

"Dream on," Maux said, and gave her a quick hug. "I'm serious," she said. "Call me if you need me and I'll be right there."

"Thanks," Dora said.

*   *   *

There was no trouble at the bank, not that Dora expected any. Dora had a key and knew the code, and the bank manager had known Mimi since before Dora was born. He expressed his condolences in a dry way that Dora found almost bearable.

The safe-deposit box was big and contained no surprises. The diamond earrings Mimi never wore; her passport, various papers that shouldn't be in the house in case it caught fire, one of Mimi's phobias—not fire, having to get another copy of her birth certificate; and the box with Mimi's urn.

Mimi had picked the urn out ages ago in some antique store. Gabby had been appalled. "You want to have a *used urn*?" She shook her head. "Mimi, I love you, but you are just plain strange sometimes."

Mimi had just smiled and bought it anyway. Mimi had kept it on a shelf in the living room, until Gabby declared it creeped her out too much. Then it had moved to the safe-deposit box.

Dora picked it up and closed the box. She went upstairs and thanked the bank manager, and then drove to the funeral home before she could change her mind.

"I've brought—" was all she got out before the girl at reception cut her off. "Oh, yes," she said. "I'll get Ralph."

Ralph was wearing a dark-blue suit and looked so perfect in it that Dora thought he was probably asked to pose for funeral-director ad campaigns. "I'm sorry for your loss," he said, gently. "Would you like me to supervise the transfer?" Dora supposed he meant "put Mimi in the urn," and nodded.

Dora waited on the plush velvet sofa. There were no magazines.

Ralph came back sooner than she thought, but not as quickly as she hoped. He had the urn box in one hand, and a manila envelope in the other. "This was in the receptacle," he said, and Dora marveled at how naturally he said "receptacle," like it was an ordinary word like "cotton," or "mayonnaise."

He handed her the urn box, which was heavier than Dora expected, and placed the envelope carefully on top of it. He held the door for her and then accepted the box and envelope back, like a footman, almost, as Dora unlocked her car.

He put the urn box on the floor of the front seat, with the envelope beside it. "If you put it on the front seat, put the seatbelt around it." Dora must have looked puzzled, so Ralph explained, "You'd be surprised how many people don't like their loved ones riding on the floor. But if you stop short, a spill can be unfortunate."

"Thank you," Dora said. "I'll keep that in mind." She left the box on the floor all the way home.

Dora took the urn inside and left it, in its box, on Mimi's dresser. She'd find a place for it soon, but for now it felt right to put it in Mimi's room.

The envelope she took to her own room, which was mercifully free of any traces of Camille. The envelope was unmarked, the flap sealed shut. Dora pulled at it a bit too hard, and the envelope ripped in her hand. A stack of old photos fluttered out onto the bed, facedown. One fell to the floor. Written on the back, in Mimi's handwriting, was "Teddy and Hannah and Dora," followed by a smudged date. Dora picked it up. There was a man with her wavy hair and her chin smiling in the photo, next to a confident-looking woman with long straight hair. They were smiling, and the fat baby between them was smiling, too, an inscrutable baby smile.

A few pieces of paper, folded in squares, looked like they had been wrapped around the photographs. She unfolded one of the pages. It was in a man's handwriting, heavily slanted. "Mom, I know you think I won't be able to support Hannah and Theodora as a writer, but I wanted to send you this story—maybe it will change your mind…." Dora stopped reading. Her father had wanted to be a writer? She felt as if the world had shifted with an audible click. She put the letter down, and turned to the other pages. They weren't letters, but a secret life, written in the same handwriting.

It wasn't the kind of day you see in Kodak commercials, with the softly diffused sunlight making the massed roses glow; it was a little too bright, and I remember the best man squinting all the way through the service, and seeing sharp flashes of light reflected from some guest's watch. And there weren't massed roses, anyway; she wanted daisies, and that's what she got. Bright gerbera daisies, almost as bright as the day. She held them so tightly, though, that she loosened all the carefully wrapped florists' tape, so they were wilting almost before the "I do's".

If you're wondering how I noticed all this, well, when you're only going to be worn for one day, you pay attention. Even if you are lucky, and preserved well, and fit your bride's daughter or granddaughter or niece, there's a kind of "reset" button, I think. Even the oldest dress, one passed down for generations, comes to a wedding day as new as the day it was made. The newness of the new bride's feeling sort of soaks into the dress, and the other, older weddings fade off into a haze of orange blossom and ringing bells, like a face that looks familiar but doesn't bring a name immediately to mind.

From the minute I knew what I was, I started paying that kind of attention, to everything. To the girls and women who came into the store, especially. The girls giggled and preened when they tried us on. They were playing princess, or starring in some romance. They didn't really talk about their grooms, except to say how impressed the grooms would be when they saw them, in that dress. (In fact, it took me a long time to realize that such a thing as men existed at all; it was months before I saw one.) Their friends oohed and aahed. Sometimes they applauded, as if the girl were a performer of some kind. The mothers would flit around, relegated to carrying and fetching. The girls made big shows of capriciousness, first calling one of us "the one" and then switching their attentions to another.

The women were more focused. Sometimes they were just as young as the girls (and sometimes the girls were old enough to know better), but they knew themselves. The tall, elegant ones, with their hair already pulled back in bridal chignons—they didn't try on the pouffy, encrusted, cupcake dresses, or the ten-foot trains. The pocket-sized curvy ones didn't cram themselves into slipper-satin columns, or dresses so low-cut that they needed industrial-strength adhesives to avoid indecent exposure. Sometimes they didn't even try anything on, no matter what their mothers or friends pleaded with them to attempt. They'd look through the racks purposefully, and if the dress wasn't there, well, it wasn't there. On to the next shop.

My bride was a woman, although she walked like a girl, with a bit of a skip in her step. She was excited in spite of herself. She came in by herself, which was unusual, but it wasn't a spur-of-the-moment visit, and she wasn't a "tourist," someone not even engaged coming in to try on dresses for entertainment, the way other people might go to the movies. She had an appointment; she had the right underwear and shoes with her in a bag. She had her hair up in a loose knot, held with an ordinary rubber band.

We all paid rapt attention. Whenever a bride came in, all the dresses were like puppies in the pound, begging to be taken home. We weren't samples, like some stores had, dresses just to try on, never to be worn in a real wedding. Well, some of us were samples, and returns, and discontinueds—some of us even claimed to have been ordered for brides who had been jilted or died, although none of us liked to think about that. But we were all real. If a bride tried us on and liked us, we were going to be in a wedding, not hung back on the rack while our newer, fresher doppelgängers were made to order at some factory.

I myself had been part of the inventory of a fancy designer, one who had overstretched and gone out of business, leaving hundreds of us in a warehouse. We were auctioned off, not even taken out of the shipping boxes. The shipping boxes were boring; I had been glad to be lifted out of mine and hung on a rack. I didn't even mind being attacked with a steamer.

When my bride walked in, I don't think I'd ever even been tried on. The girls hadn't liked me, because I wasn't covered in little shiny bits—I didn't even have any ruffles. And I'd never struck a chord with any of the women, either. I hadn't fit their mental checklist.

But she pulled me off the rack right away. I remember trying not to get my hopes up; so many dresses were tried on, but so few were chosen.

The changing rooms didn't have mirrors—all the brides had to go out to the little dais. The girls pranced out there, still giggling; the women either sidled out, a bit self-conscious about what they saw as the absurdity of it all, or were completely businesslike. She almost strolled out; I'd never seen anyone so confident.

Antoinette—she went by "Antoinette," although her name was actually Kelly—said what she always said when a bride stood up on the dais, which was "Oh, honey, that dress was made for you!" Only this time, it felt true. I didn't fit her exactly—I could feel that I was a little big in the waist—but that was no deal-breaker. I fit her in all the ways that mattered—not just the physical ones, but the emotional ones. We felt right together. I didn't feel like a bride costume, I felt like a wedding dress.

Now, I don't want to be like some of the other dresses, who overestimate their own importance. After all, you don't need a wedding dress to get married; people get married in jeans and sneakers and overalls and giant banana costumes, for all I know. Nobody stands up during the ceremony and objects to the union because the bride and groom aren't appropriately dressed. Sometimes it seemed like the brides—the girls, especially—were so focused on the dresses because they didn't want to think about the marriage. I wanted to tell them that the dress is not the marriage, it's only part of the doorway to the marriage. We're liminal; boundaries, not countries.

But I didn't feel as if my bride needed that warning.

Antoinette fussed around her, arranging the skirt. "I'd forgotten this skirt was so heavy," she said, panting a little. (Antoinette was heavy herself.) "It's silk faille. We don't get a lot of that here; most people prefer satin. Faille's not as shiny."

"I like it," my bride said. "I like the weight of it. I want it to feel serious."

She did what all the brides did, smoothing the dress over her hips, pulling her hair down and knotting it up again. She craned over her shoulder to see the back. But it didn't feel necessary. It was like a ritual kicking of tires; the decision had already been made.

Antoinette knew it, too. "Unfortunately, the tailor's not in on Tuesdays," she said. "But if you can come back any other day we can get this pinned for the alterations; you don't need very much...."

"Oh, my mother-in-law—my future mother-in-law—is going to do the alterations, actually. She offered to make the dress, too, but she runs her own business, and I thought it

would be imposing too much. But Teddy—Teddy asked if I would let her do the alterations, if I needed any. He said she liked to do them."

I could tell that Antoinette secretly doubted that anyone liked doing alterations, much less someone's future mother-in-law, but she didn't argue. Antoinette never argued, especially with brides who wanted to do their own alterations. "Once they find out how awful it is to take apart those seams, they'll be back here. And then we'll charge them a rush fee."

I didn't think my bride would be back, though, and I was right.

When she tried me on again, she was standing on a kitchen stool, and she was laughing. There was a tall man with dark hair sitting backwards on a chair, and he was laughing, too. The woman putting pins in me was trying not to laugh. "If y'all make me laugh I'll stick a pin right through Hannah, and then where will you be?"

"Stuck," said the man, and that set them off again. I never did figure out the original joke, but they didn't seem like the kind of people who needed a joke to laugh.

When the pins were all in, I was carefully taken off and laid on what was obviously a spare-room bed. I was a little worried—I'd seen dresses brought back to the shop with butchered alterations, and it wasn't pretty. But the woman knew what she was doing. She opened up my seams so gently that I barely felt it, clipping the threads with a pair of tiny scissors, and when it came time to put me under the machine, she didn't jam me through, but let the feed dogs carry me, the needle moving in and out like breathing.

It didn't seem like all that much time, then, until the day. Hannah got dressed mostly by herself, although the older woman came in to help, dressed in a dove-gray suit. "Oh, Mimi, thank you," Hannah said, although Mimi hadn't done anything yet.

Before Mimi could say anything, another woman came in, all in a rush, nearly upsetting a little table, and catching the strap of her fringed leather bag on the doorknob. While she worked herself free, she never stopped talking. "I'm late, I'm late, I'm late, I know, and I don't know where those shoes are you wanted me to wear, and I don't think I have the right underwear, either, and—oh!—did I tell you I met someone last night at the rehearsal dinner—one of the waiters—and he's going to India next month, and—India!—it sounds so excit- ing! Hannah, should I go to India? I mean, not with that waiter, although he was really cute—I mean, just, in general?"

I could feel Hannah sigh, but Mimi took over. "Rachel, dear, it's so good to see you. You're not late, and I have your shoes and all your underthings here; remember?"

"Oh, Mimi, I wish you were my mother. My mother always yells at me if I forget my bra. Although Hannah's mother may have been like you, it's totally possible, I don't really remember. I mean, Hannah's like you, isn't she? All calm and stuff? But if you were her mother, then Teddy and Hannah wouldn't be getting married, now, and that would be, just, like, miserable."

Hannah and Mimi laughed. Rachel didn't. "What's funny?" She turned and managed to pull the curling iron off the table somehow. While Mimi rescued it, Rachel grabbed another dress, wrapped in plastic, off the door. "I'll just shimmy into this, back in a jiff!"

Hannah started "Rachel..." but Mimi stopped her. "I'll go give her the right underwear, before she runs back here starkers to get it," she said.

There's a lot of other stuff I remember, but I won't bore you with all the details, like how Rachel managed to drop and step on her bouquet twice before walking down the aisle, and how Hannah and Teddy walked in together hand in hand, and exactly how many people cried (not including babies), and what color the frosting garlands were, and who had too much champagne at the reception (Rachel). But if you ever do want to hear all the details, I'm happy to tell you.

I should tell you just one last thing, though. Most people think weddings are all about the bride (mostly because she has the best clothes), but when I was there, in front of the minister, I could just feel the love pouring off the groom. It was warm, like you'd imagine love to be, but at the same time it gave you goosebumps, and that little shiver that some people describe as feeling someone walk over your grave. I don't know if I was feeling it myself, or just feeling Hannah feel it. But I've never forgotten it.

I hope you feel it someday. I hope you are wearing me when you feel it. I'd like to feel that again.

Dora sorted quickly through the photographs, looking for a picture of a woman in a wedding gown. There wasn't one, but Dora didn't need it. She didn't think she needed anything she didn't have at that moment.

EPILOGUE

IT WAS ALMOST SPRING BEFORE MIMI'S reopened. Dora had pushed and prodded and pushed again to get the store open well before the beginning of February—Forsyth College, weirdly enough, had a tradition of costumed Mardi Gras parties—and they had made the deadline, if just barely. Dora had commuted back and forth to Lymond, graduated, and worn a dress with a very small and tasteful sash (*not*, Maux had pointed out, by any stretch of the imagination something that could be called a butt bow) to stand up in Maux and Harvey's wedding, where she had danced with Con. She had spent a lot of time next to Con, in one way or another—scraping, then painting, or then arguing about painting, followed by moving in all the boxes of stock, and rearranging them, and rearranging them again, interspersed with the occasional movie and sandwich from Lud's.

Gabby had walked through the night before the official opening, and nearly water-spotted a 1930s silk dress by bawling dangerously near it. "It's okay," she said, waving Dora off. "I'm okay. Mimi would have loved this, you know." Jerry led her outside, where she couldn't do any damage.

Con looked around the store with her. "I think it will do," he said. "What do you think?"

"There's just one last thing," Dora said, "but I'm working on it."

"What?" Con was concerned. "We've thought of everything, I'm absolutely sure."

"There's this." Dora had put a plaid day dress on the mannequin nearest to the register. She hung a little cardboard placard around the mannequin's neck. It said, "Ask me about my secret life."

Con frowned. "I thought you bought that dress last week. How could it have a secret life?"

Dora blushed. "I wrote it." Dora pointed to a few pages resting on the counter. "From here on out, every dress at Mimi's is going to come with a secret life. I'm even printing them out on fancy paper, so customers can frame them, if they want."

"You wrote this?" Con picked up the pages. He started reading.

"Hey, stop," Dora said. "You only get the story if you buy the dress."

"It won't fit me," Con said. "That's not fair." He started reading out loud. " 'It was only on Friday that I knew she was going to marry that man.' " He stopped.

"Today's Friday." He smiled at Dora. "I think I'd better buy you that dress."

READING GROUP GUIDE

1. If the outfit you're wearing right now were going to tell a story, what would it say? Do you have any items in your closet that would have interesting stories to share?

2. Do you think it's true that "the clothes make the man"? Why or why not? Would Dora's perspective and goals have changed if she had continued to wear cargo pants and raggedy T-shirts?

3. Maux has a very flamboyant personal style; she never excuses the way she loves to dress. Do you wear something you love every day?

4. What do you think compelled Mimi to begin writing the secret lives? Were they for Dora or for herself?

5. If Mimi hadn't fallen ill, do you think Dora would have learned about the secret lives or about her mother and father? What was Mimi waiting for?

6. Mimi spent a lot of time assembling Dora's closet, yet Dora never wore anything from it. Why do you think

each of them did this? Has anyone ever done you a favor so huge that it felt like an obligation?

7. Con falls in love with an ideal of Dora (as put forth by Mimi) before ever meeting her. How do you think he would have felt if he'd met Dora at Lymond? Did Dora have an ideal of Gary in her mind, too?

8. After many in-between relationships, Gabby ends up remarrying her first husband. Will it work out? Do you believe in giving second chances to relationships?

9. Mimi's family relationships are troubled: she was estranged from her son, distant from her half-brother, and even slightly removed from Dora at times. Why do you think Mimi held herself apart? Are any relationships in your life like this?

10. Do you think Dora eventually would have come home even if Mimi hadn't fallen ill? What else might she have done instead?

ABOUT THE AUTHOR

Erin McKean is the founder and CEO of Wordnik.com. Previously, she was the editor in chief for American dictionaries at Oxford University Press, and the editor of the *New Oxford American Dictionary,* second edition. Her other books include *Weird and Wonderful Words, More Weird and Wonderful Words, Totally Weird and Wonderful Words,* and *That's Amore* (which is also a collection of words). This is her first novel, and really her first book where the words are arranged in something other than alphabetical order.

Erin lives in California south of San Francisco and spends her free time reading, sewing, blogging, rollerskating, and arguing about whether robots or zombies would win in a fight (lasers optional). She loves loud prints, quiet people, long books with happy endings, and McVitie's Milk Chocolate Hobnobs.

Erin McKean